SHOT TAKER

LAS VEGAS VIPERS BOOK FOUR

STACEY LYNN

Shot Taker

Las Vegas Vipers Series

Book Four

Stacey Lynn

ONE

MAX

"Three concussions. One knee surgery. You've already had one lower back surgery and a dislocated shoulder." The team doctor peered down at me as he read through my file.

Like I didn't already know the litany of injuries I'd had over the last few years. Hockey was a tough game. I was an even tougher player. It happened.

But never during a freaking weekend I was supposed to spend relaxing and rock climbing with my teammate and friend, Alix Halvrick.

I glared at him through the excruciating pain in my head while he stood, arms crossed over his chest in the corner. He was most likely taking in every single word the doctor said, every furrowed brow as he scanned my chart and the x-ray results the doctor was going over.

If my shoulder didn't feel like it was boiling inside, I'd tear the damn file out of his hand.

I was *fine*. Or I would be. It was the very beginning of July. I could still be ready to play before the season. So my head currently felt like it was being beaten from the inside out with a mallet and every time I moved, the room spun and vomit rose in my throat.

A minor concussion. I'd had worse ones.

"What's the plan then? Physical therapy?"

The doctor glanced at Alix before meeting my eyes and when he did, I swore I saw pity in them. "You have a greater than fifty percent tear in your rotator cuff, Max. Not to mention the concussion."

"And?" I dared him with my glare to say it. Suggest I quit the game, the only thing I was good at.

He blinked first. The doctor I'd always respected and now wanted to punch, dropped his file to his side and rubbed his hand across his forehead.

Oh... was the threat of me losing *my* job stressing him out? Poor guy. Too bad if something happened to him, he had a college degree to fall back on. I didn't even have that. Nothing except hockey. Like hell I was giving it up.

"We'll schedule you for an MRI and see how things look, but I'm not going to bullshit you. The shoulder will most likely require surgery. And recovery time, plus PT... you're looking at a long road ahead."

"Fine then." I tried to adjust the way I was leaning back in this stupid fucking hospital bed where Alix brought me after I slipped, slammed into the rocks, and screamed in agony while I'd tried to re-find my footing.

Fucking rock climbing.

The small movement in my bed made the room tilt, and I grabbed the damn plastic bowl before I could throw up in my lap.

I might lose my career, but I sure as hell wouldn't lose my dignity.

"Let's do the surgery. Right now."

It was early July. I had my brother's wedding in four weeks. I still had plenty of time to get back into shape for pre-season in September. Worst case, I was back on the ice by Thanksgiving. Maybe Christmas. Plenty of season left.

For now, I was going to ignore the fact this was my last year under contract and I was looking at being thirty-one, a free agent with a roster of injuries that would make anyone hesitate.

Fuck.

"It might not be that easy, Max. With the history of your back and shoulder..."

"Don't even fucking think it," I growled at him. If I could move, hell, if I could blink without wanting to throw up, I'd lunge for the man.

"Max..." Alix said, stepping forward. "Listen to him."

"Fuck that. I'm a hockey player. That's what I do. Who I am." Shit. My goddamn head. I closed my eyes and gritted my teeth together. "I'm not going to listen to this guy suspect what he's thinking of saying without any goddamn proof."

I turned back to the doctor. "Get me the MRI. And do whatever you have to do to get me ready for the season."

"I've called Vik. He's on his way, too. I'll let you know when we're ready."

Coach Vik was going to lose his shit. Ignoring the fact I'd most likely be fined for participating in a *dangerous sport* in the off-season which was already against our contract, he'd definitely be pissed about my shoulder.

"Fine." I practically spit out the word through clamped teeth.

As soon as he was gone, I dropped my head to the pillow and closed my eyes.

"Don't say whatever it is you're thinking, Alix."

Alix Halvrick was my best friend on the team. A few years younger than me, we were always together. Mostly because the majority of the team had started falling in love and getting married. The lucky fuckers. We were two of a handful of single guys on the team remaining and we liked to hang out. Today's adventure was supposed to be a relaxing climb at Red Rock Canyon.

"This is all your fault," I muttered to him. It *had* been his idea.

He was silent, which meant I'd hurt him.

I opened my eyes enough to see him through the blur of my

eyelashes and the disco ball of colors swimming in my vision. "Sorry. Fuck. I didn't mean that."

His blond brows furrowed together and he was chewing on the inside of his cheek. All of his usual playfulness had been left at the canyon, because there was no happiness in him when he said, "The doctor is not wrong about your shoulder. Your rotator cuff, Max. That's serious. And your head…"

"It'll be fine."

Because it'd have to be.

I was thirty. My career only had a limited number of years left. But it was the only thing I knew.

If I didn't have hockey, who in the hell was I?

No one. Just some rich asshole without a college degree and a handful of stories, meaning I could someday say, "Back when I played pro hockey."

Fuck that.

I wouldn't leave the sport until they had to drag my dead body off the ice.

COACH VIK SWIPED his hand over his bald head and stared at his feet before raising his face. As soon as his eyes met mine, my teeth ground together.

It'd been hours. I'd sent Alix home, only to have him return showered and now pacing the small area on the opposite side of my bed, wringing his hands together so fiercely it was a wonder he had flesh left on them.

"Surgery," I surmised, based on the ravaged look on Coach's face. Not because he thought of me as a son, but because I was a weapon. I was the man who helped him win games and keep him as the coach of one of the most winning teams in professional hockey history.

"To be determined," he said and took another swipe across his bald head. It shined beneath the harsh lights of the hospital room and he cursed. "We have some other options we can try first along with physical therapy to see if we can get it healed without surgery. If you're careful with the shoulder, keep it in a sling and meet with your physical therapist daily, we might be able to avoid surgery altogether."

I'd pulled up my phone and scanned Google regarding rotator cuff surgery when Alix left after my MRI. Bad idea. Not the worst I'd ever had, but definitely not the best. Besides the fact I could barely read due to the concussion, everything I read about shoulder surgery only made my headache worse.

"What options?"

Our coach glanced at the doctor, his brows lined with stress. "There's stem cell replacement where they take some cells from your hip and inject it into the site. There's what's called platelet-rich plasma injection. Those only take a few hours, and results can be seen in a few weeks."

"Great. Let's do those then." I looked to the doctor. "Today. Next week. Whenever."

"Max—" he started, but I was rolling with this idea. So they jab me with a needle in my hip, shoot it up into my shoulder. I didn't need specifics. It'd take hours. Results in a couple of weeks. Perfect.

"And if it works, no surgery, right?"

"Possibly," the doctor stressed. "If we do other therapies first and see if the tendon can heal itself, at least partly, it'll decrease your chance of surgery, or at least rehab time after and *maybe* increase your chance of full recovery."

Coach glanced at the doctor who sighed before Coach turned back to me. He settled his hand on my good shoulder. "It's not the shoulder we're most concerned about. Max, we've talked about this."

"No, we haven't. And we won't."

Alix stopped his pacing long enough to scowl at me. "Listen to him."

"No." My lip curled into a sneer. "I'm not listening to anyone suggesting I might not be able to play until it becomes the only option."

If these options worked, there'd be months to play after.

Worst case... no, there would be no worst-case scenario.

I would play again. Before the end of the year.

"Get me the contact info for the physical therapist, and whoever I need to call for the other treatments. And get me the hell out of here."

TWO

KIM

The drive across the island, heck, the tiny little puddle jumper I had to take from the main island to this small, private one with one resort, served to remind me how much of the world I had yet to see. Twenty-nine years old and this was my first time in two years seeing beaches so white it could have been snow and blue skies and water so bright and teal-colored, there had never been a crayon in my mega count box as a child that could recreate this.

The sky. The brightness of the sun. Heck, even the green tropical plants and trees were so much more vibrant than I'd pictured.

So much brighter when they weren't under the constant smog and haze of Los Angeles.

"We are almost there, miss."

"Thank you." I grinned at the driver in the rearview mirror. The Rasta-liveried male with long dreads in his black hair smiled back at me with a happy smile and slightly yellowed teeth.

I couldn't fathom what it was like for him to live here. To live anywhere like this. My stress levels took a nosedive into the Caribbean Sea as soon as my puddle jumper of a plane cleared the death-defyingly short runway.

Thank goodness because after running myself ragged for the

last six years, so intent on making my mark in my law firm, and particularly the last case where I sat first chair, if I hadn't had this chance for a vacation, I might have gone into cardiac arrest.

My phone vibrated in my hand, and I all but rolled my eyes as my mom's name appeared.

"Hello?"

"Oh thank goodness you're alive."

My breath fogged the car window I had my forehead and nose pressed so close against to see the tiny, winding dirt road. In the distance was a smattering of bright yellow, tiny homes, barely visible between the thick covering of trees and surrounding foliage. Villas. Not only was I at this incredibly gorgeous location for the next week, I had my own private living space.

This had to be heaven on earth.

"I called you before the plane took off," I reminded her.

"I know. I know. But they're so small and scary I just wanted to make sure you weren't in the sea somewhere."

I chuckled. My mom was the sweetest. "I'm still alive."

"Well, good. Because Bridget would lose her mind if you weren't here and threw off the numbers of the wedding party."

She laughed. Although it was no joke. Bridget and I got along so well because we both personified Type-A personality to a perfectly scripted T.

"We wouldn't want that," I said, laughing with her.

Since Bridget's mom and mine were sisters and best friends, my cousin and I grew up practically sisters. Sure, our lives took drastically different turns over the years, and there were times when we had nothing in common and didn't really get along. Like when she started liking boys and grew boobs and I was still playing with dolls.

Fortunately, my boobs finally grew in—somewhat, anyway, and I finally started noticing boys. Since then, while Bridget and I were never *besties*, we were closer than most cousins I knew, even if we grew up living in Ohio and Virginia. We saw each other several times a year plus every major holiday.

"We'll get her sorted and relaxed. I promise."

"If anyone can do it, it's you," she replied.

"I'll be there in three minutes, Mom."

"Can't wait to see you. Love you."

I ended the call, and ignored the text message alerts. This was why I understood Bridget. I was now on hour thirty of being awake, pulling an all-nighter to ensure all my cases were either wrapped up or in good hands while I was gone. I'd worked so much on the plane rides down here, I hadn't managed to fall asleep for more than ten minutes.

Yeah... I needed this break. Let's just hope I could actually *relax* enough to enjoy it.

That worry fled as the car turned toward the resort.

"Holy crap on a cracker," I muttered. The black, wrought iron private gates of the Tunstago Bay Resort came into view.

"Pretty place, isn't it?" the driver asked with that same friendly smile and jovial tone in his voice.

"It's incredible," I sighed, still in awe of the luscious landscaping, towering palm trees, the vibrancy of the flowers popping out of the bright green leaves. The main building he drove me toward had signs for multiple restaurants or tiki bars pointing in various directions. A *private* beach I'd read about. Small, secluded—and clothing not allowed—was an offshoot of the main beaches along the coast.

I couldn't *wait* to go there. Strip off society's demands that women keep their bodies covered, but not too much or we were a prude but not so little we were a slut and asking for sexual assault. There would be freedom on that beach, with others who had no problems exposing their creator-given flesh without hesitancy or fear of being an object. Or even better, a beach to myself. I certainly didn't need to see any of my family—or any of Marshall's—in nothing.

As the taxi pulled to a slow stop outside the main registration building, it came as no surprise to find my mom and dad were already there. My mom, dressed in a bright red bikini and a black flowy cover tied and wrapped around her waist, looked as stunning at the age of fifty-five as she did when she was my age and younger. My dad was no slouch either, dressed in his teal board shorts and plain white shirt. He'd been a linebacker in college, played football where they met at Ohio State, and even though he was originally from Iowa, he had no problems staying in Ohio so they could get married and live the life she always dreamed of.

He was as head over heels in love with her as he'd always been.

They were pretty much the only two people in the world who gave me the slightest bit of hope people could get married and still be happy thirty years later. But they were the unicorn, not the standard. I had the proof of it in piles of cases in multiple five-drawer file cabinets in my office.

"Hello, beautiful," my dad said, opening my door and holding his hand for me to exit. I grabbed my purse, and once I was on my feet, I was wrapped in his warmth and the fresh summer scent of coconut and sunshine. Probably the sunscreen Mom made him wear.

"Hey, Dad."

"It's been too long."

I hadn't been home since Christmas. Hell, I'd barely managed to spend more than eight hours a day outside the office since then, and most of those hours were spent when I'd gone home. I patted his back and grinned into his chest at his chuckle.

"My turn, my turn," my mom said, practically bouncing on the balls of her feet. She was much like Dad. Full of love and kindness. Very much so like her sister and Bridget. Bubbly. Craved the small-town and stay-at-home-mom kind of life.

We were so drastically different in that aspect of our lives, and while she'd never understood my need to have such a demanding career, I'd always had their full support.

"Hey, Mom." I hugged her back with the same equal vigor and excitement she threw into life and loving her family. We might not have understood each other, but I never went a day without feeling her love, even when I was twenty-six hundred miles away.

"This week will be so much fun. We're going to force you to relax, even if we have to tie you down to do it."

See? They knew me.

"Keep my drinks filled and the rest should take care of itself."

My dad shot me a doubtful look, and I pushed his shoulder playfully. "Stop."

He threw his hands out to his sides. "I'm just sayin'… I think the last time I saw you *chill* was in middle school."

He wasn't wrong. I went to admit it, but Dad laughed and grabbed my suitcases the taxi had left on the curb.

"Come on. We'll get you checked in and take you to your villa. We already have your favorite tequila in your room and wine chilling in your fridge."

My parents really were the best.

An alert dinged on my phone as my dad grabbed my keycards at reception. I fought the urge to glance at it.

Lost.

Peeked.

Fortunately, it was a spam risk call.

"None of that," my mom teased.

She was right.

"I know. See?" I did what I promised myself I'd do as soon as I arrived.

I powered off my phone and slipped it into my purse. Work and real life could wait.

At least until I'd slept and had a drink.

THREE

MAX

"It is so damn good to see you." I squeezed the hell out of my parents, my arms thrown around both of them. We had no idea where my height came from, but I towered over them both.

My dad slapped my back hard enough to leave a sting when he pulled back. "You too. You taking care of yourself?"

His brows knotted with concern, and he clamped his hand over my shoulder. I was trying to ignore the fact that in two weeks I'd have more scans done. Four weeks into physical therapy and I still couldn't swing my stick at full speed, and the first day I'd gone to the team's practice arena to try skating, I'd almost doubled over in pain. It was getting better, though.

The sling was in my suitcase for days I needed it, and that meant I'd have to be a spectator in golf instead of beating the crap out of my brothers like normal.

Sucked, but I was focused. I was getting back on the ice by Christmas or I was fucked.

"Of course I am." I grinned. The worry didn't ease in my dad's eyes.

"You're lying."

"I'm not. I'm taking care and doing my PT and brought all the equipment I need to keep it up."

"Any pain?" my mom asked.

"Only when someone touches me," I teased, scowling playfully at my dad.

He jerked his hand off my shoulder like I'd electrocuted him.

"Max." My mom laughed and slapped my chest. "Don't tease him like that. You'll give him chest pains."

"Chest pains," my dad huffed and gave me another quick hug. My parents were the best people on the planet. "I'm too damn young for that."

With my oldest brother, Maxim, recently turned thirty-three, I chose not to inform my dad that at nearing sixty, he wasn't at all too old for that.

But Marcell was the kind of man who'd believe he was thirty until the day he died.

"Damn straight you are," I said and gave my mom another kiss on her cheek. They were so far away in Virginia, and most of my season kept me traveling. I could go months without seeing them. I hated it. To say my family was close was like saying the ocean was large. Massive understatement. "And I was kidding about the pain. I was joking. No pain at all."

He didn't need to know the truth. That some mornings I hesitated after taking one pain pill, debating a second. That I groaned rolling over in bed and the first few days after the rock-climbing accident I'd spent drunk, pitying myself, imagining the worst-case scenarios in the dark shadows of my condo.

Alone.

It hadn't at all helped the concussion recovery, so on day three I'd tossed the alcohol, chugged some Gatorade and got focused on healing.

"Good. That's good." Because as much as my dad worried and cared enough to ask, he'd always left my love of hockey and the tenacity to get to the professional level up to me.

My parents were simple people, from a small, coastal town on the Atlantic, who loved each other and everyone they met without hesitation or judgment. They lived an easy life, with little hiccups along the way, but when it came to us kids, they'd always thrown their support behind our dreams one hundred and ten percent.

They kicked serious ass.

My mom took my hand in hers and even though I wasn't a kid anymore, I held her back. "Thank you so much for doing this for Marshall. He and Bridget are so excited that we get the island to ourselves. Truly, you didn't have to do this."

"Sure I did. It's what they wanted and I could make it happen." Besides, my older brother was awesome. Only one year older than me, we'd always been best friends. I'd do anything for him, so when he mentioned his construction business had slowed in the last few months and he was worried about giving Bridget everything she wanted, I volunteered.

"Marshall's planning on paying you back."

"And I'll punch him in the face if he says it to me. It's their *wedding* present."

Because you know, everyone could go around renting a private island for their wedding. To me, it was nothing. I was a single guy who made millions and didn't exactly live an extravagant lifestyle. I had my new Suburban, a fantastic condo with a view of the Vegas Strip and mountains beyond. I hadn't yet seen the need to splurge on a home when it was just me, or fancy cars when I only had two spots allotted to me in the parking garage. Sure, someday I would. When I did though, it'd be on land. Lots of it where I could have some horses, maybe a small hobby farm to work in the off-season. Simple dreams like the kind of life I grew up with. Hell, maybe someday I'd retire and move back to Virginia and be closer to family.

I just needed to make sure I still had a season or five left in me to make it all happen.

Pushing that thought far out to sea, I followed my dad to the registration desk.

Palm trees and tropical plants took the center stage. Beyond that was an inside bar, outside, another bar with covered patio dining and seating. And past that, was one of the resort's infinity pools, and then the beach and sea in the distance.

"Gorgeous," I said. "Bridget has good taste."

She'd found the resort and island after I offered. While Marshall would want to make sure he didn't take advantage of my money, Bridget had been so excited I heard her scream all the way out in Vegas... and not through the phone. Girl had a set of lungs on her.

"Especially in men," my mom said, and then cringed. "Well, at least this time."

Considering she had a son, Nathan, from an earlier relationship and her first husband was an epic loser, the joke fell flat. "Where are the boys? Is everyone else here?"

"Malcolm and Shelby took them swimming, but they should be back soon. I think they're at the east pool area."

Made sense. My oldest brother Malcolm and his wife Shelby had a son just a year younger than Nathan. Cooper and he were great friends. I snagged a map of the resort and met my dad at the check-in desk.

"We gave you the largest villa on the far west end," my dad said.

"That was supposed to be for Marshall." My damn family. If I couldn't spoil them every once in a while and thank them for their unending and constant support, what in the hell was I supposed to do with my money?

"And he insisted. Anyway, they're tucked into a smaller villa, but he said it's more private. Nathan is staying with Bridget's parents for a few nights and then with us once they take off on their honeymoon, so it works. Honest."

My dad slapped my shoulder. I bit back my growl. Frustration with Marshall for not just letting me do something nice for him mixed with pain. Perhaps I shouldn't have taken the sling off. It reminded people to stay away more than I needed it, but no way in hell was I wearing that thing unless I had to. Eyes were supposed to be on Marsh this week. Not me.

I was still irritated as the concierge handed me my key and showed me on the map where my villa was. Dad marked off where everyone else was staying, including Bridget's side of the family, most of whom were on the east side while us Mikolajczyks were on the west.

"Is there a plan for tonight?" I asked, gathering back up my bags. I could have used the valet, but I managed my own gear while I traveled nine months out of the year. I'd be a pussy if I couldn't handle a few suitcases on my own. I threw the duffel awkwardly over my good shoulder and grabbed the handle of my suitcase with my other.

"Dinner at six. I think Bridget's mom has slipped agendas for the week under everyone's doors though. There are some large family activities we've reserved and then smaller options so we don't get bored. But most of the week is ours to do as we wish."

Great. More time analyzing the pain in my body. Was it worse? Better? I'd gone through so many scales of one to ten every day over the last month, cataloging the severity of my shoulder, I saw numbers every time I closed my eyes.

"We'll let you get to your room. If you don't want to wait until dinner to hang out, we're going to try and find Coop and Nathan at the pool."

I could use a shower. Maybe a quick nap. "I'll text you," I told my dad.

After another hug, and then a hug and kiss for my mom, I left them to find their way to the pool and took off toward the path where the villas were numbered and marked.

The house, not a villa, was two stories and had three bedrooms, complete with a gourmet chef I'd scheduled to prepare my breakfasts and snacks with all my dietary needs for the week. It might have been a vacation, but I needed as much health in all forms for my body. I couldn't afford to let a single day slip.

The view outside my villa was insane. Bright blue water, white beaches. A line of trees provided me privacy on both sides. From the map, I knew Morgan, my youngest sibling and only sister, was next door and there was nothing on the other side. But the villas were so secluded, I couldn't see her front door from the path.

"Glorious," I said and dumped my bags in the main floor bedroom. I should have kicked Marshall out of his place and forced them to take this one. Even without having to worry about Nathan for the week, he and Bridget would get more use out of this space than I would. Hell, I'd probably never step foot upstairs. What was the point when everything I needed was right here?

An hour later, I was showered, dressed in my swim trunks, pacing my villa. Restless. So much for the nap I attempted, and the last thing I wanted was to dig out exercise bands or pain meds.

A day off wouldn't hurt anything. I'd been working my ass off for the last month. Hours a day, stretching, building muscle, repairing, resting.

This week was my brother's wedding, and I'd earned a day off, dammit. Besides, the silence and solitude would drive me insane.

I'd grown up with too much noise, went to college and lived in a house with eight other hockey players. I traveled with a team, hung out with them as much as possible.

I could sleep on a bus with thirty guys screaming. Hell, I could probably fall asleep on the bench during a game if I tried. Noise and activity and people were my best friends.

Grabbing my keycard and phone, I left the villa via the sliding doors and stepped onto the beach. My slides were in one hand, phone and keycard in my other and I found my way to the pool where the shouts of Cooper and Nathan followed by deeper voices I figured belonged to some of my brothers, paved the way.

FOUR

KIM

Birds chirping and a strange rumbling sound pulled me from sleep. I peeked an eye open and then flung to sitting, my hand to my chest as I took in the strange place.

"Shit." It took a moment for it all to sink in.

The plane rides. The resort. Bridget's wedding.

That's right. I was in the Caribbean at Tunstago Bay Resort for the wedding and a week of vacation.

"Damn," I muttered and willed my racing heart to slow. I didn't do well sleeping in strange places. The nap must have done me in and as I glanced at the clock on my bedside table, my eyes widened.

"Holy shit." I'd slept for three hours. I *never* napped that long. A three-hour nap was close to what I got in a full night's rest.

I stood from the bed where I'd essentially collapsed as soon as I entered. My bags had been abandoned in the living room area where my dad set them before they left earlier. My purse was on the small dining table. For a moment, I itched to find my phone. Turn it on and scroll through my alerts and to-do list before I squeezed my hands into fists and resisted the urge.

This was vacation. I had one week to chill the hell out before I threw myself back into work where I'd deal with nasty, oftentimes public, divorces and domestic violence cases that made me lose more faith in humanity by the day. Particularly this last case.

A professional football player who not only cheated on his wife multiple times, but she finally left him when she ended up with a black eye and broken jaw. From my experience, it was the rare athlete who played a game based on adrenaline and fueled by anger who *didn't* beat his wife at least once.

All things I didn't need to think about on my vacation.

"Nope." I shook my head and headed straight to the fridge.

Grabbing a pre-packaged cheese and meat tray, I pulled off the plastic top and popped a chunk of gouda into my mouth before grabbing the wine bottle. I'd have a glass of wine, unpack, and then I'd go find Bridget.

Her maid of honor and other bridesmaid, both college friends of hers and friends who had been around since the first husband, who shall never be named, weren't arriving with their husbands until tomorrow. Knowing Bridget, she'd spend the next twenty-four hours freaking out about their flights arriving on time, their dresses and suitcases getting lost by the airlines, and anything else her beautiful, anxiety-riddled mind could conjure.

Which meant I didn't have time to dally. My first sip of wine hit my tongue with a refreshing, crisp taste of pear and apples. Perfection. I closed my eyes, lingered on the brief moment of relaxing.

Then I got to work. I unpacked, pausing only long enough to trade in my travel clothes for my cobalt blue bikini and white swimsuit wrap that tied around my waist and to sip my wine and eat my crackers. Sandals in one hand, I refilled my glass of wine into a stemless steel wineglass with the resort logo stamped on it, slid my keycard into my bikini top, and headed out.

Bridget's nerves would most likely be unraveling, and as her bridesmaid, it was my job to help her out.

Kimmy to the rescue.

I snorted at the thought and at the first step outside, when the salty, breezy warm air hit my face, took another moment to inhale deeply.

Heaven. I was in heaven, or at least pretty darn close to it.

Since I left my phone in my villa, I didn't exactly know where Bridget would be, so I headed in the direction of the main resort building. We had the entire small island to ourselves, so the beaches were silent, and since others hadn't yet arrived, the villas were dark and closed up. At least those that I could see. We were all so private from each other.

It wasn't long until a squeal pierced the air, followed by another, high-pitched screech and I grinned, recognizing Nathan's tiny little voice that could carry all the way back to the States if the wind blew in the right direction.

The boy was loud. Got it from his mama. I always teased her when she'd say something about it. He was also super sweet, had a compassion for others rarely seen in kids, at least those I'd spent time around, and he kicked ass at baseball. Athletic to the bone.

I smiled as I heard him squeal again, my steps speeding up as the sounds of funky island music and deeper voices grew louder. Following the path, I caught the sign for the pool area. Of course. Made sense.

Stepping through the gated entrance that required my keycard, I was just sliding it back into my bikini top when a squeal that could only rival Nathan's pierced the air and made me flinch.

"You're here!"

I barely had time to glance up before Bridget slammed into me. "Oomph." My arms wrapped around her on instinct.

"I'm so glad you're here! Did you nap? You look tired. And oh, shit, I spilled your drink. We need to get you a new one."

I pressed my hand over my cousin's mouth and her blue eyes popped wide open. "Breathe before you pass out. I'm too small to catch you."

Her brows tugged in and as I dropped my hand, her lips were

pinched. "You're not small. You're perfect. Come on. You have to meet everyone. Marshall's entire family is here, including his brother who plays hockey," she whispered in my ear, although it wasn't a whisper at all.

Bridget had a set of lungs on her that could rival jet engines at take-off.

Thankfully, the rest of the small crowd, Marshall's family, I figured, didn't hear.

"Hockey?"

"Yes." She rolled her eyes and wrapped her arm around my back, guiding me straight to the bar. "He plays in Las Vegas. Max. I've told you about him, remember?"

"He has like eight siblings. How am I supposed to keep them straight?"

She hip-checked me. "Five siblings. Marshall makes six. And how do you forget something like that?"

Since I wasn't clear if she was talking Marshall's siblings or how his brother played hockey, I didn't answer. I also wouldn't waste my breath reminding her how I felt about professional athletes. Arrogant, cocky assholes, *almost* all of them. And that almost was only because I refused to judge an *entire* sect of people based on the many I'd dealt with. Before I could say anything, she propped us up at the bar and immediately ordered a refill of my pinot grigio.

Once I had a sip, I scanned the area. The pool was gorgeous with a swim-up bar that was now closed but I assumed it was bustling when the resort was open to the public. Nathan was in the pool. Marshall and one of his brothers in there with them.

"Damn... is that the hockey player?"

"Max," Bridget said and nodded her in the direction. "Sexy as hell, isn't he?"

He had sandy brown hair I caught right before he ducked under water. As he popped back up, the hair, longer on top, cut short on the sides, whipped back as he flipped it. Water flew everywhere and when he smiled at the boy in front of him, my uterus squeezed.

Wow. Sexy as hell did not describe him. Full, thick lips. A bright smile that said he didn't take life too seriously. Muscles on his shoulders and arms with veins that popped as he lifted them, ducked beneath the water and came back up. It all happened in slow motion. Large hands pushing his hair back. The sun hit his face, making him glisten. And all that water flew through the air. Rolled down his chest.

He was... *wow*...

"Hey!" Bridget squealed and jumped back right as water landed on our toes. Nathan popped up from the water and grinned back at his soon-to-be stepdad. "Again!"

"Watch it, Marshall!" Bridget yelled, no heat in her cry.

"You'll live, princess," said Max, the guy I was practically drooling over.

I covered my hand with my laugh. "He has you pegged, doesn't he?"

My gaze glued to him as another boy swam right to him. "My turn!" the other boy shouted.

"Who's that?"

"Cooper. Malcolm and Shelby's son. They're over there." She pointed to the couple, where there were two more guys with other girls on lounge chairs. The guys all had a beer in their hands, the girls held fruity-looking umbrella drinks I'd switch to soon. "Next to Malcolm are the younger brothers, Mason and Maverick. Their dates are Abby and Anna."

"Sisters?" Because they looked alike, both blonde bombshells and big-boobed.

"Not that I know of. Sweet though, I've only met them recently. Neither have been dating them long."

The boys in the pool screamed again and a splash grew closer to our feet. I swiveled back to the mayhem going on in the pool, the playful shoving around of Max and Marshall.

And Max. Those muscles, the slight grimace he made as he threw one of the boys into the water and rolled his shoulder. When he stood to his full height in the pool, the water brushed over his navel revealing a chest I could explore for hours. With my tongue—and teeth.

"I bet he could do things to a woman in bed I've only begun to dream about."

"I don't need to know what you dream about in bed." Bridget poked me playfully in the ribs and I jumped out of her way. "And if it wasn't my wedding week, I would absolutely tell you to have fun with that beast of a man. But for me? Please don't."

"I was kidding." Even if the man looked like he could be the kind of guy to make all my fantasies come true, and I only had a week with him, I would admire him from afar. I didn't need the headache, and that was assuming he'd even be interested in me.

"You're the only two single people here this week. And I know he's sexy. Hell, I like looking at him almost as much as I love looking at Marshall, but remember Zack? I don't need that level of drama this week."

My wineglass almost slipped from my hand. "You're not honestly bringing him up. That was *years* ago."

"It was two." She rolled her eyes. "And he ruined Christmas dinner with his massive jealous fit."

So my history with guys wasn't the best. Ironic considering what I did for a living, you would think I'd have a better handle on noticing red flags as soon as they popped up.

"That wasn't my fault." I'd gotten a call from an old law school friend, we talked once a year around the holidays just to keep in touch. He and his partner were in New York, and since I was in LA, we never saw each other. "And Paxton is gay."

"Well that didn't stop Zack from flinging over the dining room table, smashing it into Mom's chandelier, and ruining our dinner, did it?"

Yeah. That'd been pretty mortifying. More humiliating,

considering until then, I'd thought Zack was perfect. We'd been together six months before I flew him home for Christmas to meet my family. Later, I learned he'd been high out of his mind, which really, only made the situation worse.

How had I missed all of that?

"So you're suggesting Max is a sexy hockey player with drug and anger issues and you're concerned I'll be the trigger that flips his switch?"

"No." She rolled her eyes like I was being an idiot.

I wasn't. Petulant, maybe.

"Max is a great guy, but it's a week and then what would happen anyway? I'm just saying you're the only two single people here. You might not want to spend it alone, but I'm asking for my sake, *please* don't."

Outside of admiring his physique, maybe a fantasy or two popping into my head, it wasn't like I knew the guy. This whole conversation was pointless. I was here for Bridget, and to relax. Not get tangled up with some athlete whose ego was probably larger than any other body part.

I chalked it up to her bridezilla tendencies and sipped my drink. "The only thing I'm concerned about is making sure you have the wedding of your dreams, the one you've always deserved to have."

Because God knew her first wedding and marriage exploded like a bomb and left more carnage than Hiroshima.

"Besides, you're forgetting my mantra. No athletes in my life or my bed. Ever."

She looped her arm through mine and tugged me to her. "Good. Thank you. But that doesn't mean we can't stand back and enjoy the beauty we've been blessed with this weekend."

"You're insane." I laughed.

Max swiped at his hair again in the pool, laughing at something his brother said. And oh yeah... sexy barely described him. His shining, light brown eyes, so bright from here, crinkled at the edges.

Water clung to him in ways I wanted to lick off the ridges of his abs when he jumped out of the water.

Yeah... he was beautiful to look at.

But Bridget was right. This week was about her, not my libido.

Besides, I'd always promised no athletes. They were nothing but trouble.

Even if I imagined he was trouble wrapped up in a very pretty package with a sparkly bow.

FIVE
MAX

"Do it again!"

Cooper's seven-year-old voice rang through the air. His smile was bright and wide and his blond hair was almost as white as the beach. Despite the burn in my shoulder, I couldn't resist him.

"All right, kid."

"Farther and higher this time," Nathan said. His arms were around my shoulders and his legs around my waist. A brief, mild twinge of pain sliced through my shoulder as he climbed onto me and I ignored that too.

One day off. I'd get back to therapy and being careful tomorrow, but there was no way I was denying my nephews the pleasure of their awesome uncle. Besides, they weighed less than fifty pounds soaking wet. It wasn't like they could do serious damage.

"Don't forget you're next," I warned him and launched Cooper into the air. His limbs spread out wide and he splashed into the pool. Far enough from the edge he was safe, close enough his splash sprayed all over Bridget and the girl who had just arrived.

Sexy, tiny little thing with long hair pulled back in a ponytail. But there was no hiding the curls in it, the length or thickness of it.

I imagined when it was down it'd fall to her waist. She looked young, at least younger than me.

"That's Bridget's cousin," Marshall said, moving in the water next to me. Somehow, he'd barely had to lift either Nathan or Cooper since he joined me in the pool while the two kids were climbing me like monkeys on a tree in search of the last banana in existence. Not that I minded.

Throwing these guys around and being with my family after so many months away was my favorite thing.

I was more often used as a jungle gym when I came back home than anything else.

"Her name's Kim. I've only seen her a handful of times, but she and Bridget are super close."

I could hardly take my eyes off her. Next to Bridget, who was five-ten, this girl seemed almost miniature-sized. She had to tip her chin up to look at Bridget in the face. How small would she be next to me?

How easy could I throw her around?

How would all that hair look while she was *riding* me?

Damn.

I dunked under the water and when I popped up, I swiped water off my face. Ridiculous thoughts. All of them. I was here for family.

"Thinking about her, aren't you?"

"Shut up, Marsh. And no."

Lies. She looked damn cute in that teeny bikini top, toned stomach on display. Her bottoms were covered with a wrap, giant white bow at one hip I wouldn't mind peeling off with my teeth.

"Liar," Marsh said, and damn it. He was right. Maybe it'd been too long since I'd gotten laid. I'd dated Maisy last year, but she and I broke up a long time ago. I hadn't had sex since then. At least six months? I was just horny. That was why I could feel a tightness in my groin as I looked at her.

"Again!" Nathan screamed, coming close to bursting my eardrum.

"Easy, killer," I said, and slid him around to my front. "Grab Cooper," I told Marsh.

Once the boys were in our arms, I grinned at my brother. "Ready?"

"To cause the mayhem all us Miko boys are known for?"

"Yes!" Nathan and Cooper both shouted. "Mayhem!"

"No!" Bridget cried.

So we were known for being over the top. Sue us.

I counted slowly, keeping an eye on Marshall out of the corner of my eye. "One... two..."

"Three!" all four of us in the pool screamed, and even though Bridget was paying attention, she was too slow to move.

Both boys landed so close to them, water flew in every direction, soaking the cement around the pool, and most importantly, both Bridget and her cousin.

"Maxim!" Bridget shouted. "You got us soaked." Her hands went to her hips, her body banging, which I registered quickly and kicked to the curb. She was my brother's almost-wife. "You suck!"

But she was laughing, shaking water off her hands and brushing it off her bare stomach.

Her cousin, though, she looked stunned, bright-eyed and lips parted, and I had a brief moment of believing that's what she'd look like as soon as I slid my thick dick into her before she smirked and shook her head.

"So... not interested at all, huh?" Marshall asked, swiping pool water off his face. "And before you lie about it, Bridget already gave me the talk to give to you. No fucking her cousin this week."

"Seriously?" My brows rose on my head. "What kind of animal does she take me for?"

"She doesn't think you're an animal, she loves you, but she doesn't want drama this week and you can't tell me it doesn't follow you."

Irritation spiked. "Drama *follows* me?"

"You know what I mean. Everyone knows you. Hell, I'm guessing half of Bridget's family will be starstruck once they get here." His grin wiped away and he chewed his bottom lip. "Bridget's already been through hell. I want this week to be perfect for her. She has enough on her mind, so, please? For me... leave the cousin alone."

I hadn't listened to my brothers tell me a damn thing since I was big enough to kick their asses. The fact he even thought he had to say this pissed me off.

"I'm here for the wedding, to relax, and keep working on my PT, asshole. Not to fuck the bridesmaid."

"Don't be an ass." He splashed me again but this time I was ready and as his arm came out, I grabbed it and moved. "You little—"

"Not so little anymore," I grunted, right before I got him in a headlock. My brothers and I had broken more bones and furniture and given each other more fat lips and black eyes than I'd come close to experiencing in hockey.

Marshall might have built houses and renovated buildings for a living, but he was no longer a match for me.

His hands went to my hips and he ducked his head, but my arm was already tighter and my legs braced for him. He went flying, upside down into the pool, splashing into it flat on his back.

"Do not hurt him or give him a black eye before my wedding!" Bridget shouted from across the pool deck.

I flipped two fingers from my brow in her direction and winked. "Aye-aye, Captain."

"Again, Uncle Max and Dad!" My heart pinched as Nathan called Marshall, Dad.

He wasn't his bio dad, but that loser was long gone. Marshall had only been in Nathan's life since he was four, but I couldn't remember a time when he hadn't called him Dad.

"Maybe us old guys need a break."

Nathan scowled and shook his head, right before he swam to Marshall's back and started climbing up until he was sitting on his shoulder.

"Chicken time!" he squealed, and Cooper's cold, wet hands landed on my own shoulders.

"Chicken time," I confirmed, grabbed his hands and lifted him up my back, and scowled at Marshall. "Ready to lose, big brother?"

He grinned before glancing at my shoulder. "You sure you can do this?"

Another spike of irritation. I knew what I could handle. This was nothing. Besides, I had pain meds in my bag if I needed them. And the sling that was now on my dresser, mocking me.

"Backing out before we begin because you're afraid I can still kick your ass even if I'm not a hundred percent?"

"You wish." His worry narrowed his eyes. "You sure, though?"

Damn straight I was. "Best three out of five."

Five games later, we were laughing, my stomach hurt, and my shoulder was throbbing from Cooper constantly shifting his weight.

"All right. All right. Good game, guys," Marshall ceded the loss, still glaring at me. "I'm still calling foul play on that leg play."

"It was an accident." I shrugged.

So I played a little dirty. On the ice and off of it.

As the thought hit, my eyes strayed to the woman who was still with Bridget. They were now lounging under a shaded umbrella with Bridget's parents and another couple, laughing, sipping drinks with bright pink umbrellas in them.

My eyes stalled on Kim, despite Marshall's warning. Her eyes slid to mine and widened. She sipped her drink, eyes locked on mine before dipping to my chest.

Yeah... I could play dirty, and with the way she was looking at me, raking eyes I couldn't tell the color of all over my body, I had a feeling she might like it that way too.

I SLID up to the bar to grab a drink with my youngest two brothers. Since I spent most of the afternoon with Marshall in the pool, I hadn't talked to them much. By the time I got done swimming, they'd already headed back to their villas.

I had turned in myself, took a shower to wash the pool water off me and popped a couple ibuprofens before icing my shoulder. It had been sore, but not bad. Maybe a four, which was better than the initial eight. A couple hours of rest and stretching had helped and now it was down to a two if I ignored the fact the pain meds were masking some of it.

During dinner, I'd spent most of the time with my parents and Morgan. Mason and Mav had grabbed their own table with their dates, so I'd barely spent any time with them yet.

"What's going on with you two?" I asked.

Maverick and Mason were a few years behind me and only one year apart. They were actually Irish twins, being the same age for two weeks.

And no, my family wasn't Catholic. We got that a lot when I was growing up. There was a night someone had asked my mom that when I was young, when Morgan was still in the baby carrier, and she'd smirked at them, clearly irritated. It was a look my mom rarely wore unless there was blood flowing from someone's nose.

"Not many better ways to stay warm on cool winter nights," she'd explained.

Once I was old enough to know what she meant, I'd gagged. No one needed to know that about their mom.

"Nothing. Just shooting the shit. When are you coming home?" Mason asked me, his attention barely on me, but the cute blonde huddled up with Morgan at the table where my sister, as usual, was reading, glasses perched on her nose and a glass of red wine nearby.

"Don't know yet. Thought maybe this visit would make me so tired of you all I wouldn't bother."

He punched me in the kidney.

"Kid," I growled. So he was twenty-six. As the youngest brother, he got the most crap growing up. Although he was also the brattiest, so he deserved it. Somehow, he'd never learned the art of *do not ever tattle on your brothers*.

"Don't lie. You love us too much to go without your monthly check-in."

More like weekly. I grunted in response and tapped my glass against his. "Probably early September," I admitted. I wouldn't give him the satisfaction of knowing I already had my flight planned as soon as I could fly after my surgery if I had to have it.

"How's grad school going?"

"Not bad. Ready to be done. Should have just gone to work for Marshall full time after college. Too damn old to still be studying."

"I hear that. When are you done?"

"Winter. Was going to take my last couple classes this summer but figured it'd be better to have the hands-on work with Marsh during good building weather and finish up school after."

"You excited to be working for him? Kind of a hard ass, isn't he?"

"Shut your trap," said Marshall, the hard-ass from behind me. Like he could sneak up on me.

I'd clocked him while he had skirted around the edge of the restaurant to do it.

"Total hard-ass," Mason agreed.

We chuckled and I bought us a round, handing Marsh's to him but didn't let go. "You ready to run into the ocean and disappear yet?"

"We can get a boat for you tonight after dark, I'm sure," Mason cut in.

"You're both dicks. And no." He took a swig of his drink. "I want this week to be done, be back home, and get back to life though."

That I could understand. There was definitely nothing like the feeling of being in your own home. For as much as I traveled, I craved being in my own space. I just didn't like being there alone.

Bridget flounced up, holding Kim's hand and tugging her along behind her. The pretty little thing had her hair down and the breath had stalled in my chest when she walked in for dinner earlier. At the pool, her hair had been pulled back into a ponytail bundled at the back of her head so I hadn't seen the full length of it or the thickness. It was untamed now, wild and free. I'd been right, too. It did fall to her waist. A waist that was so tiny I could probably wrap both hands around it and touch my fingers together. But what drew me in even more than her hair or the petite size of her frame, was her teeth embedded into her bottom lip as she glanced my way.

"Hey guys, I didn't get to introduce you all to my cousin earlier. This is Kim."

My brothers introduced themselves, but I held back as Marshall leaned in and gave her a quick kiss on the cheek. "How're you doing? We haven't seen you in a while."

"I'm good. Busy with work as usual." She shuffled on her feet, popping the bottom lip from her teeth to answer him, and damn if it wasn't one of the sexiest things I'd seen in a while.

But was she just nervous in general, or was she nervous because of me? I guess there was only one way to find out. I held out my hand toward her.

"Hey. I'm Max, well, Maxim, but everyone calls me Max. Marshall's favorite, best-looking brother." I winked at her playfully.

Her cheeks turned a light shade of pink as she looked up at me, tilting her head back to meet my eyes.

Next to me, Marshall guffawed. "Please. You have no idea what you're talking about."

"Kim." She slid her hand into mine.

Kim's handgrip was firm. Shockingly so for being so petite, but she shook my hand like someone confident in her body and her place in the world.

Another attractive quality I'd never paid attention to in women before.

"Nice to meet you," I said.

She glanced at Bridget, who wasn't smiling nearly as wide as she usually was.

I took that to mean we'd both gotten the same lecture earlier.

Marshall had to be an idiot. Didn't he know when you told me *not* to want something, it only made me want it more?

Bridget's eyes darted between us and a smile curled at her lips. "I thought it would be good for you and Kim to meet," she said. "Especially since you'll be partnered together in the wedding and everything. Did you know my cousin Kim is one of the best lawyers in California?"

A lawyer? She kept getting more interesting. And also, how would I have known that? "No—"

"I'm going to murder you in your sleep," Kim said, cheeks now blushing bright red.

I grinned at both of them. Looked Kim up and down. A lawyer was impressive. She looked too young to be doing it for too long, but Marshall told me at the pool that she was only a couple years younger than Bridget, which meant we were about the same age.

"What kind of law?"

"Oh she puts deadbeat assholes to shame and sends abusers to jail." Bridget threw her arm around her cousin and tugged Kim to her.

I was right at the pool earlier. She was short, tiny, with very few curves which wasn't really my type. I was a big guy. Liked my women to be able to handle me both in bed with my size, and outside of bed with my personality. But I did enjoy this bashful side of Kim.

I also would've considered myself an ass or tits man in general, but my eyes kept being drawn to all that hair. The earlier vision of it spread out all over my pillows came back and slammed into my gut in a way I felt deep in my groin.

I hadn't exactly promised Marshall I'd stay away from her, but I did want to respect their wishes. It was their week, and Marsh was right, Bridget had been through enough hell.

"Oh look!" Bridget exclaimed and grabbed Marshall's arm. "My parents are waving at us. They probably want to talk to us about the dessert tonight." She looked at both of us, wiggling her brows at her cousin before giving me a sly smile. "You two be good, okay?"

Marshall flashed me a sympathetic grin as he followed his fiancée back to her parents.

But also... what the hell? Because none of this seemed to go along with keeping us away from each other. When they were gone, I looked down at Kim. "I have to admit, I'm a bit confused. I was assuming we both got the same speech earlier."

"Speech?"

"Yeah, you didn't?"

"Oh." A blush hit her cheeks and that bottom lip found its way back between her teeth. "I promised no drama."

Huh. Not exactly an agreement to stay away from me. I could work with that.

"So what's with it just seeming like she was throwing us together right there?"

Kim laughed and took a sip of her drink. "Either the wedding is truly making her crazy or she was dropped on her head a few times as a child."

"Are you sure she was dropped and not pushed? Maybe by a cousin?"

"I plead the fifth." She grinned then, and it was stunning. No, she was stunning.

"So... if I'm speaking with the best lawyer in California, I should probably know more about you. You know, so we can get to know each other before we have to walk down the aisle together." Since that had been Bridget's excuse. "Maybe during a dance?"

There were few people dancing, but the music was chill enough we'd have to touch. And man... did I want to touch her.

She scanned the floor, saw a few other couples out there, and dropped her shoulders. "I'm not sure that'd be best."

Probably wasn't considering what Marshall asked of me earlier and given Bridget's odd behavior a few moments ago, but it was only a dance. I slipped my hands into my pockets and rocked back on my heels.

"Why not?"

As I asked, her gaze dropped and then slowly rose, almost raking over my body with a heat in them that made me want to stand straighter and tell Marshall he could go fuck himself.

A cute blush rose on her cheeks before she blinked, realized I'd caught her eye-fucking me, and looked back at the dance floor. "Never mind. I guess it's okay."

Huh. Not at all the consent I was looking for, or used to getting, but in truth, it'd been years since I'd been turned down for anything.

"We don't have to."

"No. It's good. Come on." She held out her hand, small and dainty fingers, which was a word I didn't know I knew until right then, and wiggled her fingers, nails a neutral color. "Dance with me?"

She grinned, and all the heat from earlier was gone. I wasn't sure if her change was simply because Bridget told us to stay from each other, or because of me.

Regardless...

"All right, Kimmy. Show me what you've got."

SIX
KIM

Max was enormous. I mean, I shouldn't have been surprised given the size of Marshall, but compared to the rest of the Mikolajczyk boys, well... there was no comparison at all. He towered over his brother, the firefighter for Christ's sake, and his biceps? Larger than my thighs. So yeah, the last thing I needed my first night in town on a tropical island, alone, was to slide my hand into his *again* when the first touch of him almost brought me to my knees.

Thank God my skirt covered the knee wobble I'd felt when I'd tried to be polite and kind, holding out my hand when it was clear he'd totally zoned out to Marshall as he introduced me.

Hell, I wasn't even certain he'd registered my first name, but that certainly didn't stop me from standing, following him to the makeshift dance floor beneath a wide outdoor pergola and thousands of strung, blinking lights, placing my other hand at his hip, and start moving my feet with his.

His *large* feet. Which made sense. He'd need some serious-sized feet to hold up the rest of him.

"You can dance," I whispered.

We were an appropriate distance apart, his hand holding mine out to the side and his other above my hip. Formal.

"Surprised someone my size knows how?"

I glanced up, struck by the jut of his jaw, the arch of his cheekbones. There was the bridge of his nose, crooked, the only slight imperfection on him that completely fit. Then those eyes. Bright and gleaming.

He was *teasing*. Not the least bit offended I'd judged him.

"More surprised any man under the age of fifty knows how to really dance."

"Didn't think a bump and grind would fit with this song." He chuckled.

My stomach squeezed.

His hand holding mine tightened.

Gracious. I could barely manage a dance with this guy. How in the hell would I keep my feet while walking down a wedding aisle with him?

"My mom taught all of us. Used to watch my dad and her waltz around the house all the time. By the time we were ten, we were joining her in the standard box step."

That was sweet. Reminded me of my own, although I never saw mine dance. "They did?"

"Yeah. Living room, kitchen, backyard. There didn't have to be music playing, they were always dancing. They can do one hell of a swing dance too, but *please* don't ask them. It's embarrassing. Especially when my mom's wearing a dress."

I pictured skirts flying ass over teakettle and all the boys in the family forced to witness seeing the color of their mom's underwear, and flinched. "Gross."

He burst out a laugh, Adam's apple bobbing. Corded throat muscles tightening.

Glorious. That squeeze in my stomach spasmed lower.

Oh, man. I was in *trouble*.

It'd been months since I was with a man. Since Zack, there'd been a couple others. The latest being Trevor. We dated for a couple months before I realized I was bored out of my mind, and he was a bit of a snob. Yeah, we had a lot of similar interests. Same morals. Both of us practiced law, which was where we met. But where he went the corporate route, I went into family law. After hearing one too many comments about how I didn't need to fight so hard for the women I represented, I realized he was just the regular kind of entitled asshole I'd always hated. And truthfully, he never put a great amount of effort into pleasing me in bed.

Not like Max could probably do. And not like I was going to find out... although I had only promised Bridget a drama-free week.

I never promised to keep my hands off this guy.

"Yeah, so please. Spare me a weekend of misery and do not, once, mention swing dancing."

As he said it, I caught his parents out of the side of my eye, dancing. His mom laughed. His dad's booming laugh was louder, happier. He flung out his wife, twirled her back in, and both of them gazed at each other like they'd just met and were in the throes of that intense, initial lust.

"It's cool they're like that," I said, smiling at his parents and giving his mom a brief wave when she met my eyes.

"They're crazy. Loud. Insane. All of us are but Morgan." We were moving in a circle pattern, three steps, nothing too complicated, but the flow was easy.

"She's nice."

"If you can get her to close a book and have an actual conversation. It's a feat in itself."

"Really? Because I talked to her earlier and she was sweet. Although now that you mention it, all we talked about were books."

He chuckled. "Of course it was. See?" He'd maneuvered us so he could point with his finger outside.

There she was. Morgan. Sitting outside, glass of wine on the table next to her, book in her lap. Frankly, I wouldn't mind being her. It looked like a peaceful way to spend the night.

"Maybe she enjoys being alone."

"Gross." He visibly shuddered, refocusing my attention on him.

"Not for you, I take it?" I enjoyed being alone in my quiet house with nothing but music and a book. But that was probably only because I rarely had downtime.

"Hell no. I went from our loud, wild, and crazy house to college roommates. Even when we travel now, I beg for a roommate."

Right. The hockey thing. I had no idea how I kept forgetting whenever he set those eyes on me.

"Well that explains your moves."

"My moves?"

"Yeah. Your confidence and dance skills."

He chuckled. Shook his head, and seriously, this guy was so damn attractive I no longer knew what I was saying. Did I just call him *confident?*

"You think I can dance because I play hockey?"

"In my experience, most professional athletes are pretty good at knowing how to move their bodies."

Kill me. Kill me now. Those eyes of his, the color of my favorite scotch, glimmered and that smile vanished. Wiped away straight into a look I could imagine him showing during a different dance... a more horizontal one.

"I didn't... I didn't mean..."

He chuckled again and held me tighter. "I know what you meant, although I'm curious now how much experience you have with professional athletes."

Really, none in the way he was implying.

"I... um. Well..." As I stumbled, I caught sight of Bridget. Off to the side with her mom and Marshall at her other side, hand to her lower back. She was talking to her mom, but her eyes were on me and as ours met, she shook her head slowly.

She was possibly certifiably insane. Because like Max, I hadn't quite understood why she'd practically thrown us together earlier. Was it a test?

If so, we'd definitely failed.

He cleared his throat, and just like that, all the sounds of chatter and music rushed back to me. Oh dear. I'd gotten so lost in *him* I'd lost sight of where we were. Who was watching.

What was I doing? And had I actually leaned in closer to him? His hand felt hotter at my back, his own body heat scorching.

Yeah, I was attracted to the man, but this wasn't me. I didn't decide to have flings with groomsmen. I liked monogamy. Long-term, stable relationships. I'd never been the woman to have one-night stands and meaningless sex. For as much as I was opposed to marriage, sex without emotion and trust never did it for me, either.

A week with this man wouldn't bring anything good to me, and the last thing I wanted to do was upset Bridget.

Which meant...

"I should go," I said, and stopped so suddenly Max stepped on my foot.

"Oh shit. Sorry. But, what?" He was still holding my hip. My hand. I was still feeling his warmth and blanket strength.

"I should go," I repeated. "Thank you."

I dragged my eyes to his. I'd been having fun with him. Not only was he attractive and could dance, I could see conversation with him being easy. Not that we'd had much of it.

"Off the dance floor, to the bar, or...."

It was barely ten. Way too early for my night owl sleep mode to kick in, especially after the three-hour nap I had earlier. But that was exactly where I was headed. "I've had a long day. I should turn in."

"Then let me walk you back."

"You don't need to."

His hand was already at my lower back, escorting me off the dance floor. He towered over me, but most men did. Still, it wasn't his height alone, it was the breadth of his shoulders, the thickness of his arms and abs. Hell, all of him was *so much*. The warmth of his hand seared my lower back, and somehow my body followed him even if it was the wrong decision to make.

"I don't really care that we were able to rent out this resort so it's mostly private. A woman never walks alone, ever."

That was *sweet*, if not a wee bit misogynistic, assuming I couldn't take care of myself. I focused on the sweet part.

"I was shocked we had the resort to ourselves. I can only imagine how much my aunt and uncle had to dish out for this. Probably half of their retirement."

He'd always done well as a VP at a nationwide mortgage company, but when I learned we were having the wedding here, my jaw had hit my tiled floor. Hell, my parents and I could have shared a villa. Not that I wasn't enjoying my space, but...

"I paid for it."

"What?" I asked before I could reel back in my surprise.

"Yeah. I had Marshall and Bridget narrow down their dream location choices last winter once he started talking about doing something small with family only."

"Wow." It was dark and we were outside now, but I could hear the waves rolling to shore and the rustle of palm trees. "That was... that's incredibly nice of you."

Although with his career, he probably used cash for kindling in his fire pit.

Max shrugged his broad shoulders like it was chump change. "He's my brother. I wanted him and Bridget to have everything be perfect, especially given her history."

Okay... so maybe he was more caring than misogynistic.

"Yeah. Nathan's dad... I was so thrilled the day he signed over his rights and walked away. Better for everyone. And now I hear Marshall's planning on adopting him?"

It'd be the best thing to ever happen to Nathan. Marshall had been more of a dad to him than his own sperm donor had since the day he was born.

"Papers are drawn up. They need final signatures, but I think they're going to do it as soon as their marriage certificate is filed."

"That's so great. For all of them," I sighed and didn't realize I'd curled up against Max as we walked until I noticed I was wrapping my hand around his arm. Crap.

I released my death grip on him and pulled away, only to find my hand clamped in his. He didn't say a word and we found the paved, lighted paths that broke off toward the villas.

"I'm this way," I said, so much quieter because *he was holding my hand*. Like we were on a date. Like he wanted to.

What in the hell was going on?

And more depressingly... when was the last time a man did that? Ooze such confidence and just took what he wanted. They were all the things I despised and were turned off by in daily life, in my career. As a woman in law, particularly family law where I represented a lot of domestic violence victims, arrogant men who did whatever they wanted without thought of respect to their female partner, made me want to bash their faces in.

But at night, especially in my darkest, loneliest time, they were the things I craved the most—someone to take control. Take care of me so I didn't have to worry about chasing my own pleasure but allowing it to take over. Someone who could handle the dichotomy of my need for control and power during the day, but the need to let it go in the safety of my home.

When was the last time I was with a guy like this one? So strong, muscled, and big everywhere—in his attitude and confidence *and* his physical presence?

Never.

I'd never been attracted to men like this. They'd always turned me off.

And yet Max, this guy, who held my hand and simply *talked* to me like he saw me as a person, maybe, hopefully one he was attracted to... he was doing the absolute opposite.

I slowed to a stop once we reached my villa. In my small clutch

I'd had around my wrist all night, I pulled out my keycard as we neared it.

"Thank you for walking me home. Or, back here, I guess."

I swore his eyes gleamed with amusement in the faint light.

He glanced at my sliding door, the living room lit up behind the closed curtain because I'd left it for safety's sake. "I had a good time with you tonight. We'll see you tomorrow?"

"Bright and early on the boat." I grinned.

The itinerary that had been in my entryway laid out a week-long activity set, starting tomorrow with an all-day boating and fishing trip.

I was most excited about the fishing part.

"Okay then. Sleep well." His hand squeezed mine, and I glanced down to where they were interlocked. My fingers finding the spaces between his earlier like it was the most natural thing.

What in the hell was I doing?

"I will. You too." I flexed my fingers and he let go, but he seemed to do it slowly, hesitantly.

Silly of me.

I knew how I was with my mousy hair and small frame and barely existing curves, and I knew exactly the kind of woman he probably spent time with.

So I was attracted to him, big deal. Attractive, tanned, and muscled men were a dime a dozen in LA.

He loosened the grip he had on my hand and trailed his finger along the back of mine, tracing a vein that popped out to my wrist. I fought a shiver. Lost.

Gasped.

"Night, Kimmy," he murmured.

He stepped back and disappeared into the dark before I could tell him I hated the nickname Kimmy.

Because I was still focused on the whip of attraction sliding through me at the deep, sexy rumble in his voice.

"I'm so screwed," I whispered.

Later, after I'd tried to forget him without any luck, paced the villa, I took off.

"Fuck it." I whipped off my shirt and skirt. Shoved off my bra and underwear and then tugged on an oversized T-shirt and robe.

Grabbing my clutch with my phone and keycard inside, and a towel, I popped my AirPods into my ears.

The private beach I wanted to visit was quite a walk away, but screw it. It was dark, all my family and Bridget's and heck, even Max and Marshall's were still at the main building's restaurant when we left. No one was around to see me anyway.

With my flip-flops in one hand, my other holding my towel and purse, I pulled up one of my playlists made for relaxing and sought out the private beach.

My toes dug into soft, cool sand and I dropped the towel, gave a quick glance to ensure I was alone, and tore off my shirt and robe and flung them to the sand.

The moon kissed my skin and my feet sank into the wet sand as I moved closer to the gentle, rolling tide. The roar of the waves was quieter now.

Hair on my arms stood on end as the chilly water lapped around my ankles in a seductive caress.

My nipples pebbled from the gentle breeze.

So I told myself.

And when my fingers trailed my stomach, where I was alone, on a secluded beach where no clothes were allowed, I *might* have dragged my fingers through my wetness, thinking of Max Mikolajczyk....

Because damn.

He was unforgettable.

Which meant I was in all sorts of trouble for the week ahead.

SEVEN

MAX

"Max. Harder..."

My eyes flung open as she cried out. Hand tangled in her hair and my heart raced so damn fast I clasped my free hand to my chest.

Only... my hand wasn't in hair. And there wasn't a woman beneath me.

Instead, my hand was wrapped around my hard dick, and I'd clearly been pumping it based on the precum pooling at the tip.

Damn.

It was a dream. Had to be.

I had come home last night after walking Kim to her villa, grabbed a drink from the fridge, and settled myself on my patio only to see her hurry by later with a robe wrapped around her as she headed toward the nude beach.

Fuck. My. Life.

She wasn't anything like the women I usually got tangled up with. No, her wild, crazy curly hair that had brushed my hand at her lower back was long. So long.

Sexy. Natural. The curls were tight in some places, loose in others. It almost made her seem like a mess, someone who didn't care or was too wild to be tamed.

Yeah. I'd dreamed that was it. Her. Wild and untamed.

I liked women. All kinds. Still, I usually enjoyed women most who came to me, approached me with a confident swagger knowing who I was, so damn sure I'd choose them.

But one, what in the hell had that gotten me except flings with women who ended up using me. Or... throw me away for another player with better stats as soon as they saw them.

Not that I was still bitter about *that*.

And two, "Why in the fuck am I thinking of this?"

I was here a week. That was it. I went back to my life. She went back to hers. The flings were getting old and so were the initial conversations of asking about hobbies and likes slash dislikes and families.

I wanted something real. Like my parents had. Like Malcolm and Marshall had.

I wanted a woman to love. To take care of.

Which meant there was no point in thinking of Kim. Especially given Marshall's warning.

Hell, she was practically family.

Although that didn't do anything to dissuade my dick from thinking of her. Or my hand from gripping that dick. Or from spitting on my palm for lube and jerking off. And when I came, reminding myself I wanted more than a fling, it didn't do a damn thing to prevent the fact I shot my load all over my stomach thinking of the pint-sized woman who headed to a nudist beach in the middle of the night, and who was absolutely, unequivocally, not my type.

"Goddamnit." I cleaned myself off, used the bathroom, and threw on running shorts.

I couldn't push myself like I wanted, and the uneven run on the sand could be hell on my back, but if I didn't expel more of this energy, I'd be a raving lunatic later today when I had to be stuck on a boat with her.

And I was *never* ever going to think of the way she'd headed toward the nude beach last night, strutting her tiny little ass wrapped in a robe, phone in her hand, flashlight on to light the path. She hadn't even seen me from my spot on the balcony. Hadn't bothered to look to make sure no one followed her.

What would she have done if I *had* followed her?

Bad idea.

I shoved my AirPods into my ears, cranked up my music—heavy metal music that screeched in my ears and probably made my eardrums bleed—grabbed a cup of coffee, and once I tossed back enough to wake me up, I shoved into my running shoes and hit the beach.

The sun was already hot, bright blue cloudless skies above that melted with the water on the horizon, so I couldn't tell where one ended and the other began. The sun beat down on my shoulders and back while I stayed close to the shore. I had no idea how many miles the distance would be if I ran the whole thing, but I didn't have to worry about that once I hit an embankment of rocks that jutted out into the water, creating a natural pier. My steps slowed and my chest heaved as I climbed to the top. Beyond was nothing but trees and rocky terrain. I'd been jogging over a half hour, probably somewhere between four and five miles.

The run hadn't cleared my mind from shit. I propped my hands on my hips, and maneuvered through the rocks out past the shore, panting, chest heaving, and sweat dripping down my back.

Kim would probably love this place.

"Fuck," I grunted through labored breath and got the hell off the rocks.

I didn't need this shit. A woman slithering into my brain when there was no point. I just needed to stop thinking of all that hair wrapped around my fist, maybe brushing along my cock if she put her mouth on me. Holding that hair back so I could get a view of her lips stretching around the head of my dick.

As I jogged back to my villa, my calves starting to burn from running on the sand, and my shoulder starting to ache from swinging my arms, the sun rose higher and the heat grew hotter.

Focus. I needed to refocus on healing my shoulder and getting ready for the occasional headaches that kept creeping up.

I had a rare week with my brothers and sister and parents where none of us had to run off to work or I didn't need to hustle ass to catch a plane to get to my next game. There would be no holiday meals eaten two days early because I had a Christmas Eve game in Washington or Vancouver or wherever I could end up. No fires for Maverick. No construction emergencies for Marsh or Mason, and no finals for Morgan to be hitting the books over.

Not that it was stopping her yet from reading almost constantly. I'd long since been convinced that when Morgan opened a book, whether for school or fun, she slipped through a portal into another world.

My family was what I needed to be focused on. Spending time with my brothers, my sister, my parents. Sure, part of that was helping out Marsh so he and Bridget had the week and wedding of their dreams, but anything more than that?

Well, I needed to tuck those memories and thoughts of Kim into a little black box and give someone else the access key.

I mean, seriously. She was just a girl. Just a woman who I wanted to see...

"Yo!"

Mason jogged toward me on the beach. Out of all my brothers, my youngest one looked almost exactly like me. At least, me of four years ago. Cocky as shit, floppy sandy blond hair bounced on the top of his head as he jogged toward me. No shirt, just like me. His body wasn't nearly as defined, or large, but our height was the same, along with our light brown eyes. He was also the most like me in personality out of any of my family members, so I wasn't the least bit surprised he was out running, looking like he'd maybe started off in the other direction.

"Did you know there's a fucking nudie beach here?"

Of course. Of course, that's what he'd focus on. "Yeah." I slowed to a slower jog until we were both walking. Like I needed the reminder of Kim heading toward the clothing *prohibited* beach—not even optional. FML. "Clothing prohibited is the correct term, though."

"Whatever." He slapped my shoulder and then flung his arm over me. Because what I needed was my brother hanging on me while I was still thinking of... nope... *not going there....*

"We should check it out."

"I have no desire, absolutely none, to see your dick or your ass."

"Aww. It'd be like looking in a mirror, you know? Except one that makes everything seem better. Bigger."

I hip-checked him, laughed as he stumbled and had to brace his hand on the sand before his ass planted on it. "We talking about what you're looking at now?"

"You fucking wish." He leaped off the sand and wrapped his arms around my neck.

Why my brothers, any of them, thought they could beat me in a wrestling match was beyond me. No one had beaten me since I turned eighteen.

For being smaller than me, his strength took me by surprise, but it only took a few minutes of us play wrestling before I had him in a headlock, swept his feet from beneath him, and plopped his ass in the sand.

As I did, a shooting pain gripped my shoulder and I shoved my hand over it, rubbing it.

"Shit. Fuck, Max, I'm sorry."

I rolled my shoulder and kicked sand at him. "It's fine. But stay down there before you're really embarrassed."

"You suck." He kicked sand at my thighs.

I threw my head back and laughed, squinting as the sun blasted me in the face. "You wish, dipshit. I'm not the one wanting to go to a nude beach with my brother."

As I stopped laughing and held out my hand to haul him to his feet, a flash of red caught my eye.

There she was.

Kim.

Standing at the railing of her villa. Coffee mug in hand, bright yellow like the one in mine, resting her shoulder on a support beam, and that hair.

Goddamn, that fucking hair. All piled on her head like she'd just rolled out of bed. Her pajamas, visible beneath the opened hotel-issued robe, were the things nightmares were made of.

If you were me.

Fantasies, if you were anyone else. Red. Fire fucking engine red, lace and satin visible from the distance, and without a doubt, those shorts didn't conceal the small curve where her ass met thighs.

I swallowed down my groan right as Mason hip-checked me. A quick glance at him told me he hadn't noticed what, or who, had stolen my attention.

Thank God.

I'd never hear the end of it.

"Have you eaten?" I asked him.

"Was going to order room service. Charge it to the fucker paying for my room." He grinned shamelessly.

Not like I'd care. Or didn't expect it. "How about I take you and your girlfriend out to breakfast instead?"

Anything to get my mind off all that red satin. Curly hair. Tiny body.

It was going to be one hell of a long week.

Holy hot guy and brother on a beach.

What a sight to wake up to as I stepped outside my villa, planning on drinking my cup of coffee and sitting in one of the loungers before I had to get ready for our day on the boat.

My eyes had caught sight of Max before his brother shouted for him, and I was bewitched.

He had more going for him than his decent personality, his muscles, and good looks thanks to the package I'd caught sight of swinging in his shorts. Apparently Max didn't wear underwear when he ran. I wasn't sure if I should curse the heavens for sparking my libido to life so early in the morning or drop to my knees and thank our gracious Mother Earth for allowing specimens of men like this to exist.

And while on my knees....

"Nope." I popped my lips together. We were *not* going there. Not this morning. Not after I'd taken a seat on the beach last night, my bare ass and thighs to my towel, the sun long since set, the gentle glow of the resort behind me through the thick privacy of trees, my flesh, *all* of it being kissed by the air.

I had most definitely *not* imagined I was being kissed by something other than the sweet, salty air. Did not once consider the gentle roar of waves lapping against the shore could be rumbled, masculine whispers in my ear. And I most definitely, did *not* trail my fingers down my abs, my skin pebbling in the wake of my own touch as I found my center, wet, and absolutely *no one*, not a soul non this earth would ever know I brought myself to climax thinking of Max, wondering what could have happened had I not let myself be scared off the dance floor.

"Damn it," I rasped. My body already primed by the sight of Max and his brother wrestling in the sand.

They stood, and Max's attention landed on me. I felt that heat in his gaze as he slid his eyes down the length of my body from thirty yards out. The sun behind him made him glow like a Greek mythological creature, and his skin glistened from the heat of his run. It was possible I saw his stomach abs clench as his gaze reached the lace lined top of my pajama set and I took a sip of my coffee so quick, so large, it burned my tongue.

Good grief. Men like him should be locked away from the general female population—those of us that were single, alone, and could barely remember what the touch of a man like him could do to us. My thoughts alone were wild enough.

He could probably throw me across a room. How would he handle me in a bed? Or why was a bed even necessary?

Yeah, I needed to get out of there. No good would come from lusting after my future cousin-in-law's brother.

Was that even a thing?

I lifted my hand, waved, and as Max opened his mouth, possibly to call out to me, I spun on my heels and hurried inside.

The sliding door locked behind me, and I hurried to the bathroom. A lovely dose of ice water pouring down over the top of my head would do the trick to douse the flames he created.

This week was about Bridget. That was my role, ensuring she was happy.

My own needs could wait a week.

I WAS WRONG. Absolutely wrong.

My own needs could absolutely *not* wait a week. And thank the Mother I'd promised Bridget no drama instead keeping my hands off Max. I wasn't sure that would have been a promise I could now keep after this morning.

The boat we were on was more of a yacht than anything I'd imagined. Three levels with a huge, flat area at the back where the fishing was done. I had so far spent most of the time upstairs on the tanning deck. Down below was a full kitchen and seating area. We even had an onboard chef who'd been bringing us drinks and snacks to eat through the afternoon.

Anything I'd imagined last night, the play fighting I witnessed this morning between Max and his brother—Mason, I thought— none of it came close in comparison to the mouth-watering, mythical experience of seeing all *five* Mikolajczyk men spread out on the lower level of the boat, wearing only a variety of colored swim trunks slung low on their hips, casting massive fishing poles into the teal waters. Laughing. Slapping each other's shoulders that caused ripples upon ripples of muscles stacked on muscles to pop and delineate their spines. Their hips.

Those damn smiles.

"Pretty, aren't they?"

I jumped at the question, hands curling around the railing on the upper level where most of us women had been relegated once the fishing gear came out. Not from the men, but from my mom and aunt who declared, "Let's go, girls. Let the men do their thing."

Except I wanted to be *there*. Doing that *thing*... men not even included in the thought.

"Anna?" I asked, because I'd met them at dinner last night, but between Anna and Abby and all the Miko boys with the M names, everyone was blurring together.

"Abby." She smiled and then pointed. "Mason's girlfriend. Sort of."

"Sort of?"

She shrugged and kept grinning at what I figured was Mason's ass. "I mean, yeah. He's friends with my roommates. We've gone out a couple times, but we're not exclusive, or serious. He didn't want to show up alone and my roommates were all too busy, so I said I'd come."

"Oh." My brows rose. "Because last night you seemed interested."

She laughed, not a '*throw back loud, had too many drinks in the sun*' kind of laugh but like we were besties.

Yes... there was a difference.

"Oh come on. Who would miss this chance?"

I mean... when she put it that way... only a fool would. "Do you like him?"

"He's a good guy. He and Maverick both are. And he's hot as hell, don't get me wrong. But he's...." She shrugged and turned to the water, pushing her lips to one side. "Hard to explain? I don't know... there's a wall there I can't breach and to be honest, I'm not sure I want to."

"It's their twin-not-twin-thing," said Anna, as she approached us smiling.

"You too, huh?" Her back was to the sun and through my sunglasses, I had to squint to see her clearly.

"Those brothers. They're something else. But word is they have no plans to settle down. We've only been together for a few weeks, but like Abby said, no way in hell was I passing up the chance, especially once Mav told me Max paid for the whole thing. Mav offered to pay for my ticket but I insisted on at least splitting it. Hot as hell all those boys... but they definitely have bricks and mortar for walls. It'd take a woman strong enough to dig, sweat in her eyes, for *years* to get close to figuring those two out. I'll enjoy this while it lasts, but I'm not expecting to be around for the holidays or anything."

"Word." Abby clanked Anna's glass and the two girls laughed.

My eyes widened as I peered back at the men. They made it sound so easy. *Enjoy them.* Who'd be the fool to say no to that? I had been, last night—but I also hadn't been able to stop thinking about Max since then.

"Just them?" I asked because I couldn't imagine. Max had been open and kind. Confident. He was easy to talk to and he'd been a gentleman, sure, but walls? Layers? Bricks?

As if he sensed my train of thoughts, Max chose that moment to look over his shoulder. He was shoving his fishing rod into the holder at the edge of the boat.

I lifted my margarita glass as a hello and he grinned, shaking his head like I was a cute little puppy.

"Get your ass down here, Kimmy. Come and fish with me!"

Abby bumped my hip next to me. "Go get him, girl, and enjoy the ride."

The girls laughed.

I brought my margarita to my lips.

Max was still smiling up at me, a challenge in those eyes.

Danger flashed in my mind.

This was exactly what Bridget asked me not to do but when I turned back to her, she had her head tilted to the sky, a sun hat and sunglasses shading her face.

She said not to sleep with him... didn't say anything about befriending him or fishing with him.

"HEY," Max said, and I swore his eyes warmed at the sight of me, before dipping to the hot pink bikini I wore before coming back to my face. "Are you girls having fun up there?"

I was still trying to recover from the look in his eyes it took me a moment to process the question.

"I've been jealous, watching you men fish, actually. Teach me?"

"Happy to. Come here."

He grabbed the bait they'd been using. Some of the largest shrimp I'd ever seen tossed in a bucket with crabs. Alive. Pinching and climbing all over each other. Yeah, I'd let him bait the hook for me.

Once he had the bait on the hook, he handed me a black strap. "We haven't been using this, but you might need it. Do you mind?"

"What is it?"

"A bracing strap. Goes around your back so a fish or shark doesn't yank you and the reel into the ocean." His eyes gleamed with laughter.

My own almost popped out of my head and I glanced back at the water. Raging. White-capped waves sprinkled the teal water. "Um. Maybe I'll watch instead." I could swim, but I hadn't considered that a risk.

He laughed. "You'll be all right. We wouldn't let that happen. Can I strap you in?"

Oh... the thought that brought to mind... "Yeah." And dear God. My throat was dry. "Is there a water bottle in the cooler?"

They'd been drinking beers, but I had the sudden need for hydration.

He gave me a look, heated me straight to my already suntanned toes, and I swore his own voice was gravelly as he said, "I can do that."

I was strapped and secured in seconds and while I stood there, my hands wrapped around the reel, Max grabbed me a water and brought it back like nothing had passed between us.

But then his hand settled at my hip as he stood behind me. "Need my help casting?"

I needed his help for something vastly different. Hot damn,

how I had gone from *I'm not the one-night stand* kind of girl to *please, give me everything you have* in a night. It was the salty air screwing with me. Had to be.

"Please."

We casted. Caught nothing. Soon, I was involved in all the shit-talking with the brothers and Max never left my side or my back while I reeled in empty line after empty line, but still... this was so much more fun than sitting above, *watching* them fish. Now I had an up-close and personal view of the Mikolajczyk men in all their splendid glory.

None of them came close to Max, though.

I was gazing at his shoulders next to me as he bent down to bait his own hook when the tip of my line made a jerk so hard I stumbled forward a step.

"Holy crap," he said, and was instantly next to me. His voice was a deep rumble in my ear. "Tug it. Hard."

Oh dear...

I listened, brain muddled.

"Now reel it in. Nice and slow."

"I can't." I laughed at how difficult it was. I *caught* a fish. The weight of it bent my pole in half. I had to brace a foot at the back of the boat and found myself leaning back into the support strap at my waist just so I could reel it in.

"He'll fight for a while, keep at it. Need some help?"

"Maybe in a minute," I gritted out. Damn. This fishing thing was tough, and it took me a minute to realize all other action had paused.

They were all staring, gaping at the bend in my line.

It felt like hours, probably minutes, or seconds, but the weight of having to reel in whatever I caught made the muscles in my arms tremble.

"Help," I gasped, and his hands covered mine. His entire body encased me from behind, and together, we reeled in the fish. The guide was there, helping. The other guys crowded around and soon, there were whoops and hollers and *holy shits* exclaimed as my fish was pulled into the boat.

I dropped the reel from my hands and shook them out. Red lines marred my palms.

"What is that?" I asked, gaping down at the monstrous green fish with the odd-shaped head and tiny mouth, and beady eyes flopping on the boat's floor.

"Dinner," Max said, and I glanced at him, his smile so damn wide and happy I could get lost in it. "Mahi-mahi. You just caught us dinner."

Wow. To all of it.

"Seriously?"

"Hell yeah, I'm serious. The resort will prepare and cook anything we bring back."

Well, cool.

The guide and Max unhooked the fish, and then I was standing, holding some four-foot-long and forty-pound fish in my arms while the women cheered me on from on top of the boat and the guys congratulated me and took my picture.

It was whisked away into a cooler in the boat floor's surface.

As soon as the chaos muted, my hands were still shaking.

"I think I need a drink," I told Max.

"I'll come with."

I was so high on the moment, the insanity of the fact I caught a freaking fish in the *ocean* I didn't even stop to think about telling him I could handle it myself.

We left as the guys were casting their rods, determined to catch more so we could all eat dinner tonight.

"You did great. And that look on your face when you stumbled." He chuckled and opened a beer before handing it to me. "I thought you were going to fall right in."

"Thanks for thinking it'd be funny," I retorted and that first hit of a cool beer on my throat made me close my eyes and let out a sigh. Just what I needed.

When I opened my eyes, Max was still there, eyes on me, intense, licking his full upper lip before he brought his beer to his mouth and swallowed.

That bob of his Adam's apple. All those muscles, turning a golden tan from the afternoon sun.

It had to be sunstroke possibly making me forget all the bad things I knew about athletes. But I wasn't looking to date or marry the guy…

And before I could double think and talk myself out of everything I'd been debating since the moment I set eyes on him in the pool yesterday, I said…

"Listen. I know what Marshall and Bridget said, and I'm absolutely not looking for a relationship, but if we're alone…"

His eyes gleamed. Lips kicked up and *oh dear,* he was so freaking cute.

Max's voice lowered and that deeper tone rumbled right through me as he asked, "Are you suggesting a what happens in Tunstago Bay stays in Tunstago Bay-type scenario?"

Oh yeah, I was, definitely. It'd been the only thing I thought of. But now that he was there, in front of me, so tall and broad-shouldered and so, amused, well, my courage was tiptoeing the hell away from me.

"Maybe. Or more of a let's see what happens and no promises kind of thing, maybe?"

"I like my idea better," he said, and his voice had grown even lower. He reached out and dragged a fingertip down the length of my arm. Bare skin to bare skin and his calloused skin scraped against mine causing a delightful, and surprising, shiver. "What do you think?"

I had no thoughts whatsoever. Only carnal images. Flashes of pleasure and sweat and skin and passion.

But no sane thoughts.

"Um." I licked my lips. Suddenly dry. Desperate for lip balm and space and you know... a redo of the last thirty seconds where I became a moron would be fantastic.

"I'll let you think about it." His tone implied there should be no thinking required.

"You seem so sure it's going to happen."

"Yeah. You beneath me. That's what is going to happen."

"And if I like the top?" I didn't. It wasn't my favorite, but I couldn't resist challenging him, as if he just assumed I'd be beneath him.

"Then hop on and take me for a ride whenever you're ready."

"What about Marshall?"

"You promised no drama, and I happen to be very anti-drama. We'll be good."

"As long as no one knows..."

"Yeah." His thumb brushed along my spine and then his head was dipping, lips coming closer. I tilted my chin up to see what he was doing but he just chuckled, pressed his lips to the top of my head like I was a cute little child and when he pulled back, he was smiling at something behind me.

No... not something. Someone.

"Yo. Morgan."

SHIT. I hadn't realized she was there. Here. I turned, cheeks setting on fire. Had she *heard* us? I caught her face on her iPad screen, eyes bunched in concentration, and glasses perched at her nose. So much for no one knowing...

She didn't even look up at the bark in her brother's command. "What?"

"Come here."

"I'm reading."

"And if you're not here taking a shot with me in the next thirty seconds, I'm throwing your iPad to *Jaws*."

She adjusted her glasses and groaned. "Better chance of seeing a nurse shark here than a great white, but nurse sharks are bottom dwellers —"

"Can it, Einstein," Max said, laughing. "That wasn't what I meant and you know it. It's a *vacation*."

"Fine." She hugged her iPad to her chest and tossed off the blanket covering her legs. She had on a black bikini, a wrap tied around her waist that swished along the floor as she came our way. She smiled at her brother, a look that matched Marshall's almost exactly. "What are we drinking?"

"What else when we need to celebrate Kimmy's awesome catch? Tequila."

Perfect.

And I didn't even think to tell him how much I hated that nick-name. Again.

NINE

MAX

This was turning out to be the best vacation ever. A week with my brothers, bullshitting each other on the beach and boats. Jumping into the pool with my nephews. Spending time with my parents.

Bonus: I got to help my brother *and* Kimmy. People might have called me selfish, thought I only cared about hockey. But look at me, being the great philanthropist of the week. Let's be real, when she first approached me, hesitantly suggesting we *hook* up, she was literally asking for my help in getting off.

See? I was a nice guy, willing to help the masses—or at least sexy, tiny little brunettes with wild hair and lips made for being wrapped around one of my favorite body parts.

The only hard thing about it, and I wasn't talking about my favorite part anymore, was the *wait*. It was killing me. I couldn't touch her in front of Marshall or Bridget. I couldn't take her down the stairs where our brothers were still helping our nephews learn to fish, and I couldn't whisk her off the boat immediately for that private time she mentioned.

What if I like it on top?

Hell on earth was being forced to have that visual in my head, surrounded by my siblings and parents, and not be able to do a damn thing about it. And it was like Kimmy knew, because for the rest of the afternoon, she avoided me. She always made sure there were at least two people around us, never came within touching distance, but every time our eyes met, I could feel the heat and desire radiating from behind her dark sunglasses.

Needless to say, I'd needed a cold shower once we returned to the resort and headed back to our villas. The sun took its toll, and I crashed as soon as I saw my couch, so damn small my feet hung over the armrest, but I hadn't cared until I woke up, my neck sore, my bones aching and my sweaty skin practically plastered to the leather furniture.

After peeling myself off, I took that cold shower, took care of other *things*, and then dressed in a white linen, short-sleeve button-up shirt, and pulled on a pair of gray boxer briefs and navy shorts. Also linen, because it was hot as fuck down here and the linen kept my balls from sweating too bad.

Dressed, hair done, swept to the side and held in place with only a small amount of cream, I slid my phone and keycard into my pockets, my feet into brown leather slides and headed toward the restaurant, this time a quieter one, closer to my villa and my parents. There'd still be music, probably no dancing, but most importantly, at the end of the night, it'd hopefully involve ending it with Kimmy.

On top of me just like she suggested.

I WAS STANDING at a bar-height table, dinner now done—mahi-mahi for all who wanted it thanks to Kimmy kicking off an incredible afternoon where we each hauled in a fish—with an old-fashioned drink in one hand.

"I can't believe you came here without a woman," Malcolm said to me. His wife Shelby had just left to help my parents put Cooper and Nathan to bed. It was the first time I'd spent time alone with my oldest brother, and this was what he chose to start with?

I sipped my drink, gaze catching on the only woman I was currently thinking about, sitting with her parents and Bridget's.

"I'm not dating anyone. Why would I bring someone?"

"I thought you were. Marcy or something?"

"Maisy." We dated for six months. I knew going into it she was more puck bunny than long-lasting girlfriend material, but she'd been fun. Bendy. Adventurous. At least for a time. "And no. I broke up with her a while ago."

"Couldn't handle your traveling? I can't imagine that'd be easy."

Malcolm was more straightlaced and stuck-up than the rest of us. I blamed the fact he was the oldest of six kids and probably felt like it was his job to look after us. But the man was only three years older than me and acted older than our dad. Hell, even tonight he was wearing a suit coat.

We were in the Caribbean for fuck's sake, and the guy could *not* relax. Although I'd give him some credit, he wasn't wearing a tie.

I snorted. "Please. Not all women are as needy as Shelby," I teased. "She was a social media influencer, model, brand ambassador..."

At my explanation, his eyes glazed over. "A what?"

"Social media...? Never mind. You're too boring to get it."

"You're a jackass." He laughed. "So she didn't have a real job then."

This moron. "Just because she doesn't work in an office in a suit from eight to five doesn't make it not a real job."

I mean, for years after I was drafted, Malcolm still asked how my little games were going. As if making millions playing a professional sport wasn't a job worth doing. I was pretty sure my oldest brother was born with a stick up his ass that only lodged tighter the older he got.

He was a good guy. Just had so much tunnel vision on how life should be. We were raised in a small coastal town that'd be slowly dying if it wasn't for the tourism industry. Malcolm could never imagine doing anything else except go to work, probably fuck his wife missionary on Tuesdays and Thursdays and maybe Saturday nights after the weekly date night to the steakhouse or an Italian restaurant, but only if it was early enough she wouldn't be too tired at church the next morning.

Then lather, rinse, and repeat the next week.

Boring as hell, but he liked it so I wasn't judging. It simply reminded me we were complete opposites, which made conversations like this difficult.

"Anyway." I'd skip over the explanations he'd zone out to. "I started realizing she was only posting pictures for her job, with outfits she was paid to model when I was in them, then tagging my team, or me, or whoever else. She was with me for the increase in followers and that was it."

Years ago, I'd been burned enough to put up with shit like that. The girlfriend I had when I was living with a host family in Philadelphia taught me enough regarding that. It was a shocker, and a hell of a reality when I truly learned how deeply I could be used by people simply because of a public contract. Hell, if I could find someone who didn't like that I traveled like Malcolm suggested, then at least I knew they liked me for me.

"I don't get it," Malcolm said, and I swear, for as smart as the guy was, he could be so simple.

I took another sip of my drink. "She was with me for what I could do for her, not because she liked me. Why would I stay?"

"Well, was she loyal?"

I sighed. "Is that really what you like most about Shelby?" I asked him.

Hell, maybe he did. Malcolm had probably drafted a spreadsheet when he was twelve. A pros and cons list. A matrix system and boxes to check for his ideal woman. Shelby was pretty in an average, conservative way. She had a good sense of humor and was so sweet she could give me a toothache. I doubted she ever challenged Malcolm in anything and loved staying home with Cooper. Their life looked storybook perfect. I couldn't say I wasn't jealous from time to time, but that didn't mean I wanted their life. I wanted something more than dinners on the table when I walked in the door and a wife who always smiled because she was once told to make the home a haven for the hardworking man.

Hell no. I wanted a woman with her own passions. Her own dreams. Confidence in her own sense of self-worth she'd shove me in place when I overstepped. Calling me out on my own bullshit. I wanted desire and off-the-charts chemistry that wouldn't fade but only deepen with years spent together.

Hell... maybe I was the one who wanted too much.

As I thought it, Kim rose from the table with her family and headed toward the bar. She was wearing another long skirt, this one white. Fell to her ankles again until only her gold sandals and hot pink painted toes peeked out while she scooted around the tables. She had on a simple tank top, bright blue as the sea outside, and her hair was pulled back at her ears, all those thick wild curls swayed and bounced as she walked.

God, she was something else. So natural compared to women I was used to like Maisy, and yet even the way she walked showed her confidence.

She wouldn't be the woman who was satisfied with a life of missionary, but I bet she'd love the way I could take advantage of her with my size and strength while we worked that move.

"There's nothing wrong with loyalty," Malcolm said, and I swear his lips thinned a bit.

"It wasn't a dig at you. But it's not the *best* thing you like about her is it?"

"Of course not."

"Then why ask me?"

"Maybe because you travel so much out of the year and you

always hear about professional athletes cheating, or their spouses, that the travel can be a strain on them long-term, and maybe I want you to have something stable. Someone who makes you happy."

"So in your eyes, a woman who's loyal is good to stay with even if the only reason she has the loyalty is because of my pocketbook or what I can do for her? What about what I need?"

"You want a wife. Loyalty isn't a bad thing, Max."

God. We hadn't seen eye to eye since I was thirteen and surpassed him in height. My sixteen-year-old oldest brother had *hated* the day I rubbed that in his face. I might have even made him wrinkle his polo shirt while we fought over it.

I was also over this conversation. Sometimes talking to Malcolm was painful.

"Again, I didn't say it was. But I still want more. Passion. Laughter. Adventure."

"Those all fade."

I stared at my brother. The furrow of his brows, the tightness of his posture. Yeah, Malcolm was always uptight, but this seemed more. Worse. "You've been married nine years and only have one child. If your passion has evaporated and there's no laughter or fun in your home, then I'd rather be single. I'd rather be alone than have a lifetime of mundane living ahead of me. Think on that, Mal, or at least ask Shelby if she's good with knowing you only see her as loyal and stable. She's your *wife*, not your Golden Retriever."

And hell, even they had more happy energy than Malcolm did. As I thought about it, more than Shelby had shown so far this week, too.

But my brother's marriage wasn't my problem, and he certainly wouldn't listen to me for advice when I'd always been perpetually single.

And thank fuck I was, because the woman currently tripping my trigger was still at the bar, sending a surreptitious glance in my direction that only promised all the passion and adventure my body could take for the rest of this week.

I drained my glass, shook it to indicate I was getting another and left my brother to stew by himself. I'd never understood him. Probably never would, but that didn't mean I didn't love the guy.

"I'm getting a refill. Need one?"

He stared at his half-filled glass like he was in a different world. Hell, knowing Mal, he was probably back in his office at the bank rethinking spreadsheets.

"Malcolm?"

"What?" His head jerked back to me. "Oh. Uh no. I'm good. I think I'm going to head out. Go find Shelby."

Probably the smartest call he'd made all night.

"See you tomorrow, brother." I slapped his shoulder, forgot about him immediately and focused all my attention on the girl ahead of me.

The one who was glancing around with a nervous smile, and then I watched as she tucked hair behind her ear... which wasn't there because it was all pulled back.

Yeah. She was nervous.

With good reason.

I was about to rock her world.

TEN

KIM

I'd barely been able to engage in any conversation all night. From Abby and Anna's comments on the boat and then the *idea* I'd brought up to Max, and him instantly being on board, the only thing on my mind was scooping up my scattered nerves and courage to go through with it.

I mean, I didn't have to. Obviously. I could change my mind at any time. My prerogative and all of that.

Only, changing my mind wouldn't change the physical ache in my core every time I caught sight of Max.

No, it'd be good for my mental and physical health to see this through.

My nerves mixed with lust heated further with every step Max took toward me, and I tightened my grip on my fresh glass of wine as he reached me.

He was... so... *manly*.

"Didn't look like you were having a great time with your brother."

He rolled his eyes and requested an old-fashioned. Asked me if I wanted another, but since I had a fresh glass, I told him I was good.

"My brother and I," he finally said once he had his drink, "are too different to see each other's perspectives on things. Don't get me wrong, we love each other like crazy, but I'm pretty sure we speak different languages."

And yet they'd spent all day together on the boat, having fun. "How so?"

"Because I play a *game* for a living and Malcolm thinks I haven't grown up, and I'd rather take a puck to the face than have to sit in an office and be choked by a tie all day."

I laughed, unable to help it. "That's quite the visual."

He laughed with me before his expression darkened and sent a thrill to the very top of my thighs. One look from him and I was already pulsing in places. *Crazy.*

"You know what else has been quite the visual today?"

"What?" My throat grew tight and warm and I took a hefty swallow of my drink.

It didn't help a darn thing as Max's crisp amber eyes bored into my skin, traced the length of my body like a featherlight touch and he hadn't moved a muscle. If his looks alone could cause such a frenzy, what in the world would I do when he put his hands on me? Or that mouth?

"The idea of you being on top. Tell me, Kimmy. When you're riding me tonight, will you scream my name or just shout out to God?"

A full-body shiver rolled through me, impossible to hide, and Max smirked in victory.

I set down my glass of wine on the bar. There had to be more in his villa—because no way in hell were we going to mine when I was right next door to my parents. "I'm going to go."

His face fell, jaw slackened in surprise. Maybe confusion. I fought to hold in my laugh. "Oh. Okay. Did I...?"

Care that he'd come on so strong? How sweet of him.

I tortured him for the time it took to remember the look of his glorious body on the beach and the boat. "Are you coming?"

He set down his drink, pushed off the bar, and smirked. "Not until you do, sweetheart, at least twice."

"Ew. No. I despise nicknames. I'll allow Kimmy since you're so insistent on it, but never sweetheart."

"Honey?"

Gross. That was worse. "I'm not a food."

He chuckled. "Babe?"

I scowled. "That's only used for men who have so many women on their roster list they can't remember them."

"Ouch." He laughed and pulled an invisible sword from his chest. "Kimmy it is, then. So..." He leaned in, and I caught the faint scent of what had to be his body wash or shampoo. Mild, fresh with a hint of mint to it. And geez. The man even smelled *hot*. "My place or yours?"

We were doing this. We were absolutely doing this. I must have lost my mind on that boat earlier. Perhaps the sun fried my brain cells for me to think this crazy idea was worth mentioning.

But what the hell. Bridget and Marshall didn't have to know. There'd be no drama involved.

"Yours. Absolutely."

He glanced around the room. My parents were still there with my aunt and uncle, but I didn't see Bridget. *Perfect.* Most of his siblings had left as well. "Do you think anyone will suspect anything if we leave together or do we need to sneak out of here, be all clandestine and shit?"

"I figure no one will pay us a lick of attention at all, and if they do, I'm not sure I care."

"Confidence. I like it."

It was a stupid compliment. It really was. And yet still, the way he looked at me with approval, unashamed with my need or my desires or caring what people thought, well—a warmth pinched at my chest I hadn't expected.

Which meant I'd have to not be more stupid than I was already being.

This was a week. Five days really. This was sex and pleasure and nothing else.

Hell, we wouldn't have time to even get our hearts messed up or connected to each other. I could even ignore my personal ban on athletes and celebrities.

After all, there wasn't a chance in hell I'd fall in love with a player in a week.

THE RESTAURANT where we'd had dinner was off to the northern side of the resort, on the complete opposite side of mine. As soon as I realized he was leading me in the direction of the beach where I'd spent time thinking of him, my knees wobbled and I almost fell straight into the sand.

"You okay?" he asked, holding my hand tight and settling me on my feet.

"Yeah, just, you know... the sand. I um... nervous, I think."

He paused, glanced at the dark, quiet beach. We were on a path, hidden from the rest of the villas so we had complete privacy. "I don't want you to misunderstand, because I think your idea is a great one, but if you're having second thoughts, we don't have to." He shrugged and his easy smile returned. "Or we can have a few drinks. There's no pressure."

He was wrong. I was feeling pressure. In my lower stomach, there was a deep pulsing heat that would drive me insane if he didn't relieve it soon.

There was no way my fingers could do a better job than him.

"I'm not nervous about that." I bumped into him and then tugged him forward. "I was thinking about your villa. And its location close to the private beach."

"Ahhh. Yes, my brother, Mason, was awfully excited about that find." He cleared his throat and sent me a look that almost scalded my toes. Lowering his voice, he dipped down. Silly, considering we were alone. Until he opened his mouth and almost whispered, "And I wasn't going to admit it, but I saw you. Last night."

Oh. *Ohhhh...*

"You did?"

"Wrapped in that robe heading straight toward it and I'll further admit I sat on my patio and watched you. When you dipped behind those trees, it took a lot of effort not to follow you."

Well, thank God he hadn't. Who knows what he would have seen. Although, if he had...

"You would have seen me naked. Possibly thinking of you..."

He blinked. Blinked again and then his jaw jutted forward. "You made yourself come, on a fucking beach, naked, thinking about me?"

Oh damn. He sounded almost feral. Ragey.

"Was that... bad to tell you?" Because I would have thought it was hot as hell.

"Fuck no. Just means now I know how we're starting the night."

He bent then, and his hands hit my waist. In one rapid move, I was ass up, squealing in surprise, and then his large palm was at my ass he'd boosted onto his shoulder. The sandy path blurred as he hurried double-time, my hips dug into his back and my hands clung to his hips.

"I can't believe you're carrying me like this."

"Quiet, or Bridget will hear you shouting."

"Well shit. You know how to turn a girl off."

An echoing slap registered right before the lingering pain registered.

"Did you just... spank me?"

"Yep, and before you get all hurt over it, that's the smallest thing you need to be worried about me doing to you tonight."

Oh *shit.* That sounded fantastic.

"OH WOW." My head spun, dizzy from being upside down for so long and quickly set on my feet. "Your place is so much nicer than mine. Larger and everything."

His hands were at my waist still, steadying me, but I was peering around him to see a... "Stairway?" I gaped up at him. "You have an upstairs? Shouldn't Bridget and Marshall have this one? I mean, it's amazing..."

I was acting like the small-town girl who'd never traveled out of Philadelphia. And I lived in LA for crying out loud.

"Yeah. Marshall made me take this one. I'm still pissed at him for it, too."

"Why?" Because what the hell? How did Bridget turn down this place?

"Because I paid for them."

"Oh... that's right." I spun in a slow circle. I hadn't even realized he'd gone to the fridge. In his hand was a bottle of white wine, somehow, the same kind I was drinking earlier, and a beer in his other.

Obviously the guy had money, loads of it. I wouldn't even lie. I googled him this morning before the boat trip. He was currently starting year five of a six-year contract, making seven point three *million* freaking dollars a year. This was nothing to him. A drop in the bucket. Hell, the cost of this for a week for him was probably equal to the excitement I felt when I found a handful of quarters in my junk drawer. I did pretty damn well for myself outside the monstrous school loans for law school I'd be paying off for the rest of my life, but his income was excessive. *Millions.*

He cleared his throat, poured me a glass of wine and slid it across the counter. Clearly, he didn't want to discuss this.

"So, am I supposed to be impressed by that?" I asked, hoping my tone came out as teasing as I wanted it to.

His beer froze halfway to his mouth and then he cracked a smile. "Yeah. A little. But I'm hoping that my money is the least impressive thing about me by the time this week is over."

Funny enough. We could agree on that. I tipped my glass in his direction. "Me too. Cheers."

"Cheers." He clinked his beer bottle against my wineglass and tension mounted.

I was in his villa.

For sex.

Hopefully, hot monkey sex that would end with us both satisfied. Multiple times, if the Mother favored me at all.

Tension mounted, rolled in like the tide until it threatened to smother me while Max took a small pull from his beer, and dropped his gaze to my breasts, my stomach, to the skirt beyond that hid everything and he licked his lips with his tongue, catching a drop of his beer.

Oh dear sweet heavenly bliss.

The urge to jump this man and climb him like a sequoia was so fierce I drained the rest of my wine, set the glass on the counter, and took a step toward him.

This was my idea. Time to get to the good stuff.

I splayed my hand to his chest, and he was so tall I had to tilt my chin up to see him clearly. The heat from his body, the steady and strong thump of his heart, sent a shiver of anticipation racing through me.

I was going to have *sex*. Hot sex. Mind-blowing sex. Max's arrogant little grin and the gleam in his whiskey-colored eyes practically whispered it along my skin.

"I'm not sure where to begin with you," I admitted, my hand moving across his chest. He flexed beneath me, making those pecs of his I'd admired all day curve and beneath the brush of my thumb, his nipple hardened.

The man was a mountain of possibilities.

"Then how about I start?" He bent, his lips hovered inches from my mouth, and I inhaled the sweet scent of the beer he'd just drank right as his hands wrapped around my waist and lifted.

My ass hit the cool counter, chilling me through my skirt. The move put us closer to eye level and his lips were still *there*. So close to me, so full and thick and plump my tongue darted out and slid along mine to wet them.

His eyes darkened, dropped to mine. He leaned in and kissed the corner of my mouth before whispering, "Are you okay with kissing?"

Oh. Consent. What a gloriously sexy thing on its own. "Anywhere you want to kiss. Yes."

He chuckled softly, more of a warm rasp of amused breath right before his hand slid up my side, cupped my shoulder, and slide to my throat. One hand wrapped around the back of my neck, forcing me to tilt my head back.

"I plan on tasting you so often over this next week I'll have every inch of you memorized," he muttered and then his lips were against mine. Warm. The faint taste of beer mixed with my wine, but he kept the kiss light, exploring me and pressing his lips against mine, nibbling my bottom lip until I parted them on a surprised gasp.

The tip of his tongue slid inside and *oh dear goodness and all that was beautiful in the world*. Mother Earth *loved* me for this moment alone. His kiss was divine. Sparks of pleasure ignited as soon as I gathered my courage and met him stroke for stroke. The intensity between us crackled hot enough to start a wildfire.

"Oh," I whimpered, and my fingers pressed into him. My knees turned to jelly, and how did I already need him to hold me up?

This was a kiss, but what a glorious kiss it was. Quite possibly, my best first kiss.

"Damn," he muttered, tearing his mouth off mine, sliding it to my jaw, back to my ear. "I don't know how I'm so turned on already."

Thank the Mother I was doing the same thing to him. I was unraveling and we'd barely begun.

My hands went to his neck, then his shoulders. I explored his clothed body with my hands while he explored my throat and mouth with his lips until my fingers found the buttons of his linen shirt. I undid the top one, then another. Max moved back far enough to tear off his shirt, and then all that masculine perfection was on display for me and my eyes and my hands alone.

"Wow," I breathed, so absolutely blown away by the stunning perfection that was him.

He chuckled, hands at the hem of my own tank. "Same, Kimmy. Trust me, I'm feeling that same thing right now."

How could he? When he was so *much* and I was so... not. A flash of insecurity hit me. I didn't work out. I worked too much. I was small, sure, but that was genetics. His body came from hours in the gym, more on the ice and perfectly scripted diet plans. His was honed to perfection because his career demand it.

Mine was slim, but soft in all the wrong places because I ate well to keep fueled, but I couldn't remember the last time I'd stepped foot into a gym or done an ab curl.

But as Max lifted my top and I had to raise my arms above my head to finish the task and he dropped it to the counter, his eyes said he wasn't the least bit disappointed.

"I'm almost afraid of hurting you," he said, his finger trailing the strap of my bra, down to my breast where he outlined the edge of the satin cup. His gaze met mine and his lips twisted playfully. "Almost."

A heavy swallow thickened my throat. There were so few I trusted, who knew what I *really* craved and liked. I had a week with him. Might as well take advantage. "I don't mind a bit of pain."

Surprise darkened his eyes and his tongue swiped along his bottom lip. "Yeah?"

Words escaped me. My body was too needy with the promise in that look of his. I nodded, the only affirmation I could give.

He brought his mouth closer to mine and whispered, "That makes me so fucking hard. I can be gentle. I'll give you that if you want it, but I like it a little *more* usually."

His hand was still at my bra, scraping against the edge of my flesh as he trailed his fingertip over the swell of my small breast to the center of both. He hooked his finger into the middle, between my breasts, and gave the bra a quick snap.

"Oh," I gasped, and my fingers dug into his arm and the counter. And yet, a rush of heat followed straight to my core.

"You like?"

"Yeah," I rasped.

"Show me. Will you take off your bra and skirt for me?"

Oh God. It was a question, phrased in the gentlest of ways, but there was nothing gentle about the look in his eyes or the promise in his expression.

More a command than a question, and yet still offering me that consent.

I did the only thing I could.

I obeyed.

How in the hell we went from offering up a week of sex to *I like a little pain*, I had no idea. I was still trying to gather my bearings from that fucking kiss.

One damn kiss and my body was coiled tighter than I'd ever experienced. Could *ever* remember feeling with a woman before. Yeah, I liked sex.

I'd taken time to enjoy the buffet of women at my disposal over the years. I'd had relationships and short-term flings and one-night stands on the road after a loss and I played like shit and I just wanted to feel good for a moment.

No one... not a damn woman had ever sent my blood racing as hot or as quickly as kissing Kimmy had done.

Her eyes locked on mine while she reached back and undid her bra.

Glorious. Absolutely one of the sexiest things I'd ever seen. Her nipples were hardened points, and I ached to touch them. Pinch them. Discover how much pain she really enjoyed. I wanted to swirl my tongue around them, suck them into my mouth until she was writhing beneath me, and I wanted to see her naked, draped over my lap, or on her knees clutching the headboard while I surrounded her with my size.

Hell, she was so much smaller than me, finding positions that worked for both of us could be an exciting venture all on its own. Thank God my bed had a shit ton of pillows to help us out.

"You're beautiful," I murmured, fists clenched at my sides. My hands ached to spread apart her knees, tear off her skirt and underwear with my *teeth* for fuck's sake, but I wanted her to give this to me.

Give herself to me.

It was, after all, her spectacularly fantastic idea.

"Can you kiss me again?" she asked and rolled her lips together.

"Whenever you want."

I leaned forward and cupped the back of her head while I took her mouth again. She tasted sweet like her wine, warm and wet and the instant my tongue hit hers, the same visceral reaction hit me all over again. Later, I'd think about what this meant, outside sizzling hot chemistry, but for now, I was too lost in the tiny little sounds she made as I kissed her, the wiggling of her hips as she removed her skirt and kicked it to the floor. The soft, cottony fabric puddled at my feet like a blanket, and I kissed her harder, finally slid one hand to her thigh, and spread her knees enough so I could push in between them.

I bent down, whispering *"lay back"* while I kept my mouth fused to hers and she fell instantly, slowly, allowing me to cradle her head and arched into me until I lost her mouth and slid mine to her shoulders. Her small chest heaved with her breaths as her hands wrapped around my arms. Like she needed the anchor of my touch.

"Exquisite," I whispered against her hot flesh and then did what I'd been waiting for and took her nipple into my mouth. She bucked up instantly, back bowing off the counter and her thighs spread, inviting me closer.

Only a fool would say no to that. My hand at her thigh continued caressing until her muscles slackened, nerves dissipated and pure pleasure took over. I skated my hand up her inner thighs, to her center, right where a wet spot was soaking her thong.

I brushed my knuckles over that spot, earning an *ooohhh*, from Kimmy and then pushed the gusset to the side.

"Shit," I groaned. Her sex glistened with moisture. There was a small patch of shaved hair at the top, a beacon to the spot of her that would undoubtedly drive her over the edge.

My mouth watered with the need to taste her, but I wanted to prolong this. Wanted to get her over this last hump of her nerves before the real playing began.

I took her hand in mine, and she curled her fingers around mine but I kept moving, holding her underwear pushed to the side with one hand, I ran her fingers through her own slit. "Show me what you like."

"Oh God. I can't." Yet her fingers were uncurling from gripping me and then her fingers, two of them, pressed right to her clit that was swollen. As she began to rub herself gently, showing me exactly what she liked and how she liked it, I followed the path of her fingers, swiping my tongue over them, her clit, and down to her opening and inhaled. Her sweetness coated my tongue. Everything about this woman was perfection. Made me crave more. God damn *yes*. This was better than I imagined.

I might have groaned against her.

She squealed in surprise and pleasure. I knocked her fingers out of the way and slid my own two deep inside of her. She clung to my wrist and cried out, and my tongue went back to her clit.

"Oh God. Yes," she chanted, slamming her hands to the edge of the counter, and gripped it like she was fearful of falling off.

"I won't last," she panted, and her eyes were squeezed closed like she was embarrassed to admit it.

Please. Best damn compliment ever.

I bit her clit, the sensitive flesh of her hood, and as I did, a rush of moisture made my fingers even wetter.

Oh yeah. She liked the sting of pain. Her eyes flew open and her lips parted as another *yessss* fell from her mouth.

"You do like pain. Giving up control?"

She nodded frantically. Swallowed.

"Good. Put your feet up on the edge of the counter." I helped her, spread her wide open, stopped fucking her with my fingers only long enough to get her exactly how I wanted and to double check the curtains were closed.

The villas were private, but no family member of mine or hers needed to see this if they decided to take a nighttime stroll.

It took moments, and then I was bent over her, kissing her again, loving the way she kissed me back with the taste of her on both of us, and then I pressed two fingers into her again.

"I need you to take more, so I don't hurt you, okay?"

She nodded against my mouth, dug fingernails into my scalp, and held me to her. I added a third finger, twisted, worked them in slowly and as her thighs began to tremble, I increased my speed, using my thumb to keep it pressed against her clit.

"Max. Please. I can't... so much..."

"Yeah," I grunted. My dick was so hard and ready for her, but I wasn't joking. She was small. I was a big guy. I couldn't hurt her and ruin the rest of the week for all the ideas I was quickly planning for us. "Come for me, Kimmy. Let me see how beautiful you are."

She rocked against me, and I fucked her harder. I applied more pressure to her wet and swollen clit and as she shattered, clawing at my scalp and my back and shoulder, I thanked *God* Marshall had given me this villa.

Because there was no way in hell my parents needed to *hear* that sound coming from my room for the rest of the week.

No way in hell. It was all for me.

"YOU OKAY?" I'd slid my hand to her neck and brought her back up to sitting. Her eyes were still a little glazed over. Her hair a mess, coming loose from where she'd pulled it back. She was naked for everything but her underwear and had legs wrapped around my waist.

Kimmy buried her head in my chest, kissed my pec, and hummed.

"Can't speak," she said, muffled against my skin.

I laughed and slid my hands up and down her back. "That might be the best compliment I've ever been given."

I made her lose the power of speech and hadn't even been inside her yet, and based on how sleepy she currently looked, I was starting to doubt if it'd happen tonight at all.

"Come on," I said, and picked her up. She held on to me tighter, clinging to me so her breasts were pressed to me.

"Are you taking me to bed?"

"Yeah."

Her lips brushed across my chest and her arms tightened at my shoulders. Lifting herself up, she rolled her hips until she found my dick, still hard, still desperate for her.

"Fuck, Kimmy. I'm trying to be a gentleman here."

"Stop trying so hard."

I laughed, kissed her temple, and inhaled the fresh and coconut scent of her hair. I didn't know if it was from lingering suntan lotion or her normal shampoo, but all it made me think of all over again was that beach and what she'd admitted to doing on it.

Just imagining it was hot as hell.

We would *definitely* be exploring that beach sometime this week.

I toed the door to my bedroom open and flipped on a switch. The lighting from one of the lamps near the bed cast a soft glow over the room. The bed was freshly made and topped with white linens. I wrapped my arm around her lower back and held her to me while I bent down and tore off the top comforter slash quilt thing.

I lowered Kim to the bed, making sure her head hit the pillow, and hovered over her, keeping all my weight on my good side. Carrying her had created a dull pulsing in my shoulder but I'd deal with it tomorrow. She clung to me, almost unwilling to let go, and pressed her body to mine before finally relaxing and releasing her limbs.

"I kind of like the idea I can pick you up and do whatever I want with you," I admitted, trailing a line of kisses down her throat. I slid one hand beneath her ass and lifted her until she was pressed to my crotch.

The sounds she made only made me harder and watching her eyes roll back was sexy as hell.

Damn... I'd planned on a week of relaxing and instead I got Kimmy.

Definitely the better option so far.

"You need to take off your pants," she said, already grabbing at the sheets beneath her, writhing against me. "And get inside me."

I laughed against her throat and nipped her playfully.

"No hickies before the wedding." She wiggled, trying to get away from me.

"After the wedding?"

I'd send her home with my mark on her. I didn't like that one bit. I wouldn't get to see it fade, wouldn't get to replace it so everyone—man, anyway—could see she belonged to me.

Except she didn't. Wouldn't.

Shit. I needed to remember that. One night of good sex didn't make her mine.

"We'll talk then," she rasped and slipped her hand to my neck, up to my hair. It was short there, and her nails scraping on my skin sent a delicious little shiver down my spine.

"Deal." I pulled back and settled her on the bed again, tugging on her underwear until she lifted her hips. If she was nervous before, she wasn't now.

No, she watched every movement I made with rapt attention and then focused on me as I stood from the bed, unbuttoned my shorts, and shoved them to the ground. My dick, hard and longing to be free, pushed through my boxers and I wrapped a hand around the tip, sliding my fist over the drop of moisture there.

Kimmy's lips parted and her tongue slid along her bottom lip.

"Want a taste?"

"Yeah."

Fucking hot damn. She was *perfect*. I leaned over her and pressed my finger to her lips. As soon as she got close, her tongue darted out and swiped the taste of me away before she sucked my thumb into her mouth. I felt that warm, wet suction shoot straight into my balls and when she hummed around my thumb, my dick jumped.

"Shit." I shoved down my boxers and pulled my thumb out of her mouth. "You are driving me absolutely crazy."

"That's the plan." She grinned, stretched out her body like an offering and I almost lost all self-control but fortunately, remembered.

"Condom," I grunted and pointed a finger at her. "Stay right there."

I hurried to the bathroom and grabbed a box I always made sure to keep on hand in my toiletry kit and tore one off. The rest got thrown on the nightstand next to the bed and before I reached the bed, I was already covering myself, sliding the condom on, and then climbing onto the bed above her.

As soon as I did, she spread her legs, welcoming me. A quick check with my fingers showed she was still wet. *Dripping*, and as I pushed two fingers slowly inside of her, spread them to help stretch her out, her hands flew back to the headboard behind her.

"Yes," she hissed and arched into me.

I was dying. Absolutely dying to be inside this woman and

finally feel her. "Ready?"

She nodded and closed her eyes. That wouldn't do.

I wanted to see the awe and every look she made as I sank inside of her.

"Watch me," I demanded and her eyes fluttered open before dropping to do exactly what I'd told her.

I grabbed her knee and spread her leg far to the side, bending it as I pushed it toward her. The move would open her up and once I had her ready, I slid the tip of my dick through her slick, wet heat.

She shivered as I brushed against her clit. Gasped when I first pressed against her center. And then I slid in.

Kimmy bit her bottom lip, eyes widening. I kept one hand wrapped around my length, feeding it inside of her, and right as my swollen head was inside her, she let out the most rapturous groan.

I wanted to do this. Every. Fucking. Day. For the rest of my life.

Good God, the way this woman moved. Took. *Gave.*

As I slid inside her, I bent down, wrapping my arm beneath her thigh to keep her spread open.

Kissing her, I asked, "You okay?"

"So good." Her words were dry and raspy.

I was two seconds away from coming like a teenager who first glanced at a pussy.

Her hands released their grip on the headboard and reached for my hips. "Just... give me a second," she said once she was stuffed full of me.

I glanced down and *fuck.* I could see myself move inside of her. Pressing a hand to her lower stomach, another animalistic groan fell from her lips and she rolled her hips, finding that perfect spot she needed against me.

I pulled out slowly and pushed back in. My dick was slick with her and I had to bite down on my lip to stave off my own deep sounds.

"Ready for me now?" I asked, holding back as heat gathered in my spine. My lower back. My balls.

"Yeah."

I moved then, pushing inside of her with more force that had her hand flying back to the headboard. Later, we'd do other things. Her on top, taking all of me while she rode me. I'd flip her over and take her from behind. I'd be inside of her until she was so sore she kicked me out, but now, I wanted this to last. I moved slowly so as not to hurt her and ground my hips when I was deep inside to send a spark of pleasure through her clit. Every time I bottomed out, she vocalized her pleasure, and soon her legs were shaking.

I reached down and sat on my heels, fucked her slow and hard, and pressed my thumb to her bundled nerves that was so damn swollen and wet. I'd never seen a more beautiful sight.

"Come for me, Kim. Come on." I pushed against her and slammed in deep and as I did, she ground out my name as her walls clamped around me.

"Jesus," I groaned and had to slam a hand to the mattress.

A shot of pain flared in my shoulder but I ignored it. This was too much. *She* was too much. I continued moving through her climax as she gorgeously shattered beneath me and as soon as she was done, I slammed inside of her and came, grunted out my own form of cursing her name into her throat and fisted her hair while my balls emptied deep inside of her.

"Holy shit," I sighed, once I could finally form words again.

"Wow. You *are* big everywhere."

I laughed, kissed her sweat-lined throat, and held her against me. "I'm not really known for lying. Too damn playful for that."

"That was not playful." One of her hands skated up and down my chest and I shifted to my good side, elbow to the bed so I didn't crush her. "That was incredible."

"It was."

It really was. The best ever.

As she laid beneath me, sated and soft, I wondered again if it was just the sex, her size, or if it was simply *her*.

TWELVE
MAX

I woke up to a mess of tangled curls smothering me, the scent of Kimmy's shampoo all over me, and her tiny little body wrapped around me. One of her legs flung over mine, her arm draped over my stomach, holding me to her, and her head burrowed in the crook of my neck.

Outside of the throbbing in my shoulder from last night's activities... what a fucking great way to wake up.

I stretched slowly, trying not to wake her but as soon as I moved, she flinched, jumped a bit and as her head moved, she kicked her leg off me and relaxed her grip on my side.

"Sorry. Wow. So sorry."

I palmed the back of her head to keep her from scooting farther away. If I didn't have my other arm trapped beneath her I'd bring that leg of hers back over mine. "I wasn't complaining. I liked waking up and having you suction cupped to me."

She chuckled and relaxed. "Thank you for that lovely visual."

"Trust me, this visual *is* lovely."

"You're insane."

"And yet that's not what you said last night. Pretty sure you used the words amazing. Incredible."

She slapped my stomach and I grabbed her hand, resting it on my abs. "I was mind-numbed by your dick."

A laugh burst from me and echoed through the bedroom. Hell, yes. I liked this woman. Bonus points to her being great in bed. Her confidence definitely carried over.

She burrowed her head into my chest and groaned. "I didn't mean to fall asleep last night and I just realized I'm going to have to do the walk of shame past all your family and most of mine."

Ignoring the fact sleeping with me brought her shame... "They won't care."

"I care. There are some things my parents don't need to know, and if Bridget sees, she'll be pissed."

Damn. I'd forgotten the warning. Not that I'd agreed, but the last thing either of us wanted was to upset the bride.

"I have an idea and it only involves Morgan. Trust me?"

"Not any further than I can throw you."

Interesting idea. "How strong are you?"

"Max..."

"Okay. Hold tight." I pushed out of bed, covering her body back up as I reached for my phone.

"What are you doing? You can't call her. It's so damn early."

It was seven-fifteen.

I snorted. "Please. She's been studying since before the sun rose." Like I already knew would happen, Morgan answered immediately. "Hey. I need your help."

"With what? And why are you awake?"

Telling my sister about the insanely hot sex I had was never going to happen. "I need you to bring some clothes. Just shorts and a shirt, tank top or something simple. Can you do that?"

"You want my *clothes*?"

"Yup. Thanks, sis."

I hung up before she could ask too many questions. My baby sister liked to learn. Everything about everyone. Hell, I still wasn't convinced she hadn't heard mine and Kim's conversation on the boat yesterday. As a bookworm, she could be practically invisible. We all knew if we needed to hear the family gossip, it was Morgan who had it.

Hell, she probably color-coded and cataloged it in neat little file folders inside her brain.

Besides, I didn't need to wait and hear if she'd do this for me. She would. Morgan loved me.

In the bed, Kimmy stretched and groaned. The sheet fell down until one of her nipples showed, drawing my gaze to the rest of her covered tiny body.

The way she let me move her last night rushed back and while Kimmy still had her arms above her head, stretching up toward the headboard, thankfully attached to the wall so we didn't bang the shit out of it last night, I pounced.

"What are you...?"

"Quiet," I murmured and pressed my lips to the column of her throat. I braced most of my body weight above hers.

"Hi." She arched and tossed her head back into the pillow and her soft, small hand slid to my lower back while I teased her flesh with soft kisses and playful bites and worked my way down her body.

"Your sister..."

"Will be here soon, so you might want to come before she hears you scream."

"You can't."

"Bet." I flicked my tongue across her nipple, relished in the breathy little gasp she made and the way her nails dug into my flesh. "You should know better than to challenge me. I'm an athlete. I'll always rise to the occasion."

"That's not the only thing that's rising," she moaned and rolled her hips into mine.

Hell no it wasn't. I'd been hard since before I was awake enough to be aware of her body clinging to me.

"I'll take care of me later," I murmured, and went back to work, because now I had a goal.

A victory to win, and I always came out on top—even if Kimmy definitely took to that position with champion gusto.

I kissed her slowly, playing with her nipples. And fuck yes, her responses were otherworldly. Every pinch of her nipple caused a hitch in her breath, a clench of her thighs. And before long, I trailed my finger down to her clit. Her sex.

"So fucking wet," I murmured and pulled my mouth off hers to taste the rest of her. The salt of her skin from sleep and the air, the lingering scent of whatever flower shampoo or perfume she'd used yesterday. Morning sex wasn't actually my favorite. Hell, I didn't spend the night with many women. There was always something to do—a game to leave for, a practice to get to. But this? Lingering in bed with a woman who could drive me absolutely crazy in minutes?

My new favorite thing. Possibly more than coffee or scoring a goal.

Damn.

She was getting to me in less than a day.

I pressed a finger into her, felt the wet, soft walls of her clamp around me, and quickly added another. I was down to minutes, and I meant it. Kimmy's cries were only for me.

Like she knew my train of thought, her hands clamped to my shoulders and dug into my back. Her legs spread, thighs tightened and she rasped my name and a *please* and a *yes* and a *right there, oh holy shit....* And if I knew one thing about women, it was when they said *right there* it meant to stay the course. I twisted my fingers, rubbed them along that spot inside of her that caused those whimpers to turn guttural, and as she cried out my name, I bit down on her nipple and sucked hard.

Kimmy shattered, her orgasm an all-body experience of nails biting into my skin, hips bucking wildly and she bit down on her lip to stay quiet.

Which would not do.

I pulled off her breast and pressed my mouth to hers, took her mouth while I continued dragging her orgasm from her. She came beautifully, long and hard, and when she finally shivered and moved away from my hand, I slid my fingers out of her and skated my hand up her side.

"See? Told you."

I grinned down at her. She laughed. "Okay, Max. You win that round."

A knock hit the door and I kissed her quickly. "Perfect timing too."

She was still breathing heavy, skin flushed, eyes glazed.

"Stay here," I said, and pressed my hands to her hips.

Damn, she was small enough, tiny enough I could practically cover her entire abdomen with one hand.

My dick was still hard and I spent the quick trip to my door thinking of hockey stats and my late grandmother wearing her floral kaftan dress as she bent over our oven wearing nothing beneath... an image I never should have seen when I was ten and still haunted me. Like usual, it did the trick. With one last horrified shiver at that memory, I opened the door to my sister, one hand holding the clothes I requested, her other hand covering her eyes.

She knew me well.

"Please tell me you have a girl in here and aren't trying out something new because I don't want this shirt stretched out."

"Shut up, Morgan. And thank you. You can also peek if you want."

She dropped her hand and blinked. Without her glasses on, it was a wonder she could see anything anyway. "So?" Her eyes widened and cheeks pinkened. "Oh. Good morning." She grinned at me and lowered her voice. "The bridesmaid? How cliché."

"Love you too, sis."

"Have fun!" she called out and turned away. I closed the door and spied Kimmy in the kitchen.

"I thought you didn't want anyone knowing you were here?" So much for staying in bed, but if she didn't care about my sister knowing she was here, I didn't mind one damn bit.

She was filling the coffee pot with bottled water from the fridge like she knew it'd be there. Hell, maybe all the villas were stocked the same. "Morgan doesn't seem to be the kind of girl who'd gossip or share what she saw."

"She won't." I walked to the kitchen and set the clothes on the counter. "Here. I can finish the coffee if you want to put these on."

Not that the sight of her in my shirt she must have found on the floor was a problem for me.

Her brows arched at the clothes. "I still can't believe you had your sister bring me clothes."

"I don't know if I should thank you or be disappointed you don't think I'm a nice guy, but it's either that, or you head back to your place in last night's dress, and since you have to head past Bridget and Marshall's..."

She grabbed the clothes like they were on fire. "Point made."

"Plus, you'd look ridiculous running with me if you were in other clothes."

She sputtered. It was adorable. "I... what... you want... excuse me?"

I gently shoved her out of the kitchen and started filling the coffee filter. "Running. Walking. Whatever. It's gorgeous out and I want to spend time on the beach. And you're coming with me."

"I don't run."

"Then how else will you explain it if we're seen together at breakfast?"

"Now I'm going to breakfast with you?" Her hands propped on her hips and she glared at me. Looked playful enough. She might have told me she didn't like being bossed around outside the bedroom, but maybe still wearing my clothes made it acceptable. "What makes you think I want to spend more time with you?"

"You do." I only glanced away from her to hit the start button on the coffee machine. "Mostly because I know you want more of what I did to you last night, at least three times, and this morning..."

"Okay!" She laughed, whipped me with the shirt in her hand, and jumped back before I could grab her, yank her to me, and lift her up on the counter and eat *her* for breakfast right where I had her last night.

Damn... that was fun. Definitely should have used my mouth instead of my fingers when we were still in bed.

"Breakfast it is, you beast."

She spun on her heels and headed toward my bedroom. I enjoyed the view for just a moment before calling out, "You can call me a beast later. You can be my beauty. I can have you trapped, maybe restrained—"

The door slammed shut. But truly, the ideas *that* brief train of thought brought to mind.

Too damn bad I didn't have any ties with me. But I was a resourceful guy.

If she wanted me to be a beast, I could find other ways to tie her up and have her chained at my mercy.

Oh yes...

This week was going to be *great*.

I left all my independent, feminist sensibilities on the mainland.

That had to be the reason why I was now wearing Morgan's clothes. They were a bit too big, but Max had been right, much better than my dress, and I was walking with him on a beach toward one of the restaurants for a *morning-after the best sex of my life* breakfast.

This definitely called for a mimosa.

Fortunately, the beach was quiet. Everyone must have still been sleeping, maybe taking the morning to relax. As far as I knew, today was for ourselves, although there were a variety of activities we could partake in if we wanted. I had to do a quick run-through later for hair and makeup with Bridget and the rest of the bridesmaids, and tomorrow she'd scheduled a spa day for all of us, including getting our nails done, but the rest of the day was mine.

"Does Marshall have anything planned for the guys today at all?"

"We'll go golfing tomorrow, but nothing today."

"I was going to go snorkeling this morning. Would you want to come with?"

It'd been one of the few activities I'd really wanted to do, but going alone, or with strangers hadn't exactly appealed to me. My mom hated water and Dad would come with me if I asked, but who wanted to enjoy the Caribbean Sea with their dad when I could have Max instead?

"Hell yeah, I'll come with you. I wanted to do that anyway. Any chance you'd want to do the parasailing stuff?"

Suspended in the air with a thin rope and only the hope it didn't snap and send me flying into the waters, the parachute drowning me or a shark eating me?

"Not a chance in hell."

"Spoilsport," he teased, but at least he was good-natured about it. "Shit," he muttered and his hand briefly touched my lower back before pulling back.

"What?"

"Bridget and her mom. We can go somewhere else."

Oh shit was right. Because my aunt had already spied us and was waving her hand high in the air.

"Come and join us," she called out.

Bridget must not have been paying attention because she jumped when her mom yelled, catching sight of me and Max.

Her eyes widened in surprise before her lips pressed down.

Crap.

"Damn," I muttered, already feeling my scalp burn with embarrassment.

"Make up an excuse or run for it?" Max whispered, making me laugh.

"Too late. And I'm blaming you for all of this. I'm warning you now."

"I can leave," Max said, quietly next to me. "Pretend I just got a call or something."

Sweet of him to offer to save us an inquisition, but hell if I was going through it alone. "The hell you are. Your bright idea of going out for breakfast is what got us here. We could have had room service, stayed in bed... but *no*...."

"Room service. Damn, I was off my game," he teased and I knocked my elbow into his side.

We reached them and I gave Debbie a hug. The sweet scent of coconut tanning lotion invaded my nose so severely my eyes burned.

"Good morning," I told her and turned to Bridget who wasn't near close enough to either of us for a hug.

"You too, honey. What are you two doing out here?"

"I caught Kimmy when I was getting ready to go out for a run. Thought I'd share breakfast with someone instead."

Oh, how easily Max could lie. And that grin. Debbie smiled at him and gave him a hug and might have swooned.

"How lovely. Food is always better with good friends and family. We were just getting a table, so I'll go ask them to make it for four."

"I'll go," Bridget said, covering her mouth with her hand to hide her laugh as she caught my look of embarrassment. Of *all* the people to run into, it had to be the one who'd practically thrown me at him. "Be right back."

Considering we had the entire resort for ourselves, it wasn't like there was a wait and we were quickly seated at a table, menus in front of us, drinks requested—coffee and mimosa for me with a request to keep them coming, the mimosa not the coffee.

I earned a side-eyed look from Max at my order.

I shrugged and sipped the ice water with lemon. "So, what are you two doing today?"

"Greg and I are going to go play a round of golf after I eat, and Bridget and I meet with the florist later this afternoon."

"Oh, that'll be nice. Do you need any help?"

This week was about her, not my now raging libido thanks to the brute of a man sitting casually next to me. Like he hadn't just made me scream his name less than thirty minutes ago.

"Oh no." Bridget waved her hand in our direction. "I think you probably have enough things to do today. Mom and I can handle the flowers." She leaned forward and propped her elbow on the table, chin to her fist. Hand to God, she waggled her eyebrows at Max like a moron. "And you? What are *you* doing?"

At least she wasn't *too* pissed I was blatantly ignoring her request. But that meant playful Bridget would come out to play and sometimes, that was worse.

"Snorkeling. Laying low." His knee knocked into mine beneath the table. "Might see if I can get some of my brothers to go swimming with me."

"Oh. How nice and relaxing. I'm sure you've had such a *hard* night. Relaxing would be good for you."

"I don't know," Max said and a glimmer in his eyes that said *I was in trouble* sparked. "I think you'll find I have a lot of energy. Not a lot of time needed to relax, you know?"

Bridget blushed. At least she hadn't lost all sensibility. I stared at my fork wondering how much trouble I'd get into if I stabbed Max in the thigh with it. It was off-season, right? He'd have time to heal. "Well, since I have a Miko-man of my own, I do believe I know what you're suggesting."

The waiter returned with our drinks. My hand curled around the stem of the champagne flute. I could douse my cousin with it. Force her to flee our breakfast to shower off the sticky orange juice. But that'd only give her more fodder to use against me.

The breakfast from hell. Why'd I agree to this? Breakfast was my least favorite meal of the day.

I blamed Max's huge dick.

At that thought, I took a large sip of my mimosa and narrowed my eyes at my cousin. She was hellfire. Straight from the seventh ring of hell. Especially when she grinned like a lunatic and suggested, "Oh, I know! If Kim isn't doing anything, I'm sure she'd love to go snorkeling with you and your brothers."

Like it hadn't been my idea in the first place, not that she knew that.

"How about it, Kim?" Max asked, and there was that twist of

lips I wanted to smack right off his sexy, chiseled face. "Would you like to go snorkeling? That'd be fun if you don't have any plans."

At the question, his hand gently grazed up my thigh, fingers curling around to my inner thigh and stopping just beneath the hem of my shorts.

Yeah. Stabbing him was looking more like a possibility. I plastered on a fake smile considering the amount of embarrassment I was currently facing, although thankfully Debbie, sweet as pie, seemed to be missing all of it while she was still scanning the menu.

"I'll consider it," I muttered, and reached down to peel his fingers off my now burning flesh. "My day is free until we do the hair and makeup later, right?"

"It's yours to do as you please." She sipped her own mimosa. And that might not have been acceptance that I was going to do whatever I wanted anyway, but it sure seemed like it.

He grabbed my fingers before letting go, squeezed, and then turned back to Bridget. "Looks like we're all taken care of then."

"Yes," she hummed around the rim of her own mimosa glass. "Seems that way, doesn't it?"

"So what's everyone going to eat?" Debbie asked, lifting her gaze from the menu.

Bridget and Max exchanged the most salacious look I could imagine and then when they turned to me, we all burst into laughter.

I HEADED toward the dock where four boats, much smaller than the one we were on yesterday, gently swayed against their holdings with the waves. After breakfast, I'd said goodbye to Max on the beach before heading back to my own villa, finally getting a shower. There, I'd checked my phone for the first time since my arrival two days ago.

A plethora of messages awaited me. Fortunately, there were no emergencies and all of it was something other people in my firm copied in could handle. My assistant, Ethan, was a godsend. His first text to me had been **don't check your email. I've got it all covered. Just send me pictures of all the oiled-up and suntanned men on the island and we're even.**

But now, as soon as Max stepped off a boat, ducking as he hopped down to the dock, there wasn't a single thought racing through my mind except *Damn... this man is fine...*

No way in hell was Ethan getting a picture, either. I'd owe him one.

"Hey. You're here." He grinned, coming straight toward me where he slid my beach bag off my forearm.

"Right on time. Aren't I?" As I looked around, I couldn't find the boat's tour captain.

"You are. Let's go."

"Um." My sandal-covered feet cemented themselves to the wood dock. "What?"

"Yeah. Come on." He grinned at me over his shoulder and hopped back onto the boat. There, he dropped my bag and turned back, holding out a hand so he could help me get on board.

"Where's the captain? Or driver or whoever?"

He gave me that cocky grin and shrugged. His tanned muscles were already glistening in the sun, and those perfect V muscles at his hips dipped beneath his white and teal floral swim trunks. "You're looking at him."

"Excuse me?"

"Yep." His fingers wiggled, gesturing for me to come nearer, but nope. I was good on the dock. Feet mostly firmly planted on land. "Trust me. While you were doing whatever you were doing all morning, I came down here, talked to the resort. I was able to pay the captain and tour guide to give me lessons on the boat and show me where we were headed. He said it was safe."

"Safe." With a man who didn't drive boats for a living taking me out to sea where I could be eaten by a shark.

That was the very opposite definition of safe in my book.

He chuckled. "Yeah, come on. I got approval or paid him off, whichever, you know? Trust me."

He was so damn arrogant. So damn sexy with all that skin and that smile. "You have to be joking about this, right?"

"No. It's not like I didn't already know how to drive the boat. I just had to sign some waiver—"

"*I* didn't sign a waiver."

His smile fell at the same time his hand clasped on to the metal pole next to him. He scanned my face and I shuffled on my feet under his scrutiny. Was I looking like an idiot? Because... this was crazy, right? Resorts didn't just *give* their boats to people.

"I'm teasing you... sort of. The boats are available to rent if you can prove you're knowledgeable, and yes, I did have to sign a waiver as well as an acknowledgment I'd cover any damages. There's a map on board and some bobbers off the coast we can't go past. I figured we could snorkel inside the area to be safe, but if you'd really be comfortable with the captain and the original plan, I can go get him."

This guy... he wasn't mocking me. At all. A little more playful than I was used to with men, certainly, especially spending so much time around lawyers, not to forget the asshole athletes I'd school in court. Yet when it came down to it, so far Max *always* ensured I was comfortable. Consenting.

I was pretty certain there wasn't a sexier quality in men than that.

Definitely better than the gaslighting and feigned interest I'd received from others.

If he wasn't a professional athlete, I might just like the guy.

He pulled himself up. "I'll go get him."

There it was. No hesitation, no mocking, or trying to get me to just *get over it.*

He'd happily go up to the resort and change what he'd planned for us. For me.

"No." I settled my hand on his chest as his eyes met mine. "I want to do this."

"You sure? Because I'm okay with the guide and all. I'm not gonna lie, I thought being alone with you would be sexy and fun, but if you're not..."

I pressed my hand to his mouth. "I'm good. Startled, but honestly, yeah. This could be fun."

His smile was as wide as the island. "As long as I don't tip the boat, right?"

"As long as."

Shit. I'd thought I'd screwed that up for a moment when Kimmy's face blanched at the idea of me driving the boat. I kept my eye on her while I untied the boat from the pontoons keeping it from slamming into the dock. I stayed close to shore, that had always been my plan. The guide, Ramon, showed me an area where we could swim and snorkel that would ensure we saw lots of marine life. All safe, or at least very low risk of anything nearby that could harm us. It was the ocean. There was always a risk.

As the boat slowly sped up, Kimmy slid into the small bench seat next to me and tugged sunglasses down over her eyes. She wore a teal and cream ballcap, her hair threaded through the back opening into a bun-type wrap thing, and on the front of the hat *Jeep Life* was embroidered in a dark pink color.

It matched the color of her cheeks, and there didn't seem to be any hesitation or fear left in her.

"You own a Jeep?" I tapped the brim of her hat.

"Teal. Like my hat."

She turned to me, bright white teeth in her pretty smile.

Pink lips I couldn't resist. So I didn't. I kissed her softly and quickly before pulling back.

Her tongue swiped a path where my lips had been and she shook her head.

"Bridget mentioned deadbeats and abusers on the West Coast. Where do you live?"

She rolled her eyes and scrunched up her nose. "San Bernardino and they're not *all* deadbeats or abusers. I practice family law, mostly divorces and child custody arrangements. Some of them get pretty ugly."

Her lips flattened like she didn't want to talk about it more. I could understand that.

Didn't exactly scream a lot of happy memories.

"This might make me sound like a jerk, but you look too young to have been practicing long enough to be that successful."

"I'm twenty-nine." She peered at me then and slid her sunglasses down to the tip of her nose. "And it doesn't make you sound like a jerk, it makes you sound sexist. Would you think the same thing of a male player on your team who ended up being named MVP or invited to the all-star tournament his rookie year if he's like, twenty?"

Well, shit. She was right. I'd never considered that about players. Their age had nothing to do with their skill. And fuck... because that was exactly what she was saying.

"Point taken," I admitted and felt about as large as an ant.

She shrugged. "It doesn't make me mad, it's more irritating that I'm so used to it." She slid her glasses back up her nose and looked back at the water.

I pulled back on the accelerator to slow the boat as we neared our destination.

"I'm sorry. Truly." Because she was right. What a dickish way to look at women and their accomplishments. If someone treated Morgan like that, or belittled her based on her looks, I'd have to be physically restrained before they ended up with a black eye. Or worse.

As the boat slowed and bobbed on the gentle waves, Kimmy

asked, "Want to hear something that I think is funny but might make you mad?"

"What?"

"When I go to court, I wear this one pair of high heels. Like, *super*, high. Six-inch spikes to give me more of a height presence."

"That's bullshit."

"I know. Bullshit I have to, right? But that's not the funny part or the part that'd make you mad."

"What is it?"

She leaned back in her chair and stretched her arms over her head. With her bikini and the visual of six-inch spiked heels I now envisioned digging into my ass, I had a hard time staying focused on the conversation.

"I have a glass jar in my office that's full of men's business cards and phone numbers."

Excuse me? My eyes narrowed and my jaw clenched. "Okay..."

"They're from the asshole deadbeats and abusers Bridget talked about." She turned to me with a sly smile. "The men give me those cards after I've just kicked their ass in court. They see me in my heels, picture my legs, and those idiots actually still think because they have money or decent bodies, I'd actually want to sleep with them or be taken out for dinner all because they suddenly think I'm pretty."

She had to be kidding. "You know all the shit they pull."

"Men have a certain level of audacity that's surprisingly pitiful. I mean, imagine, you've just lost complete custody of your children and you now have a protective order of restraint you can't be within a hundred yards of your ex-wife, but you still think you're such hot shit you hand *me*, the *bitch* who just secured all of that, your number and tell me 'if I want a real man to give you a call.'"

Unfuckingbelievable. "Men don't do that."

She threw her head back and laughed. "Oh, the fuck they do."

"Damn." I mean, on behalf of all men, I wanted to apologize to her, but I'd just also been put in my place. She was laughing though, and I thought of that glass jar of cards and numbers she kept.

To remind her of how shitty men were?

Possibly. Mostly, I wanted to travel to LA, get my hands on that jar, and then get those same hands on every man who was such a massive jackhole.

"Come on." Her hand settled on my thigh, warm and tan and slim, and brushed up and down my swim trunks. "If I can laugh about it, you don't need to look ready to murder someone."

"You've thrown me for a loop with how crappy men can be to women. I *do* kind of want to murder them."

"Well," she huffed. "That wouldn't be good for your game, probably."

Assuming I ever got to play again, going to jail for murder wouldn't be good.

She grinned then, another blinding, full smile and I touched my finger to the bridge of her sunglasses, tugging them down so I could see her eyes. They were amused, bright blue beams probably brighter because of the sun and blue skies.

And all my fears of not playing again went *poof*.

"Wanna see some fishies?" I asked, because if she could find humor in this, at least for now, then I could let it go.

"Let's do this."

THE WATER WAS INSANELY CLEAR. I could see everything. Bright-colored fish, the vibrant weeds and reefs swaying gently far beneath the waves and currents. Tiny crabs and lobsters swam near the snow-white sandy seafloor. Bright orange and yellow seahorses bobbed along the light green grasses as they ate.

I turned back to Kimmy and pointed in front of me. She was behind me, to the left, but in front of us was a stingray. Its massive wingspan gently floating, tail swishing as it swam beneath me.

She swam toward me, flippers moving as fluid as the sea, eyes bright behind her goggles and a smile appeared around her snorkel. Once she reached me, she let go of her rope long enough to curl her hands into a heart in front of her.

In her bikini, barely more than scraps covering her most intimate places, she looked as sexy in her snorkel gear as we both looked ridiculous. She'd laughed at me as soon as we sat on the edge of the boat and pulled our gear on.

I wasn't laughing now. I wanted her. I couldn't remember the last time I'd craved my hands on a woman so much. Perhaps it was the thrill of the week, of knowing we were both on the same page to have fun and get laid and do whatever, but every time that grin of hers hit me, it was a punch to the gut.

Pointing my finger up, I gestured for us to break the surface. The water here wasn't that deep, and I swam up and toward a nearby sand bar until my feet hit the sand and I could remove my flippers and be out of the water.

"What is it?" she asked, coming up right behind me and pulling up her mask.

I was speechless at the sight of her. Water dripping off her what would now be cool skin, running in rivulets, creating an enticing path between her breasts, down the delineation in her abs. Running down her slim thighs.

"What's wrong?" she asked, because I was standing there, half in the water, my dick rising in my swim trunks and not saying a word.

"Max—"

"Nothing's wrong," I muttered and reached out, cupping her jaw.

Her eyes widened and lips parted on an "*oh*" right before I pressed my lips to her and pushed my tongue inside.

God, one taste of her and I was now hard as a rock and that tiny, excited little gasp she gave whenever I'd kissed her so far shot a spark of excitement through me. One damn kiss and my flesh was no longer cool from the water but burning me from the inside out.

It was insane, *insane* the things she made me feel. As we kissed, the two of us alone out in the vast water on a sandbar, she rolled to her toes, pressed her body against mine, I bent to kiss her until I was desperate for more.

"Come here," I grunted, an animal-like sound as I lifted her up.

She clung to me, locked her hands behind my neck, and kissed me back. No questions asked, no demands of her own as I carried her out of the water.

I dropped slowly to my knees in the sand and brought her with me until her sex was against my hard length and she instantly rolled her hips.

Goddammit.

"Fuck. I want you here, but I don't have a condom."

"Pill," she rasped, lips at my throat, seemingly unbothered.

I stopped her and cupped her face even as I rocked against her. "Are you sure?"

"We'll discuss the merits of me knowing my own mind later," she sassed back and claimed my mouth.

We kissed until her thighs shook and then it was a rush of removing swim trunks and bikini bottoms and laughter as it clung to our sweaty and sandy skin and then she was there, hovering over me.

I wrapped my hand around my dick and spread the tip through her moisture. I'd usually take more time to prepare. To make sure she was ready, but as Kimmy began sinking down on my length, her head falling back and eyes rolling to the heavens, I lost all train of thought except *yes* and *take it* and *more* and *come all over me.*

Her hands splayed over my chest, head tilted down. We watched ourselves where we were connected and I pressed my thumb to her clit even if she didn't sound like she needed the help. She rode me slowly, driving me mad with need, and then she took one of my hands and settled it on her hip.

With a brief hint of insecurity, she bit her lip. "Take over."

A rush of euphoria hit me. God, it was sexy as hell when she knew exactly what she needed. "Gladly."

I settled a hand on her back, brought her down to me, and with a forceful kiss, I pulled her down as I arched up. She cried into my mouth, and I swore her hot, slick sex grew wetter as I took her. Over and over again I thrust into her with barely-held restraint until she arched back, fingernails dug into my pecs and she cried out my name to the heavens.

She came, an unending orgasm that rolled into another, and when she finally collapsed onto me, wet, sandy hair all over my face, I pulled her off and came all over my stomach.

Good thing there was so much water around us to wash off.

We were a mess.

"So maybe it's a good thing you paid our guide off after all," I teased, running a fingertip down to his stomach, stopping just above the mess he'd made.

He laughed, husky and satisfied. In the sun, his sandy brown hair shined bright, and his eyes glimmered like diamonds. "I didn't pay off the guide. I bought a private trip."

There was nothing but the sound of the ocean and birds around us. The lapping of waves against shore, the sun heating my skin. It might not have been the clothing-prohibited beach at the resort, but we'd made *great* use of the sand bar.

"The tide looks like it's rolling out." From the time we'd been on the sand bar, even more was now visible. Our boat, still well anchored, bobbed along the water with more slack in the line.

"We should get back to the boat then. The guide said some of these waters can get really shallow as the day wears on." Max pressed his hands to his hair, exhaling heavily. "I just need to remember how to walk and think first."

A laugh burst from me. I bent down and kissed his chest. "You're funny."

"I'm the best." He grinned cockily up at me, peering at me

through squinted eyes due to the sun.

I didn't feel the need to stroke his ego any more than necessary. It was large enough on its own. Pushing off him, I climbed to my feet and gathered the snorkel gear we'd discarded on our rush to the sand. One of the flippers was pulled out into the water and as I stepped off the sand bar to retrieve it, Max grabbed my hand. "Let me. That drops off pretty quick."

"I *can* swim."

"I know." Still, he waded in, and he was right. One moment it looked like he was ankle-deep in water and in the next, it was to his chest. Fortunately, the flipper was his, so he tugged it on and I gathered the rest of our gear, while I pulled my own flippers on, and waddled out to where he was, bobbing in the water.

When I reached him, he took his mask and snorkel and kept them in his hand. "Do you want to do more swimming?"

I did. Definitely. We'd only been out in the water for what felt like a short time before we were distracted, but since I had no idea what time it was...

"We should probably head back. I still need to shower before I have to meet up with Bridget later."

"All right." He reached out and took my hand, carefully pulling me to him so I didn't trip over my flippers. "Thank you for today. It was a blast. All of it."

I laughed against his mouth. "Any time, hotshot."

"Hotshot?" Brows rose in amusement.

"Yeah." I turned to dive into the water and grinned back at him. "I've Googled you. I know your stats."

His jaw dropped and before he could say anything, I dove into the water. It must have only taken him a second to quiet his surprise because he was soon right next to me, matching me stroke for stroke, but where I was trying to race him, he was swimming at a languid, smooth pace. Of course he was.

The man had a foot of height on me and more power in his legs than probably fueled my old electric scooter. He tugged on my thigh, yanking me backward, and took off. Pretty sure I heard him laughing from beneath the water.

"You suck." I paused long enough to shout at him and double-timed my strokes. It was no use.

By the time I made it to the boat, Max was already on the deck, snorkeling gear tossed to the floor and his hands on his hips.

All that water dripped off him, dragging my eyes to the waist-band of his shorts. The *nerve* of him for throwing them back on. What I wouldn't give for one more look at him before the day ended.

"Get that thought out of your mind," he groaned and bent down to help me from the ladder onto the boat.

"What thought?"

"You wanted to see me naked again. Admit it."

No way in hell. What was he? A mind-reader?

"Come on, slick," I teased, running my hand down his arm before I danced away and grabbed a towel. "It's going to take me hours to tame this wild mess of hair."

He scanned my body slowly, heating me more than the hot sun. "I like your hair wild."

"It's an insane mess and a pain in the ass to take care of."

"It's sexy."

He sounded so certain of it, I paused, mid-motion of wrapping a beach towel around me.

"Yeah?"

"I mean, *you're* sexy. But that hair? It was the first thing I noticed about you. Definitely hot."

Huh. I'd spent so much time hating my hair, the curls, the time it took to manage. I'd never considered it could be a positive attribute. I had also never had a guy admit to liking it so much. One more thing that made Max different than most I knew. I went to him and rolled to my toes. He was so tall, I could barely kiss his chin, but he leaned down, and met me halfway. "Thanks, Max. I think all of you is sexy, too."

He chuckled. "Even my stats?"

"Even those."

I WAS EXHAUSTED as I found the resort's spa and salon, a small building near the main lodge. After spending the day on the boat, the sex, and returning, Max walked me to my villa.

He gave me a kiss that melted straight to my toes and made them dig into the sand, cupped my jaw, and grinned down at me.

God. Even suntanned and sex-tired, he was still so *goddamn* sexy. It was unraveling me. Twisting me up inside.

I wasn't sure if continuing this for the rest of the week was the best idea. Every time I was around Max, he surprised me with his chivalry, playfulness, and willingness to learn. To apologize when he was wrong. He was the perfect blend of male sexiness and humility. Add in his confidence and sense of humor and I was starting to forget all the reasons why athletes had always been off the table for me.

I'd barely had time to get cleaned up and wash and dry my hair, a feat difficult in itself when I had energy. By the time I reached the salon, I was fighting the urge to crawl up onto a massage table and sleep for the rest of the day. My feet might as well have been trudging through mud as I entered the salon.

Around me was soft chatter, even more relaxing music. If I stayed awake through the hair appointment it'd be a miracle.

"Hey!" Bridget called out from where she was standing with her maid of honor and bridesmaid. "You're here!" She turned to the brunette with long, shiny hair and a happy smile. "Kim, this is my friend Carrie. Carrie, this is my favorite cousin."

"I'm your only cousin. It's nice to finally meet you," I said, turning to Carrie. She was gorgeous. As tall and lean as Bridget. Thank goodness for Gretchen who was closer to my height. Without her, I'd look like a child as I stood up with Bridget.

I took the mimosa Gretchen handed me. "I'm glad you guys finally made it. When'd you get in?"

"Right around lunchtime," Gretchen said and leaned in to give me a quick hug. "How are you? Long time no see."

"Tell me about it."

She and her husband Paul had come with Bridget and Marshall to my family's Christmas dinner.

"Months." She nodded. "You look like you're enjoying the sun."

"And another Miko brother," Bridget teased, hip-checking me playfully.

"Shut up." I rolled my eyes.

"Oh... which one?" Carrie asked.

"You're married. Happily," Bridget said.

"So." She shrugged and grinned at me. "It's like masculine, alpha-male central at this resort. My husband Brad told me he was going to make me wear a blindfold I was drooling so bad on the way to our villa."

"They had to pass the pool," Bridget said. "And everyone was there... except for you and Max."

"The hockey guy?" Gretchen said and laughed. "Nice. He's *hot*. I saw him on the cover of one of Paul's *Sports Illustrated* magazines last year and he about had the same reaction as Brad."

"You're all too much."

Bridget tugged on my hair. "Is that why you have sex hair?"

"Impossible." I rolled my eyes. "I just showered."

"I knew it!" She threw her head back and laughed. "Where'd you two go?"

"Snorkeling."

"Oh, was it fun? Paul and I want to do that," Gretchen said.

"It was..." *so incredibly sexy. With hot sex. On the beach. Orgasms in the sand.* Yeah, this vacation was one I was going to remember forever at this rate. "Great. You're not mad?"

Bridget shrugged. "Promise me no drama. And I mean it because I know you get invested easily and Max is well... Max is..."

"A fling. One week only. We have absolutely nothing in common outside our vacation here."

If only I could force myself to fully believe it. Sure, we lived far apart. He had a job I'd despise. Those two factors were enough to make me believe my statement. It was a week. A fling.

Absolutely nothing more.

"Then I trust you." She shrugged and sipped her champagne. Perhaps that's why she was in a good mood. Champagne bubbles would do that to you. "So, you have to tell us. What's he like?"

"You're marrying his brother."

"Who cares. I'm with Carrie. He's freaking hot and besides..." She grinned shamelessly and tapped her champagne flute to mine. "I'm not married yet."

"And just because *we* are," Carrie said and wiggled her finger between Gretchen and herself. "We're not dead or blind."

They all laughed.

My cheeks burned and fled to the tips of my fingers.

Yeah, Max was hot. Definitely. His body was incredible and his facial features were pure perfection.

But it was the rest of him I was starting to like a whole lot more.

And that was dangerous.

"It's just a bit of fun for the week," I said, perhaps more to remind myself than them. "No big deal."

"Please." Carrie clasped her hands together around her flute. "For *all* of us."

They giggled.

I shook my head.

And then I laughed right along with them.

They were right. I could have all the hot monkey island sex I wanted, but it'd be smart to remember to keep my heart out of it.

Four more days and then we went our separate ways, probably forever.

SIXTEEN
MAX

"Holy shit. Your *hair*."

Smooth, asshole. Real smooth. I blurted it so loud, Kimmy jumped in her chair, book in her hand, bottled water next to her.

Her hand flew to her chest in surprise. "What are you doing here?"

"Your hair is like... down to your ass."

And straight as a needle. All those curls. *Gone*. I didn't know whether to cry or run my hands through her fresh, silky-looking new 'do. *Damn...*

"I know," she groaned. "It took for freaking ever. Hours after everyone else was done, I was still stuck in that stupid chair."

"You look incredible. Beautiful as always, but it's different too." I couldn't stop staring at her. It changed her, hardened her up, or made her seem more exotic or something. I couldn't put my finger on it, but all that wild was now sleek and sexy.

She chuckled and tilted her head to the side. "What are you doing here?"

Right. She'd asked that once.

I was there because after I got back from snorkeling, I ran into Maverick and Mason on their way to the golf course and joined them. Except trying to swing a damn golf club sent such a searing pain through my shoulder, I'd had to sit my ass in the golf cart, work on PT and then rest it with a sling while they gave each other shit. My mind raced with fear.

If I couldn't heal this then, what then? Those thoughts caused a raging headache, and I'd had to leave the course after the sixth hole to go home and nap like a toddler.

I woke up, my headache a low throb, pissed off and took a shower before meeting up with the rest of my brothers for dinner. Then, still pissed, I went for a walk, and somehow... ended up here...

Kimmy didn't need to know all that. She was a fling. Not someone who wanted to hear the shit going on in my real life.

Poor little multi-millionaire athlete. Can't play games. Boo-fucking-hoo.

Please. I didn't need the pity.

Instead, I flashed her a panty-melting smile—one that'd already worked on her several times.

"Waiting for you to invite me in."

She rolled her eyes. "Get in here. What'd you do today?"

I took the lounge chair next to her and stretched out. "Hung out with Maverick and Mason a bit... took a nap. Ate dinner with my brothers."

"That sounds like fun."

Eh. It sucked.

"It was all right." A yawn hit hard and fast, surprising the hell out of me, and I covered it with my mouth, shrugging it off. Damn, I was tired. Had to be all the salty air. "I grew up so close to them I miss them like crazy when I'm on the road, and being so far away from them all the rest of the year sucks about as much."

"I can understand that. It's the one hesitation I had before I moved to California. I love my parents. And Bridget. Seeing them only a few times a year is hard."

"But you like living in California?" I shifted on the lounger and turned my head in her direction. "I miss living so close to a beach."

She grinned and shook her head, looking out to the sun setting on the horizon. "I think I get out to the beach once a year. Even that Jeep I love so much hasn't been off-roading nearly as much as I'd like. My clients are... demanding."

She frowned as she said it, glanced at me, and then pressed her lips together.

I could figure out what she was thinking. Not all athletes were good guys. Most were, but the ones who weren't, dominated the headlines and gave the rest of us bad names.

Kimmy grabbed her water and uncapped it, finishing the rest in a few large swallows. "What about you? What's life in Las Vegas for you like?"

I closed my eyes as I thought about it. Hot. It was so damn hot there, especially during the off-season when I spent the most time at home. "Tiring. Sitting here right now feels like the first time in a year I've been able to relax."

"Yeah, me too." She reached out and playfully tapped my thigh. I was spread out on the lounge chair, fighting against my eyes drifting closed. Damn. I hadn't realized how tired I was until I sat down. I was so damn weird like that. I could sleep around anyone, hard to do it on my own.

"I don't want to sound rude, and it's not that I'm glad you're here... but why are you?"

The truth? *I'd missed her.* While Marshall and Malcolm talked about Shelby and Bridget and their marriages and while Mason and Maverick talked about Anna and Abby... I'd been there, thinking of Kimmy, except I couldn't say a single thing about how much I'd liked spending the day with her.

We were temporary.

A playful, sex on the table relationship, since we were both alone in the Caribbean.

I shrugged off her question and smirked. It made her crazy, that much I knew. "I didn't want to be alone."

"Because you hate it." She nodded like she understood.

"Yep. Figured you'd be alone too so I thought what the hell, let's go visit Kimmy." If she was as good of a lawyer as Bridget said she was, I imagined she knew I was lying. Fortunately she didn't call me out on it. She laughed softly, sounded like music and tinkling bells, and made my groin tighten.

I hadn't come over here for sex. I hadn't even been thinking about it and wasn't that a kick to the gut. I'd come over here to spend time with her.

"What the hell," she repeated, now smiling and showing off those full, stretched lips, which only made me think of other things...

I squeezed my eyes closed and turned my head toward the beach, groaning. "I didn't even come here to have sex, but now that I'm next to you it's all I'm thinking about."

"Well stop, because that's off the table tonight."

I peered at her with one eye. "Why's that?" Because so help me God, if it was her period, I'd be crushed. My dick would be depressed.

She cleared her throat and swallowed. "I'm a little sore. You know... down there."

My lips twitched. I mean, way to make me feel like an even bigger man. "Yeah?"

I chortled. Couldn't help it.

She slapped my bicep and made me jump.

"Don't laugh at me."

"Can't help it. I'm now thinking about how awesome I am to cause that and I gotta say, feels good."

"Well, I don't. You beast."

"Yeah I am." We were laughing, but I didn't want her *hurt*. "Can I do anything to make you feel better?"

Her eyes heated. Oh yeah. There were things I could do...

except… "Now who's thinking about sex?"

She laughed again and sat up. "Want to go inside and get a drink? I don't know if I have what you like but you can look."

"I'm good." I clasped my hands at my stomach. "Had one at dinner. You coming back out?"

"No. I'm going to stay inside to get away from you." She was on her feet, shoving my hair and head as she moved behind me. "Of course I am. Would you like some water?"

"That'd be great, thanks."

While she was gone, I took a minute to get control of myself. Just because we agreed to have sex and hang out didn't mean we *had* to do it every time we were around each other. The problem was we'd popped the seal. Now it was all I was thinking about.

I didn't have to consider game plans and watch game videos. I didn't have to bust my ass working out or count every calorie. I didn't have to remember dry cleaning deliveries that coincided with my travel schedule.

The only things I had to think about were everything I wanted to avoid. Would I play again? Would I recover fully? Is my headache really from the sun? When will this dull throb in my shoulder fucking quit? How long until I can hit the ice?

She returned and dropped the bottled water right on my stomach.

"Ooff," I grunted as it hit me and I caught it before it rolled right off. "Not nice."

She had a glass of wine in her hand and retook her place in her chair, throwing the blanket over her legs. With the quick peek I got of her short, skin-tight shorts and an oversized sweatshirt, she looked absolutely adorable.

"I miss the curls," I admitted. "In your hair. Don't get me wrong, you look good right now, but those curls of yours might be my favorite."

"It's hair." She laughed. "And you're crazy."

Growing crazy for her, yeah. Which was a problem. "There

actually is something I wanted to talk to you about."

"What's that?" Her brows pinched together as she sipped her wine.

"Earlier, on the beach?"

"Yeah."

"I didn't use a condom."

"You also pulled out and I'm on the pill."

"Still, we don't know each other well, but you should know I get tested frequently through the season. It's required, so you should know I'm clean." I *wanted* her to know. Because I hadn't asked about what she'd googled about me and found, but there was a hell of a lot out there and not all of it made me seem like the greatest guy.

She gave me a soft look that caused some strange burning in my chest. "I wasn't worried, but thank you. That's still good to know."

"Good." I opened the water she brought and we both turned back to the ocean. "You asked about what life in Vegas is like."

"Yeah. I mean, the Strip and strippers and all the shows and lights. Must be pretty crazy to be around that all the time."

I rarely went to clubs on the Strip. Maybe once or twice a year. "I live far enough off the Strip it's not a problem."

"Big high-rise in the city overlooking it all?"

She was teasing, but she wasn't wrong. "Pretty much. Haven't seen the need to buy a home when it's just me, but I want that one day. Lots of land too, to have a horse or something."

"You ride?"

"Used to when I was a kid. Our grandparents on my dad's side had stables. They took us out there on weekends and let us run free. Best thing about my childhood I remember outside hockey."

"That sounds fun. I went to horse camp once when I was ten or so, but that was it for me."

"Didn't like them?"

"I mean, I was ten and barely three feet high. They were terrifying."

We both laughed and I imagined that. How tiny she must have been.

"It was fun though. We just didn't have the access you did, so I never really got into it after."

I opened my mouth to tell her someday we could do that together and then quickly snapped my jaw shut. We couldn't. Wouldn't.

Because we had the week and that was all.

It was too damn bad I kept forgetting.

"I've got buddies on the team, Alix and Kane. We hang out a lot but not on the Strip. We rarely ever go there now."

"Where do you go?"

"Do you follow hockey at all?"

"Not for a single second of my life." She grinned, unashamed and honest. I liked that. I'd dated girls before who pretended to know about hockey thinking it'd impress me. Yeah, it'd be nice to talk to someone and have them understand but lying was an absolute game-ender for me.

"There's a guy on the team, Joey. He bought a bar a few years back. It's off the Strip, but we usually hang out there. And other than that, our season is crazy busy. We start pre-season in September, and the regular season ends in April unless you get to the playoffs, and then it can slide into June. Which doesn't leave a lot of opportunity for time off."

"I take it your team usually makes it to the playoffs?"

"Every year, we just don't always win."

"So you don't have a lot of time off, huh?"

If I wasn't mistaken, she sounded a bit sad about that. Disappointed.

That was probably me being a hopeful idiot, so I said, "Not a lot, no."

Although if she offered, I'd figure out a way to make the time. But she didn't. So I didn't.

Instead, I turned back to the water and closed my eyes. The

water lapped the shore. Palm trees rustled in the breeze and soon, my breathing slowed. This was nice. Ever since we'd gotten to the island it'd been *go go go*, and I didn't mind that, but sitting here, next to Kimmy felt *nice*. Relaxing. I exhaled a deep breath and soaked in the sounds and the warmth in the air.

Yeah… this was nice.

Next thing I knew, I was being gently shaken. "Hey. Max."

My eyes popped open to see a straight sheet of hair in my view and I followed it up to Kimmy. "Yeah?"

"You fell asleep. Come on."

"What?"

"You've been sleeping for an hour and now I'm tired. Come on." She tugged on my arm and I stood on my feet, still half-asleep. What an idiot I was.

"Shit. Sorry." I scrubbed my face. "I should get back to my place."

"Or stay."

Well, if she was offering. "Or I could do that. I'm sorry though, I came to hang out with you and I just crashed."

"I didn't mind. I just read for a while, and to be honest, it was nice not doing it alone."

"Good."

"Come on. You can use the bathroom. The resort-issued toothbrush is on the counter."

God. I was tired. My limbs were slow as molasses as I trudged down her hall, the villa so much smaller than mine with only a small living room and one bedroom. The bathroom was right outside of it so I ducked in and when I came out, I found the only lights on were in the bedroom.

Kimmy was in the bed, knees up, book propped on them, lightweight blanket draped over her legs.

"Did you lock the doors?" I asked.

"I did."

"Do you need to use the restroom or anything?"

"Nope. I did all of that before I woke you up."

"Thanks." I flicked off the light in the bathroom and removed my shirt as I headed to the bed.

I dated. I didn't mind relationships though they didn't happen frequently. Maisy was my last one and I was pretty sure she was the reason I hadn't had one since. Being used so blatantly had been a turn-off. Worse, it wasn't the first time.

I rarely thought about Charlotte and wouldn't now. Not ever again.

"He's better. He'll go pro and you'll be stuck in the minors. You can't blame me for that."

Fucking bitch. She was now married to one of the largest assholes in the league. He didn't give a shit about her. She liked the money and fame, but I figured that was all they had between the two of them.

I shook my head. It was fifteen years ago. This was why I tried to not think about Charlotte too much. Remembering how shitty she treated me made my blood boil. Maisy had been just like her only at least I realized it before she ran off with a teammate or some shit.

But getting ready for bed, with Kimmy already in it had a domesticated feeling to it. I wasn't even thinking of sex. My body was too damn tired, and it didn't suck.

I climbed into bed and turned off the lamp she'd left on next to my side and slid across the bed closer to her. I slipped my arm beneath the sheets and wiggled it until I draped it over her lap, between her book and thighs. "This okay?" I muttered, lips at her shoulder.

She grinned down at me and ran a finger through my hair. "Yeah... you want me to turn off my light?"

"I'm good." She continued running her hand through my hair, eyes focused on her book. Damn, that felt *nice*.

"Good."

I closed my eyes again and was asleep in moments.

SEVENTEEN

KIM

I woke up wide awake. There was no lingering sleepiness, no trying to remember where I was as the cream curtains with white large, green tropical trees on them came into my view. There wasn't even the surprise of a heated presence in my bed behind me. I was on my side, and while Max wasn't touching me, memories of last night rushed to the forefront. The way he'd simply shown up. I'd been so deep into my current fantasy read filled with all things faeries and vampires and wolf shifters, he'd startled me.

What surprised me more was how he didn't just take a seat, but waited until he was invited, and then how smoothly conversation flowed. Perhaps it was because we'd already been so intimate with each other, but I couldn't remember a time when I'd met a guy and had simply fallen into the getting to know you conversations with such ease and comfort.

And when he fell asleep, practically mid-sentence talking about his life?

Freaking adorable. So was his profile, the parting of his lips as he slept, and the quiet breaths he made next to me while I grinned at him and went back to my book.

My dad's side of the family flew in today and I knew we'd

spend some of the afternoon and evening together with them. But that was later, and before then I just had the spa appointment with Bridget and her other bridesmaids. Until then, I had nothing to do except ready my books.

And for a woman who'd spent the last six years working sixty-plus hours a week, a day of mostly nothing was as equally torturous as it was heavenly.

Behind me, Max stirred, brushing his legs as he moved and bumping into mine. That brief touch sent a new spark of awareness through me, and I carefully rolled to my back and to my other side. I didn't want to wake him if he was still sleeping.

He was, and even though his chiseled features softened while he slept, I still vividly remembered the strength of that body and all the wicked things he could do. My legs moved, core heating and as I did, a still, low ache reminded me in more precise detail how large and how powerful he was.

I was still sore, and that sucked, because we only had a few days left, and that meant I couldn't wake him up and have a repeat of yesterday morning...

But I could give him what he hadn't taken when I offered.

Reaching out, I slipped my hand beneath the sheet draped over his chest. As soon as I met his warm, muscled flesh, his stomach tightened. A tiny moan slipped through his full lips. I brushed my hand over his stomach, keeping my eyes on Max in case he woke up and didn't want this, but as I shifted my weight and came up to my knees, he only stirred enough to fall back asleep.

I pulled the sheet down, moving on my knees to get it out of the way completely as I resettled my hand at his lower stomach. He had thick hair across his chest, down the center of his abs. It spread out into a light smatter and I could tell he spent time keeping it shaved so he didn't look like a bear. But that would only make him more of a beast. A smile tugged at my lips as I brushed my hand further south, across the waistband of his boxer.

Another soft moan. Another shift of his legs and clench of his abs. A flutter of his eyelashes, but eyes that remained closed. I bent down, peering up at him as I kissed his stomach, peppered his lower abdomen with them until his breathing increased and as I glanced down, the evidence he was responding to my touch was tented beneath his boxers.

I brushed my hand over his covered erection and gave him a gentle squeeze, taking my eyes back to Max, only to see his eyes slowly flutter open.

"Fuck, this better not be a dream."

I chuckled against his skin and shook my head. "No. It's a returning the favor from yesterday." My mouth was already watering with the thought of having him, seeing how much I could take.

"Damn... you don't—" As he spoke, I pulled down his waistband, just enough to lick the tip of him. "Fuck. Never mind. Ignore me."

"Planning on it," I murmured, and grinned up at him.

"Take my boxers off."

He lifted his hips high enough so I could slide his boxers down. As I did, I played with his cock, thick and veined. It was no wonder why I was still sore, why that initial moment he'd slid inside me had been borderline painful. He was *large*. A girth so thick my fingers barely touched as I wrapped them around him.

"Yes," he hissed in a breath as I stroked him slowly, with little pressure so I didn't hurt him due to the lack of lube. One of my hands cupped his balls, heavy and full, and once he kicked off his boxers, I leaned forward, lowering my mouth to his cock. He watched me with rapt attention and at the last second, I slid my tongue down the length of him, around the base, up to the tip on the other side.

"Shit."

I'd reduced him to one-word curses in the span of moments. If I could, I'd give myself a pat on the back for driving him crazy. He deserved it since he did the same to me, and yet I wasn't the sadist he was, enjoying toying with me and stretching out the insanity.

With little fanfare, I brought my mouth to his swollen head and licked away a drop of moisture before sinking my mouth over him. And *oh goodness*. I'd been right. It was difficult to take him. I opened my mouth farther, the stretch creating a slight burn around my lips.

"Careful," Max muttered and his hand slid to my shoulder, up the back of my neck. He held me in place while his thumb brushed along the column of my throat. A molten heat coursed through me at the tenderness of his touch. Quickly followed by a rush of wet warmth at my sex.

"Take only what you can," he said, and that thumb on my throat drove me crazy. He could choke me or caress me, and I was pretty sure it was the dichotomy of knowing he could hurt me but wouldn't that turned me on further. I bent over him, and he gathered my hair in his fist before returning to brush that spot at my neck.

How was it possible I was trying to please him and he was driving me *wild?* With a thumb.

I quit thinking about myself, focused on him. I slid down him again, working with my other hand to take what I couldn't and as I bobbed up and down on him, his groans turned guttural, his hips strained with self-control.

"Fuck, you feel so good, Kim. Like that. Oh yeah..." He was lost in chanted praise and every word of encouragement he gave, proving how much he liked what he was doing, sent a jolt of pleasure through me until I could no longer hold back. *From the way he spoke to me.*

He had to be part magician. I let go of his shaft and moved my hand to my own sex, rolling a finger in that perfect spot. I jolted at the pleasure of my own touch and earned another *oh yeah, up on your knees so I can see what you're doing.* Followed quickly by a *shit that's hot* and *I'm close. Kimmy. Get there.*

Get there I was, faster than humanly possible. I pressed my fingers to my swollen clit, applied pressure and drew them in a circle. I came, gasping for breath around his cock, and sinking far enough to make me gag. And why did *that* feel so good? I took him deeper, whimpering around him while my own hips bucked, needing more, and soon his other hand clasped around my neck and his fingers dug in.

He came, deep in my mouth, emptying himself inside me while my own climax raged on.

Shit. How in the hell would I ever find a man who *did it* for me like Max did?

"CAN YOU STICK AROUND FOR BREAKFAST?"

After Max's morning wake-up, he'd wanted to return the favor. The look he gave me when I admitted I was still a little sore was nothing less than scalding. So much so that my cheeks were set aflame at the glint in his eyes, which definitely promised more soreness at a later date.

Then, I'd rolled out of bed, cleaned up, and when I was done, Max took care of himself while I got coffee ready. I was sipping on my first cup from the Keurig maker, his just finished brewing, and flipped through the room service menu.

There was no way in hell I was having a repeat of yesterday morning and running into my aunt, cousin, or even my own parents. The rest of our family, uncles, and grandparents, what little we had or who had been able to make the wedding, were arriving this afternoon anyway so there were still several days of a ton of family around coming up.

"Have I mentioned how much I miss the curls?" he asked and slipped by me in the narrow galley kitchen. As he did, his hand brushed along my lower back from hip to hip and his head tipped down, pressing a kiss to the top of my head.

The move was so comforting, along with him smirking at me over the rim of his coffee mug, a warm tremor cascaded through me. How very domestic of us, for people who didn't know each other three days ago.

And wouldn't... in four more. I pushed that thought out of my mind and tapped the menu. "You've mentioned the hair, yes. But you haven't yet answered my question about breakfast."

I forced myself not to think about how he'd never see the curls again. Once I finally washed it after the wedding, I'd be boarding a plane and heading back to real life. The curly-haired woman he met and decided to spend a week messing around with for fun was gone for him.

It's just a week of fun. Remember?

Right. At best, we could leave friends who created fond memories on a holiday but that was it. Heck, parting on good terms would be important given our connection to the bride and groom. It was possible I'd see him again sometime.

"I can't get breakfast." If I wasn't mistaken, that was disappointment tugging on his features. "I need to get to the course soon. What are you doing today?"

"I have a spa appointment for Bridget before lunch." I took a drink of coffee and pushed down my own disappointment. Before he'd crashed last night, I'd enjoyed talking with him. Had so many more things I wanted to know... "My grandparents and some other aunts and uncles come in today so we'll probably be close by, hanging out at one of the pools and doing dinner later."

"Good."

"Good?"

"Yeah, because then hopefully you'll be rested up and relaxed before I come to you later, because if you're up for it, I'm definitely going to want to see you."

Oh, I could look forward to that. Hopefully, I'd spend the day getting my head on straight. "Game on, hotshot."

EIGHTEEN

MAX

My phone rang as I climbed out of the golf cart at the practice green. After this morning with Kimmy, I almost felt like a dick for not sticking around to have breakfast with her and jetting so fast. But after the morning, the way I'd fallen asleep on the patio with her, how much I *felt* whenever I saw her... yeah, I'd needed to cool things down. Take a break. Get my head on straight so I could enjoy the rest of my week with the right mindset.

Unfortunately another morning run and a cold shower after hadn't distracted me from her at all. Mostly because the run had been short. The damn sun had given me another headache even with my sunglasses on.

Or possibly it was because I couldn't stop thinking about Kimmy that had sent me racing back to the cold shower. There was something so *perfect* about the woman. Outside her zip code and demanding career that would most likely ensure we never spent time together, in addition to the difficulties I brought all on my own.

After I couldn't concentrate, couldn't sit, I headed to the golf course well before my brothers and Dad would meet up with us.

I swung the putter in the air and grinned at the name on my

phone, seeing Alix Halvrick's name light up the screen with a call. He'd been grumpy when I refused to write him in as my plus one so he could spend the week with me.

Apparently he wanted a bridesmaid of his own.

Fat fucking chance of that happening. And really, thank God. Because Alix was one good-looking dude. I'd hate to have had to punch him and mess up his pretty face for a chance at Kimmy.

"Yo, dude. What's going on?"

It was only ten here which meant it was three hours earlier in Las Vegas. Unless he was with his family in his home country of Switzerland. He spent time there every summer.

"What? Can't a man wake up missing his big brother and want to say hello?"

His accent was always thicker in the morning, fading some during the day, but it also became more apparent when he was stressed.

"What is it?"

I loosened the grip on my putter I hadn't realized I'd clenched.

"Nothing. I want to see how you were doing. Thinking about you is all."

Typically I'd laugh. Call him on his big brother bullshit, but there was concern in his voice.

"I'm okay. Not a lot of pain."

"You are lying."

I scowled at him and the damn putter in my hand. The only fucking golf club I could swing. I'd bail on the golf outing if I didn't want to spend time with my family.

"Fine. It's sore, but it's fine. I'm doing my physical therapy like a good little boy and it's okay."

Except I had the sling in my golf bag. After my shower, it'd hurt more than it should have. Not a great sign but maybe I'd just slept on it wrong. The beds were comfortable, the pillows sucked.

"Good. That is good. I keep thinking about that day."

"It's not your fault, Alix. I've told you that a thousand times." Even if I had blamed him for it.

My fall was an accident, reaching too far for a grip and slipping. Yeah, we'd been wearing equipment, but that didn't mean when I'd had to hold on with one hand while my body swung because I slipped and my head crashed into the rock, it was his fault. The hike might have been, but we'd done it tons of times together.

"I am still worried. If you can't play—"

"I will. By Christmas at the latest. Lots of season left after that. Tell me what's new with you," I said, my voice angrier than I intended but I didn't apologize.

He knew it pissed me off to think about not playing at all. Probably why his sigh was thick and heavy. Yeah, I knew the warnings. My recurring headaches were bad enough. That just meant I needed more rest. Sometimes concussions took longer to heal.

It was the shoulder that was the greater concern, and I wasn't leaving the goddamn league over a fucking rotator cuff.

"I arrived home last night and from the time change, I could not sleep. Thought I would see how you are doing before I go work out with Kane. He says hello, by the way."

Training. Working out. All the things the guys on my team could do without me. Shouldn't have pissed me off. Shouldn't have made me want to chuck my putter as far as I could…which wasn't far given my damn shoulder.

"How is he?" I forced myself to ask. If Alix noted the anger in my voice, the jealousy, he didn't say anything.

"Quiet. Quieter than usual. I don't know."

Shit. "Ava?"

Kane's college sweetheart turned wife left him three years ago. He came home from an away trip and the house they'd owned was empty of her things. He hadn't been the same since. We'd all thought when he sold their home and moved into a townhome he was ready to move on.

We were wrong. The man hadn't dated anyone since Ava left and from what he'd told us, which wasn't much, she'd found a new man back in their hometown. Apparently Ava was now happy. Kane on the other hand, grew more miserable every year.

"We need to find a way to get him back into the dating world," I muttered, more to myself than Alix. "He's the kind of guy who needs a woman. Wants one."

"Maybe. I will see if I can get him to talk today. Maybe plan a night out or something."

"Good." As the team captain, we needed him. He might have been quiet, but he was a hell of a leader, both on and off the ice.

"So," Alix chuckled. "Now that work is out of the way, tell me...how is vacation? Have you scored? In other ways?"

Flashes of this morning and yesterday blared bright in my mind, and I must have waited too long because he assumed correctly. "You did."

"It's all in good fun." It wasn't uncommon for us to trade stories back and forth, but if he was hunting, he wouldn't get his kill this time. There was nothing about Kimmy I wanted shared. "How'd your trip home go?"

He sighed again. "Not so good. My dad is... more difficult than normal."

"Shit. Really?"

Alix's mom died after he was already in the States playing hockey. He'd talked before about how it was his mom who supported his love of hockey, not his father. His father believed Alix should be helping him run the bank where he was president. As far as his daughter went, he expected her to marry a man exactly like him.

Basically the guy was a dick, always trying to convince Alix to return to Switzerland and didn't give a shit what his daughter wanted.

"Yes. It is always *you have had your fun. It is now time to be responsible.* Always the same with him."

"Damn. Man. I'm sorry. How's Arya doing?"

I tucked my phone between my ear and shoulder and practiced putting while Alix told me all about Arya. How miserable she was at home, but still relied too much on their father to do anything about it. We might have been guys who enjoyed playing the field, but Alix was a damn good guy, and when it came to family, we were both protective.

By the time Marshall and Malcolm arrived, Alix and I had switched back to hockey talk and when I'd be back home. I'd sank several putts all over the green and completely been able to push aside the jealousy that had stirred in my gut about Alix and Kane hanging out without me.

"Hey, man, I gotta go, all right."

"Fine. Fine. Have fun without me. But do not think I have forgotten about the woman you won't tell me about."

I chuckled. "Some things aren't meant to be shared."

"So you do like her."

Marshall pulled up in his cart and waved as he stepped out.

I did. At least, I was starting to think I did. I'd never shown up at a woman's place, unannounced, and crashed because I was so comfortable for sure.

"Like I said, it's all for fun."

I'd do my best to keep reminding myself of it, too.

MAVERICK AND MASON NEVER SHOWED. After calling both of them, they both said they were too hungover to spend hours in the sun—hilarious in itself given how cloudy it was. Which meant they hadn't even tried to get out of their beds. I hadn't bothered correcting them. It was their vacation too.

Besides, there were worse things to do than hang out with my two older brothers and my dad, even if I couldn't play.

It just sucked while they were giving each other shit, I'd

thrown on my sling and gotten suckered into driving Dad's cart for him.

"It's not even fair," Malcolm muttered to Marshall, after he beat him on another hole. "You don't even have the time to play."

"Don't be a poor loser. It gives you wrinkles," I teased.

He gave me a blank expression. "You think I care about wrinkles?"

"I think you care about always looking good, so yeah. I bet you have more serums and lotions than Shelby."

If there was anything I could do to get under Malcolm's skin, it was calling him girlie. But he *was* the prettier one of all of us. And since he liked to give me shit for my *hobby* of a career... I could never resist goading him.

Besides, he was two strokes behind Marshall.

"How do *you* know about serums?" Marshall asked. "Because that's something Bridget talks about, and there are dozens of bottles of them all over our counter, but I zone out whenever she talks about them."

"I give a shit about looking good." I grinned at them and curtsied.

My dad, used to our constant smack talk, grabbed a fresh beer from the cooler. Shaking his head, he popped the can open and took a drink.

"And you're giving me shit about serums?" Malcolm asked.

"I didn't say I *used* them. I implied you do. And then you got all butt hurt because I pointed out you're getting wrinkles."

His entire face scrunched up. "I am *not* getting wrinkles."

I patted his shoulder and gave him a little shove as I sauntered back to the cart. "See. I told you you cared about it."

I was still laughing when both Marshall and my dad hit the ball perfectly. Two hundred plus yards straight down the fairway. Perfect set up to a birdie on the par-four.

After them, Malcolm stomped up, still scowling at me.

He hooked his shot into the trees and weeds lining the left side of the fairway.

Perfect. I wasn't even playing and I was still winning.

"I hate you," he grumbled on his way off the tee box and took a proffered beer from my dad.

MARSHALL WON.

Malcolm sulked back to the resort and my dad went with him when Marshall and I said we'd return the golf carts.

Malcolm turned into a sore loser after I pointed out his wrinkles.

The guy needed to start taking chill pills or he was going to die of a heart attack by the age of forty. Not that I'd point out that to him and make a vein pop in his temple.

"So. You and Kim?" Marshall asked.

"What about me and Kimmy??"

"She's a good woman. Really sweet."

"I know that. Kimmy is great." I couldn't quite tell if this conversation was a warning or benign, but my shoulders still tensed. Since no one was really supposed to know, I waited for him to speak again.

"You didn't listen to my warning," he said and shook his head like the typical disappointed older brother. Not that I cared.

Marshall should have known if you tell me *not* to do something, it's only going to make me want it more.

"I never said I'd follow it." I came to a stop. "Wait? How'd you know?"

Two brows arched. "Besides the way you looked at her on the boat, you two just happened to run into each other on the beach and decided to get breakfast together? Please."

"Yeah." It was plausible.

Not possible enough since Marshall started chuckling.

"Kim hates breakfast. Bridget died laughing when she told me she saw you, too. Says it's her most hated meal of the day. Plus, she also doesn't work out. If anything, she'd be more like Morgan and reading, not out walking."

He laughed so hard he almost buckled over in two. I shoved his golf bag draped across his shoulders, making him fall to a knee before he could rebalance himself.

"You're an ass."

"I know."

"Are you pissed? Or is Bridget?"

He scolded me with a look. "We have bigger things to worry about than what you two are getting up to, she just doesn't want drama. Kim has a history, I guess, of her exes or boyfriends ruining family events."

"Like I'd do that."

"Which is why I told her not to worry." He pointedly looked at my shoulder. "She know?"

"Why would she need to?"

"Because you're injured and need to be careful."

"I don't know what kind of sex you have where your shoulder comes into play but I really don't want those details."

And yeah, maybe it hurt. But only when I picked her up. And maybe when we were swimming even if it was good exercise for it. Or maybe that had to do with the beach. Although she'd done all the work until she set my hands on her hips.

"Don't be a dick. I'm worried about you."

"No need to be." And now I was getting pissed.

He kicked a rock out of the path and swung his arms behind his golf bag, looped his arms over the bag while we walked. That damn simple movement ticked me off. Because there was no way in hell I could do that now.

"She hates professional athletes, too, you know?"

I was still glaring at his arms so casually draped and his shoulders stretching it took me a second. "What?"

"Kim. She despises professional athletes. You know she just settled a huge case against Ricky Marsksam? The football player who beat his wife?"

"No shit?" She hadn't said a word. Not even when I asked about her job. Although, I'd dropped it pretty quickly, assuming she didn't enjoy talking about it.

"Yeah. Makes me wonder why she'd give you the time of day."

"Maybe because I don't have wife beater stamped on my forehead? What part of *it's a week fling thing* do you not understand?"

"I know that for you, Charlotte leaving messed you up when she chose Selkin. I know that fucked with your head for a long time, but you have a lot more going for you than playing hockey and I'm betting right now you're freaking out, wondering if you'll actually be able to play again. I don't want to see you sabotage everything because of some bitch who acted like one when you were twenty."

My head spun. "None of this has anything to do with Charlotte," I gritted, my canine teeth grinding together. Goddamn. If my shoulder was decent, I'd punch him.

"No?"

Like I'd admit I'd thought of her more in the last four weeks than the last ten years. So what. It meant nothing. *You'll never be good enough... you're not even going to college...*

"Fuck Charlotte and fuck you, Marshall. Why would you even bring this shit up?"

"Because I'm worried about you, and I know how hard it will be if you can't play again."

"I'll play again. You don't know shit."

Because I would damn it. Come hell or high water, I'd be back on the ice.

"Fine. Want to know something else I know?"

"Not particularly." He'd already said enough to have me pissed off for days.

He chuckled and flashed me a grin. "I know Kim hates nicknames in all forms. And absolutely despises being called Kimmy, yet, you call her that with no problem."

She'd told me about nicknames, but hadn't she been the one to allow Kimmy?

Maybe she didn't hate it as much as Marshall thought.

Marshall passed me and slammed his golf bag into my gut. "Think on that, maybe."

I was gripping my stomach, still cursing him under my breath by the time he disappeared from view.

So she hated nicknames. And breakfast. And athletes.

I didn't particularly love lawyers but it hadn't stopped me from thinking she was hot.

But maybe... just maybe... it *did* mean something. For both of us.

My family was a *lot*. It was easy to forget when we only saw each other at weddings and funerals for the most part. My dad's family was scattered all up and down the Midwest from Texas to Michigan's Upper Peninsula. Apparently, all of his siblings, and their kids, needed to be landlocked to be happy. With my mom and Bridget's being sisters, and the only two children on their side of the family, I always forgot how exhausting my dad's side could be.

I'd already fielded two dozen questions about my job in law, how I managed to have a work-life balance which was offensive enough because who *ever* asked a man how he managed to handle it all. I'd been asked by two of my aunts if I was going to stay home once I had kids—always assuming that was what women wanted and we could have no other goals, no other life purposes in addition to a fulfilling career.

I understood their point to an extent. Those women had been raised in small farm towns where most women *did* stay home. But they also worked their asses off on the farm. Why was me working in a law office, spending my work hours in a different building so much different than the twenty-four-hour, seven days a week job they had to balance.

I'd sat at a table with cousins I barely knew listening to them discuss the cost of cattle prices and fertilizer increasing, and then listened to every woman close to my age talk about the children they'd left in the States with their in-laws, the joys of parenting all while managing to complain about how much their husbands sucked and didn't help...

I was *over* family time.

It didn't help that after our lunch, my parents begged me to head to the pool with everyone. The weather was cruddy. Such a disappointment to the previous days—days I'd spent with Max and was desperately trying not to ruminate over, because please... I wasn't the kind of woman to obsess over anything other than my work.

Yet thoughts of him were always there, lingering in my mind. Every time he snuck back into my thoughts, my skin warmed, chasing away the chilly breeze and pebbled my skin with goose bumps.

Two hours later, after needing to cover myself with a towel and then take it off and not getting any sun and unable to go into the water due to my hair, I was done.

I turned to my mom and began packing the small beach bag I'd brought with me. "I'm going to head out."

She gave me an understanding smile and tipped her sunglasses up so I could see her eyes that mirrored mine. "Can't take it anymore, either, huh?"

So she wasn't as bad as Dad's side, but the slight irony made me shake my head. She'd never understood why I wanted to spend so much time in school and studying law, either.

"I think I'm worn out. Need a nap, maybe somewhere quiet to read."

"We'll see you at dinner, though, right?"

"Of course." I stood off the lounge chair, grabbed the handles of my tote bag, and bent down to kiss my mom on the cheek. "I can't wait."

"Lies," she teased and kissed my cheek back. "Go have yourself some fun."

"Reading a book?" I arched a brow and stood.

"It's one of your favorite things."

True. She wasn't wrong with that one. "Text me the time for dinner."

She winked and covered her eyes with her sunglasses. "Enjoy your faerie porn, dear."

I snorted and shook my head. "You're so weird."

I was halfway to my villa when Marshall surprised me, walking from the path that veered off to the main building.

Golf bag flung over his shoulders, he obviously was coming from the golf course.

Of course, it only reminded me of Max.

"Hey," I said, stopping on the path where we met. "How was golf?"

"I beat Malcolm and pissed Max off, so all's well."

"Max lost, huh?"

His lips rolled before he said, "Max didn't play. But I'm curious to know one, why you'd assume he'd win and two, why you thought he played."

"Because he...." Said he couldn't stay for breakfast because of golfing. Which meant I'd have to admit we spent the night together. Damn it. "And you guys were giving each other crap on the boat the other day."

"Right," he drawled and shook his head. Pretty sure he was fighting a laugh which meant he *knew*. Of course he did. Because Bridget wasn't an idiot and despite our lies at breakfast, she figured it out. "Any chance you know where Brie is? I tried texting and haven't heard back."

"She and Debbie had a last-minute meeting going over tomor-row's rehearsal menu."

"Great. Thanks. So, about Max."

"We were talking about him?" I cocked my head to the side.

"Yeah, can I walk with you?"

Since he had to pass my villa to get to his, I couldn't exactly say no. "It's your pitch, superstar."

He shuffled his bag draped over his shoulder so it didn't smack me in the back as we walked, and it didn't take long before he said, "He calls you Kimmy."

Not the starter I thought he was going to go with. "And?"

"You despise Kimmy. All nicknames. I've listened to you make your feminist—and very valid pointed arguments, I might add—"

"Nice save." I chuckled. So I might be known for my *rants*. You know, all things about equality, equal, respectful treatment of men toward women, not checking out a woman's breasts and then calling her pretty in a business meeting and objectifying her, or being condescending and calling her sweetheart in a professional setting. Those *rants*.

"But he calls you Kimmy. And you keep letting him."

I kicked a pebble out of the path, my skin heating even though the clouds were still hiding the sun and the air was cool. "So?"

"So you like him."

"He's a good guy. All you Miko men are." Because yeah, maybe I did. But I knew the score and my place and what this was.

At least, that's what I'd spent all freaking day reminding myself of.

"Max isn't... Max is built differently."

And *boy*, didn't I know *that*. Although I doubted his physique was what Marshall was getting at. "Okay..."

"He hates being alone. He *wants* a family. Wants kids and the whole works and I know he's been perpetually single for like, ever, and I know he's had his share of women—"

"Which is absolutely something I don't need to know and isn't my business until he tells me himself."

"Right." He cleared his throat and stopped, draping his arms over the ends of his golf bag. "The thing is, I know what he gets like when he wants something—or someone, in this case. You two have completely different lives. If you're one hundred percent sure you *don't* want anything after this week, I'm asking you to be careful with him."

There was a lot to unpack there. Mostly, why Marshall was getting involved even as endearing as it was that he was looking after his younger brother.

"I think we're on the same page."

"But are you certain? Because I know your views about marriage, and I can say they're the exact opposite of Max's."

I almost choked on the salty air. *Marriage?* Now he had to be smoking something. "That's quite the leap after a week on the beach."

He shrugged. "I know my brother."

Irritation spiked. Endearing yeah, but we were also both adults. Granted, I'd approached him first about letting whatever was going to happen this week, but he dove in with both feet with the whole *What happens in Tunstago Bay stays in Tunstago Bay.*

What I wasn't currently appreciating was the *I'm the woman, therefore a man-eater,* aspect of this conversation. "Have you given him this same speech?"

"Actually, yeah, I have."

Well then.

My jaw snapped shut.

"I care about you both. I don't want to see this blowing up in your faces, and I'm not saying you have to marry him or anything, I'm asking you to make sure you're protecting both of you when this week comes to an end."

"I got it, Marsh. But we're also both adults."

"I know, but he's going through a lot right now. He doesn't need anything else messing with his head when there's enough going on up there."

Like what? The tip of my tongue burned to ask, but I bit it back. *None of my business.*

His head tilted to one side. "Has Bridget ever told you the

advice my mom loves to dish out at every single opportunity, to every human single or dating?"

"What?"

"Never date a person you wouldn't consider marrying. That doesn't mean you have to marry every person you date, but why waste the time if it's not worth it long-term. And given your views of marriage—"

"That it's an antiquated institution that was created solely by the men in charge to benefit the men in charge and only serves to continue keeping outdated and irrelevant coverture laws in place for women who rarely receive the same matrimonial benefits to a marriage like men do, at least until they get divorced and then they're called vengeful, selfish, money-hungry bitches for demanding they finally get their equal do?"

"Yeah." He coughed but there was amusement in his expression even if he thought my ideas on it were wildly insane. I dealt with women going through divorces for a living. I'd stand by my statements until the day I died. "Those ideas."

I grinned at him. If he wanted me to apologize, we'd be here until my bones were dust in the ground.

With a shake of his head, he continued, "So maybe think about that teaching Max grew up with it and how he puts that to use in his life, would you?"

I opened my mouth to argue, because hell yes, I could argue that. He was a man who could handle his emotions and feelings— hurt or otherwise and he wasn't my responsibility. I barely knew him.

As I thought it, though, it didn't sit right in my gut. I didn't want to do anything to hurt Max. I *did* like him, despite what the end of the week could bring. He was slowly showing me not all athletes were assholes.

Amusement fled from his face and then he lifted a hand to stop me. "Before you put me on the stand, counselor, and grill me like you're cross-examining a witness, I'm only asking you to be considerate. That's all. I'm not telling you two what to do or what not to do."

Okay. He had a point there. "I can do that."

"Good."

He walked me to my villa, where we parted ways in possibly tense terms, but there was no anger. Only a slight irritation... and a possible growing worry.

Perhaps Max and I *did* need to ensure we were on the same page, because I'd been thinking that if he offered to spend time together after this week I'd jump at the chance—and him, any opportunity I could.

But not if it would end up hurting one of us in the end. Marshall was right, our long-term lives and goals looked vastly different.

IT WAS LATE, and I'd debated going to Max's villa a thousand times since dinner. So much, in fact, I'd returned to my own, slid into comfortable pajamas, in part because I didn't want to show up in a dress if I did go, and mostly to hide the food baby I was sporting in my stomach from the massive amounts of fish and seafood and steak I inhaled earlier. *Delicious* though. Worth every uncomfortable press of my abdomen against the tight-fitted dress I'd had on.

Then, still debating, I opened a bottle of wine and poured a glass. Then poured another. It was after the first sip of the second glass I realized I could get drunk while debating and that wouldn't do anyone any good.

He'd been the one who mentioned wanting to see me later and I hadn't heard from him. Granted, we didn't have each other's numbers, but our villas had phones if he wanted to call first.

But screw it. I wanted to see him and maybe we needed to talk.

Which meant when I showed up at his place, that opened

bottle of wine tucked neatly in the overnight bag I thought to grab with a toothbrush, clothes for the morning, and even a towel for the beach—just in case—I didn't even know if he was there.

Because of course I hadn't been smart enough to call his place myself.

I lifted my hand and knocked quietly. He could be sleeping. Or at a different restaurant or bar with his brothers. He could be—

The door swung open.

Right there. In front of me. Dressed in nothing but sweats shorts, tanned skin, and rivulets of water, looking so glorious it took immense effort not to lean in and lick up every last drop trailing down his chest. And his arm in a sling...

"What happened to your arm?" I reached out to touch him and jerked back. How had he gotten hurt?

"It's nothing. Old hockey injury." As he said it, he moved his arm out of the sling and pulled it off, but there was a clench to his jaw as he did it.

"Old injury, my ass. What happened?"

"Shoulder injury a few weeks back." He sighed, clearly unhappy about telling me about it and stepped back. "Want to come in?"

I hesitated and stepped over the threshold.

"How bad is it?" I asked, because he might not have wanted to talk about it, but he hadn't given any indication he was hurt. I thought of the times he'd picked me up. That first night he threw me over his shoulder. If he was hurt, should he be doing those things? And if it wasn't as bad as he was making it out to be, why was he wearing the sling now?

"It's nothing. Really."

He couldn't look at me. Or wouldn't. He shut the door behind me and headed to the kitchen. I followed.

"You're lying."

Nothing pissed me off more than a liar.

His jaw tightened and a far-off look hit his eyes before he shook it off.

I didn't give him a chance to lie to me again. "If you don't want to talk about it, fine, but don't lie to me. And if it's hurting, maybe we should—"

"It's not my goddamn fucking shoulder I'm worried about!"

He shouted so loud the villa shook. I took two quick steps back, almost stumbled over my own feet before righting myself. Holy *shit*.

"Fuck." He slammed his hand to the counter and pinched his eyes closed.

"I should go."

Maybe I'd goaded him. Perhaps I'd pushed. He'd already blown me off about it. We were a fling. It was none of my business.

And it'd never been clearer than in that exact moment.

Shit. Right when I was starting to think he was different.

"I'm sorry. So damn sorry for yelling. I don't..." He lifted his head, peered at me through narrowed eyes and then pushed off the counter to rub them. "It's my fucking head. It's killing me, and the shoulder, yeah, the shoulder's a pain in the ass, but it's not what is pissing me off. I can rehab that. Be fine even if not a hundred percent, but..."

"Concussion," I said quietly, so quietly I didn't think he heard.

But then he dropped his head again and turned toward me. "It's my fourth in three years. A minor one, but yeah... it's been weeks. Didn't even come from a goddamn game, just a stupid accident while rock climbing with a buddy."

At his age, a shoulder not one hundred percent and his concussion history....

"I'm sorry," I said, and okay. He shouldn't have screamed at me, but based on the tremble in his arms, the squint of his eyes, maybe he'd needed to unload it. "That's a lot to handle."

He laughed, but it was cold. "I'm a free agent in a year at thirty-one with a history of injuries and now this. It's more than a lot to handle. I'm looking at the end of my career, and that's if they let me play this season."

"Is there anything I can do?" I stepped toward him, remembering my wine bottle still in my arms and set it on the counter.

He exhaled slowly, blowing air out through full, puffed-out cheeks and frowned. "I'm really sorry for yelling. You didn't deserve that. Marshall made me mad earlier. My whole family is worried. I needed this week to be a break from all the thoughts racing in my head and every time my family glances at my shoulder, I want to punch something. Only I can't, because it's still too fucked up. I can't even do that yet."

"Do you want me to go?"

"The only time it hasn't worried me is being with you this week, so... no." A quirk of his lips, a tease of a smile.

My toes curled into my sandals. "Okay. Drink then?"

"I wish, but I can't with my head tonight." He grabbed a water bottle from his kitchen fridge and handed me a wineglass. "I'm really sorry," he said as I took it from him.

"You're forgiven."

I had a feeling I'd forgive him for a lot if he looked at me like that more often.

I slipped out of my sandals, set the bag I'd brought on his table and filled my glass with my wine.

"How was dinner with your family?" he finally asked.

I gave him the out. If he wanted to talk more about his shoulder or his fears, I'd listen, but if I helped him forget, I could give him that, too.

Two days and then we were gone. Maybe, at least we could leave as friends.

Except when I looked at Max, I didn't see a friend. I saw something *more*.

Bad idea. I sipped my wine to wash away the thought.

"Long. My dad's family is..." I searched for the proper term and came up empty. "They're a lot. Good, sweet people, but they're a lot to handle."

"Seems to me you can handle anything and anyone."

A spark of excitement trilled through me at the compliment. He tossed them out as easy and quick as I imagined he slapped a puck across the ice.

I turned to him and didn't have to turn much because he was right there. In front of me. All that muscled skin still wet on display. So close I could inhale the scent of his body wash. Nothing extravagant, but there was a crisp, clean scent to him I could definitely get used to being around.

Which was most likely why I opened my mouth, forgot about his injuries and worries and everything else he'd told me, and stupidly blurted out, "I don't believe in marriage."

Well, that was.... not at *all* how I was expecting our first few moments together were going to go, especially considering I'd been trying to decide whether or not to take her up against the wall as soon as she entered or have her on the kitchen counter like that first night.

Being surprised by her while wearing my sling was one thing.

The marriage statement was a whole other.

"I'm sorry... what?" I could barely hold back my laugh as she turned the shade of an eggplant.

"Oh the Mother," Kimmy groaned and slapped a hand to her forehead. "Forget... just forget I said anything, because that was... that was so stupid and I am rarely so ridiculous."

As she stumbled over her words, she hurried to the kitchen. She yanked out the cork, filled her wineglass even though there was plenty in it from her first pour and took a healthy sip—more like a chug.

"So, dinner was that bad?" Because what in the hell was happening?

I was torn between laughing and checking her for a temperature.

Somehow I didn't think my hands on her was what she wanted right now. She looked to be a downright mess of nerves.

Kimmy set the wineglass down harder than needed on the marble countertop and then braced both hands on it, straightened her arms, and gave out a low, slightly panicked laugh.

I moved and stood close, off to her side so she could see me.

Without looking at me, head still down but her hair tucked back so I could see she had her eyes closed, she must have noticed me growing closer. "Want to tell me more about your shoulder? Have you hurt it since being here?"

Not going there. I crossed my arms over my chest.

"I think we should get back to the marriage thing."

It was *so* much more entertaining than my own freak out.

"Oh please, let's not ever go back to that."

"Well, no, now you have me curious. I mean, do you not believe in the definition? Or think it doesn't exist? Or do you just not like it? Because there's a lot to wade through here."

Her eyes opened and she slid her head in my direction, amusement and mortification coloring her skin. "You're a goofball."

I couldn't disagree. "I don't know if I've heard someone say they don't believe in marriage."

Yeah, I knew people who never wanted to get married, sure. But *believe* in it? That felt like a whole different ball game.

Never mind the fact she said it to *me*. Something had to have happened.

"You'll never hear it again, either." She stood and blew out a breath so heavy I felt it from feet away. Reaching for her wine, she brought it to her mouth.

"So, marriage?"

She scowled and I smiled shamelessly. She was adorable even as she rolled her eyes.

She also wasn't still chugging it like it was the last alcohol on the planet. All good signs.

"You're not going to let this go, are you?"

I rocked on my heels. "Nope."

"Ugh. Fine. But you should know I'm not crazy."

"Crazy cute, definitely. Crazy sexy, absolutely."

That blush returned to her cheeks.

"Goof," she accused. As if I didn't know. It was only Kimmy that was being a bit slow.

Life was a game and I was usually the main player.

"Are you going to keep procrastinating? Because we won't get much further tonight than childish insults and marriage talk."

A low, frustrated growl came from her before she took another drink of her wine. I gave her enough time to drain my water and grab a fresh one. Then I reached back and slid her white wine into the fridge. Might as well keep it cool although if she kept downing it at this speed there'd be no point.

"I ran into Marshall—"

"Oh God." What had he done *now*? "No conversation is good when it starts with him. What'd he say that has you all freaked out?" I twisted off the top of my water and flicked it across the counter.

Talking to me was bad enough. I didn't need *both* of my older brothers flying into dad-mode this week. Hell, they were more dad-like than my own.

"Mostly, I think he reminded me that while this week will be fun, and absolutely has been, it's good we remember it's only the week. That we're too different for anything to last longer."

Right. Because she hated athletes. And I might not ever play again. Then what good would I be? Just a washed-up athlete who used to play hockey who didn't even go to college.

And now I had to punch my brother in the face days before his wedding. Bridget would flip her shit over a black eye. It'd set me back, what, a week or two in therapy? Probably worth it.

"He talked to you about *marriage*? Because please, don't take this the wrong way. I like you. I think you're great and I've been having a lot of fun with you, but *marriage* after three days sounds a bit like lunacy, doesn't it?"

"Obviously." She chuckled. Didn't drink her wine. Perhaps she was calming down. "I guess I wanted to make sure we were on the same page with everything."

I set my palm on the counter and leaned in, bent forward enough so we were at eye level. "I can guarantee you I have not once thought about marriage this week, if that's what you need to hear."

I had thought about having to say goodbye to her, and every time I did, my stomach flipped. She didn't need to know that, though.

"I didn't, but more, he said you want something long-term, and you should know I don't plan on ever getting married."

"Ever ever?"

"I'll spare you my thoughts on the institution of marriage and what it symbolizes for women, but yeah... I don't believe in marriage."

"Which is different than long-term."

"What?"

"You said I wanted something long-term. Which yeah, I'd like that, but that doesn't mean marriage, either and don't go crazy with this because I'll repeat, *again*, I have not once thought of marriage in regard to this week. I'm pointing out that long-term commitment and marriage are two different things."

She inspected me with the intensity I imagined she took into the courtroom. No wonder she won so much. She looked damn intelligent and serious. And yeah, maybe I was doing a little bit of objectification, but she looked damn hot doing it, too.

"Point taken." She tipped her wineglass toward my water bottle and I angled mine so the tops tipped. "So we're agreed then. This week only."

"I haven't considered anything else." I swallowed down my lie with water and wished it was whiskey.

I definitely had. All day long I had, especially after Marshall's comments to me. It still didn't mean we couldn't enjoy the rest of the week.

"Okay then," she said, and for a second, I swore she looked a little hurt.

That was ridiculous though. *She* was the one who brought this up and laid down the ground rules.

I was a team player. I could follow the rules. Eh... most of the time.

"So we're in agreement." I flashed her a wink to take the sadness out of her eyes, although I had to be misunderstanding that. "Again."

"Yup."

"Good."

I drained my water. "Need another glass?"

She looked into her glass and nodded. "Please."

I poured her a fresh glass and she wandered toward the back patio. She was standing at the railing and staring off into the dark void. Waves rushed the shore. Trees whistled from the wind.

"Today's weather was crappy," I said, because that's what we were now reduced to.

Weather talk.

I mean hell, she'd agreed to the week but she also seemed pretty damn nervous being around me. Which was silly.

Hadn't I already shown I'd respect her?

And then rock her world?

"Thank you." She took her drink and sipped on it, leaning against the railing. I matched her pose but instead of staring into the darkness, I watched her. "I hope it's not like this on their wedding day. It wasn't bad, but Bridget will cry if it rains."

"Isn't that supposed to be good luck?"

"What?"

"Rain. On your wedding day. I thought that was good luck for a happy marriage."

She frowned and looked at me. Really looked at me for maybe the first time since she'd stepped into my place. "You know about marital superstitions?"

"I'm an athlete, not an idiot."

"Point taken. That's twice tonight."

"Yeah, well I like scoring."

She snorted, actually snorted, and then grabbed her nose and bent over. "Holy shit, the wine is burning my nose."

If I was a better man, I'd help her. Instead, I couldn't help it. I threw my head back and laughed my ass off. "Sorry."

"You sound like it," she said, but it was muffled as she pinched her eyes closed and shook off the burn. Scowling at me, looking adorable doing it, she took another sip once she recovered. "So, tell me something else about you. How'd you get to the pros?"

I could have smartassed her with shit like *all skill, baby*, but she'd roll her eyes and probably throw her glass at me. "A very long, indirect route," I said and just like with Marshall earlier, I was thinking about way back then.

A decade ago.

All the shit I went through.

The plans to go to college and how those changed.

"I started playing like every other kid. Saw it on TV, loved it. But we lived where hockey wasn't huge yet, just south enough and planted firmly in college football and baseball land, but I didn't care. I wanted to play so badly, my parents found me a league. Turned out I was pretty good at it."

I thought about those years. When I was five getting started up to when I was ten. I made some travel leagues that took my dad and me up the East Coast multiple weekends a month. Five o'clock in the morning ice times. Or nine at night. Hockey was a brutal sport from the get-go.

"Pretty good at it, hmm?"

"The best," I confirmed because I was. At least until I hit the travel leagues. Then I was getting outplayed every game.

Some kids gave up. Didn't love it enough.

Not me. By the time I was fourteen it was in my blood. I never wanted to stop. I worked my ass off all year long to get better and the next season, I was outplaying some of them easily.

"I was recruited to a junior league when I was sixteen. I mean, yeah, I had to try out and all that, but it works a lot like the pros, with scouts traveling to games. Apparently one guy had seen me play in a game near D.C. and talked to my dad. So I tried out, made the team, and shipped off a few months later."

"Shipped off? At sixteen?" Her eyes widened adorably and lines sprinkled across her forehead.

"Yeah, it's pretty common." I shrugged. "There are only so many teams in the league and none were near Virginia. So I moved in with a host family in Michigan." At her still surprised expression, I explained, "They had a son who was a year older, and a complete dick. Still is to this day, but his parents were sweet people. But yeah, they took me in, I lived with them during the season. My parents came to games when they could. And when I was eighteen, I was drafted to the pros in Detroit."

"At eighteen. That's insane. What about college?"

"Didn't go. Could have. Most kids from the junior leagues end up going that route. They can play NCAA hockey unless they were in the Canadian junior leagues. But I was drafted early and high. I didn't want to risk getting hurt in college and never seeing the pros."

That nasty churn in my stomach started. I'd done all this work, sacrificed a shit ton, gave up a lot all for this. And now....

I shook it off.

"I started in their minor league farm teams. Got called up when I was twenty. Sent back down. Called back up and then six years ago, was traded to Vegas."

She peered at me with interest and an intelligence that almost made me fidget. Could she see all I wasn't saying? All I'd struggled with. All I'd lost along the way.

"You'll never be good enough. You keep getting hurt. Devon is going to make it big."

"So date him then."

"I slept with him last weekend. I just wanted you to know why."

God, that stung.

"What happened to the asshole?"

"Who?"

"The asshole you lived with."

Ah. Perfect. She had to have seen something on my face when I mentioned him. "Devon Selkin. Now plays for Boston. I'm not sure there's a person in the league who likes him, but he's a good player." Unfortunately. He couldn't have sucked. Gotten cut. Bounced from team to team. Nope. He got a full ride to Harvard and has been in Boston his entire career.

With Charlotte.

Her head tilted to that side, her eyes soft, but introspective. "Why don't you like him?"

"Because he's an asshole."

She smirked. Brows arched. God damn. Hadn't I opened up enough for the night? I didn't talk about Charlotte. Ever. Hadn't since I was eighteen.

Kimmy wasn't Charlotte. She wouldn't leave me if I did get injured or whatever. Hell, it'd probably work in my favor. I liked this woman. Wanted a shot with her after this week even if it meant moving slower than I wanted.

"I don't like him because he's an asshole," I stated, sighing heavily. "I also don't like him because when I was living with him for those two years, I started dating one of his friends. But when I was a senior, and Devon was already at Harvard, I got hurt during playoffs. Couldn't play. Charlotte assumed I wouldn't get drafted so she went to visit Selkin at school. Broke up with me the next weekend. For him."

I chugged my water.

She sipped her wine. "You loved her."

"Thought I did. I was young, though. It happens." It wasn't a lie. But it wasn't the full truth, either. Yeah, I'd gotten over Charlotte as a person, but that lingering fear of being ditched for something I couldn't control? That had never quite disappeared.

"And they're still married?"

"Yeah, and I don't care if it makes me immature or vengeful, but I secretly like the fact Devon cheats on her all the damn time. He's your typical pro athlete. A woman in every city. Probably drinks too much at home. But she got what she wanted and she hasn't left, so whatever."

Her lips pushed to the side. "I don't think it makes you a jerk or anything. I think that's normal. She hurt you."

"Yeah. Messed with my head for a long time. Mostly because I thought I did love her and she sowed seeds of doubt in my playing abilities for a while. Took a bit to get over it."

There I was, still letting her words hurt.

"You know, Max. I don't think you're half-bad."

She was teasing, grinning in that soft but confident way of hers.

I chuckled despite the turmoil she couldn't have known her questions would brew inside me.

"Want to see how bad I can actually be?"

She laughed. Okay, that was corny, but it wasn't *that* bad.

"What am I going to do with you, Max?" she asked, her voice soft while she slid her hand into mine.

"I'm sure we can figure out something."

Like... maybe longer than a week?

I was smart enough to keep my mouth shut, but I did, in fact, lead her into the room where she absolutely, one hundred percent *loved* all the bad parts of me based on her pleasured cries.

TWENTY-ONE

KIM

Bridget paced in front of me. Her fitted, white dress with a sweetheart neckline stopped just below her knees and every time she blew out a calming breath, she fought against the confines of the stitching and zipped back.

"Calm," I told her and placed my hands on her biceps. "You need to *relax*. This is Marshall... not a stranger you're meeting for a first date."

She sniffed and took a quick breath, blowing it out through her light-pink-painted lips. Her long blonde hair was gathered and set at her shoulder in a simple, offset ponytail with a bright, white hibiscus flower in it. It was the same color of the flowers we'd all be carrying tomorrow.

I spent all day with Bridget and our moms, fine-tuning every detail, ensuring everything was prepared for tomorrow. My cousin had been absolutely calm all day, but now that we were hanging out in the bridal room, every second drove her toward a nervous breakdown.

"This is the rehearsal, honey. If you freak out today, what are you going to do tomorrow?"

"Elope with Marshall before the sun rises so the actual

wedding is all fake."

My eyes widened. "You've put a lot of thought into this."

"I can't help it." She shook out her hands, pulling them from my grip, and then rubbed them together. "I have no idea why I'm so nervous. I love him, right? I mean, you're right. He's Marshall. He's been through everything with me. He's adopting Nathan for crying out loud. He's wonderful."

"And sexy," Carrie piped in.

"Totally sexy." Gretchen grinned and sipped her mimosa, flashed my cousin a wink that had her chuckling.

"And he *loves* you. With everything he has. Tomorrow is just one day. It's only the beginning and you've been through so much together."

"You're right." She blinked rapidly and nodded. "You're absolutely right. Nothing to worry about."

"I'm always right," I said and handed her a mimosa. Perhaps a bit of champagne would chill her the hell out.

She rolled her eyes. "Of course you are."

As she sipped her mimosa, her features relaxed, her breaths returned less to a panic level and more stable. As she scanned all of us, she grinned. "Your dresses all look super cute on you."

Tomorrow, we'd all be wearing floor-length gowns in the lightest chiffon and the palest teal-blue. They were absolutely gorgeous. Tonight, our dresses matched the color we'd wear tomorrow but were the same style as Bridget's. I'd had no idea she'd planned on us having matching rehearsal dresses, but admittedly, it was a cute idea. The pictures from tonight and tomorrow would be fabulous. Each of us had our hair similar to hers except where her flower was white, ours was hot pink.

Tomorrow, the men would be wearing navy linen suits and white dress shirts. I had no idea if they'd be matching tonight as well, but I was most definitely looking forward to seeing Max in a suit tomorrow. My ovaries would probably explode on the spot.

But for now, we waited in the room where we'd finish preparations tomorrow, sipped mimosas and snacked on bruschetta and some sort of seafood canapé that looked like foam but had all of us moaning with pleasure every time we popped one into our mouths.

They were absolutely *divine*.

Soon, our mothers ducked their heads in.

"It's time," Debbie said to Bridget. "Are you ready?"

It could have been the mimosa or the pep talk, or Bridget remembering she really *was* ready for this, but she was now the picture of calm, cool, and collected like she usually was.

"We're ready."

"Good. Because the guys just got done pretending to seat everyone and are ready."

"Wonderful." She gathered up her bouquet, hot pink like our own hibiscus flowers and smaller than the one she'd hold tomorrow and handed us each a white flower. We departed the bridal room but stood behind a row of hedges so the men couldn't see us.

Torture. It was absolute torture. I was desperate to peek my head around the corner and catch sight of Max. If it was killing *me*, I had no doubt Bridget was dying to see her groom, but when I looked back to her, only peace shone on her face. That and the sun that was now beginning to set.

Tomorrow, she'd get married with the sun directly overhead and hopefully, the breeze would help keep us cool, but now the shade protected us.

"It's just a practice," she whispered to herself, and then the music began to play, signaling it was Morgan's turn to start down the aisle.

"I still think it's stupid I'm going to have to walk back down the aisle with my brother," she grumbled and rolled her eyes at Bridget.

"Should have had fewer brothers," Bridget teased. "Now go." She waved her future sister-in-law off with a smile as Nathan tugged at the skirt of his mom's dress. "Mom."

"Yes, honey. What is it?"

"Daddy says I look as handsome as him. What do you think?"

Tears swelled in her eyes. They did for me every time he called Marshall Daddy. He was right, too. The kiddo did look handsome in navy shorts and a short-sleeve, perfectly pressed white shirt.

"You always look handsome," she said and bent down to kiss the top of his head. "Tonight you look more handsome than ever."

"I know." He grinned and held up the pillow he'd carry down the aisle. On it, sat three fake rings and my heart pinched.

I hadn't expected the third one, but of course Marshall and Bridget would include Nathan in this somehow.

I sniffed and caught sight of Gretchen now nearing the front of the altar after Morgan, which meant I was almost screwing up the rehearsal. "My bad," I whispered to Carrie.

"You're good, but go," she whispered back.

I took off, careful of my speed but hurrying so I didn't set off the timing further. Rattan chairs lined the aisle where the small number of guests would sit. The rehearsal was only the wedding party and everyone else there would be at the dinner later. For now, I tried to focus on stepping on sand, thankful we were all going barefoot instead of in heels. It had the unfortunate consequence of making me appear shorter considering I always wore heels, but at least I didn't have to worry about breaking an ankle.

I stepped down the aisle, careful of my steps, the timing, and then my gaze met Max's and... *holy* freaking sexy man on a beach.

He stood proud and tall next to his brothers Marshall and Malcolm, Marsh's best man. Like Nathan, the men wore the same outfit except their shirts were long sleeves, loose linen.

The effect was stunning. There wasn't a man in the Miko family who wasn't attractive, but Max, out of all of them wore his confidence more easily than he wore his perfectly fitted outfit. It took effort, vast amounts of it not to stumble when he caught me gaping at him and smirked. His thumb brushed along his bottom lip and his tongue followed.

Of course he'd taunt me. Before we'd had to get ready for this we'd spent the afternoon in his bed. His shower. We made love everywhere on the main floor of his villa and that one small touch reminded me of all the wicked things we'd done. Where his mouth had been earlier.

My lips parted in surprise at the wicked gleam in his eyes as he winked at me. I struggled to refocus and stepped up to Gretchen.

"You're so going to have to give me all those naughty details," she whispered, holding a smile in place as Carrie stepped into the aisle. Tomorrow, the aisle would be lined with both the pink and white flowers but tonight it was bare. However, the entire setup was gorgeous. Beachy and classy and soft and romantic all at once.

"No way in hell," I whispered back, nudging her with my elbows.

Max was mine, even if it was temporary. I wasn't sharing a single detail about him, or the things we did, with anyone.

"Spoilsport," she fired back.

I grinned at her, smiled at Carrie as she reached us. We all quietly chuckled as Nathan made his way down the aisle, proud to be carrying that pillow in front of him until he reached the altar and stood in front of Marshall. The music changed, and we all turned to see Bridget hit the opening of the aisle.

I caught a glimpse of Marshall. The shock on his face at seeing her and it wasn't even her wedding dress. His eyes turned molten. His chest seized and he rocked back onto his heels.

Yeah... there was no need for Bridget's earlier nerves at all.

This man *adored* her. As she stepped toward him, my uncle holding her arm next to him, her answering smile was the exact same. Relaxed and heated and excited all wrapped up in one beautiful bride.

The love on their faces, the desire in their eyes, the truth of how both of our parents had such happy marriages... it was one of those rare times when I wondered if my thoughts about marriage were all wrong.

Or at least wrong enough to consider it happening someday.

Because there were people who did it well. My parents. Bridget's. And hopefully, Marshall and Bridget would follow.

THE REHEARSAL WENT off without a hitch and we were escorted back into the main lodge for the dinner part of the evening.

My dad's side of the family was there, and Gretchen and Cassie's husbands along with Cooper and his mom, Max's younger brother's dates. Everyone who didn't need to be at the rehearsal surrounded where we were seated at the bridal table.

My heart stuttered when I saw the room. The head table was set up so we were seated next to who we walked down the aisle with. No separating the groomsmen from the bridesmaids which meant I'd sit right next to Max. He was already at the and when I grew closer, he pulled out my chair and slid in next to me.

"You look so good in that dress I want to rip that zipper down your body..." He leaned in and whispered. My body shivered from the heat in his eyes. "With my teeth."

He finished with a snap of said teeth clinking together and set his hand at my thigh before turning to face the rest of the table.

No one seemed to notice my cheeks turned the color of the flower in my hair but I ducked my head.

"I can make that happen later as long as I get to return the favor."

He tightened his grip on my thigh. "Deal."

If I wasn't mistaken, his voice had some gravel in it.

My uncle's voice bellowed through the microphone, breaking the spell I seemed to fall under more and more around Max. I turned to my Uncle Greg while Max's touch burned through my dress like a brand. As I listened to my uncle congratulate the happy couple, tell stories of Bridget's childhood, embarrassing stories that included myself, Max's hand moved, fingers first gently brushing along my dress.

I thought he was simply brushing his thumb over my thigh until the hem of my dress fluttered against my skin. He inched it higher with minimal movement on his part. I shivered at the contact. The warmth of his fingers and then his palm seared my skin with a heat so fierce I grew warm and wet inches from where he played.

Reaching for my glass of wine, I shot him a look of disbelief, but if he caught it, he didn't show it. His focus was on my uncle, grinning as Greg welcomed Marshall to the family.

At one point, he choked up, covered his emotion with a cough. "You have been the best thing to happen to our family since Nathan came along."

Bridget leaned into Marshall who had an arm draped around her waist. He squeezed her tighter and kissed her temple.

Greg cleared his throat again.

I might have been the only one in the room unaffected by Greg's emotions. I blamed Max. His fingers were slowly creeping higher, his pinkie mere centimeters from the satin edge of my thong.

"Stop," I whispered, and covered his hand with mine, stilling him. "You cannot turn me on while I'm trying not to cry over my cousin and your brother."

"Why not? I'm turned on whenever you're around me. Especially in that dress."

To prove it, he slid his hand out of my dress, took my hand, and placed it right at his groin.

Where... holy shit, he wasn't joking. He was hard beneath the zipper of his shorts. I should have pulled away. Should have put a stop to this game. Sensible and independent and intelligent Kimmy would have.

At some point, that part of me must have gone on her own vacation because instead of doing what I should have done, I traced my finger along his length. Max swallowed harshly and reached for his water.

But his hand didn't stop covering mine. In fact, he applied pressure. I squeezed him gently, covered my hand over his and found his head through his shorts. Obvious. Thick. A heat beneath my palm through his linen shorts.

His stomach clenched.

I squeezed and groped him again.

He drank his water.

I focused on my uncle, closing out his speech.

"To Marshall and Bridget!" Cheers rang out, and I slipped my hand from beneath Max's despite the urge to finish him, right there, where he'd have to hide it.

What insanity took over me, I had no clue. This had to be island Kim who was so vastly different than lawyer Kim who rarely pushed buttons and crossed lines.

I raised my wineglass in the air and clinked it against everyone else's at the table, congratulated Bridget and Marshall. When the toasts were done and everyone tucked into the salads that were delivered on queue, Max leaned over.

"Point made on the teasing. My dick is now stone with no hope of going down for the rest of the night."

I grinned around the rim of my glass. "We'll take care of that later."

"You bet your cute, tiny ass we will." He kissed my cheek, and I jumped, then froze.

I hadn't been prepared for anyone to see. Sure, Bridget and Marshall suspected, even assumed. But...

My parents.

I'd promised no drama.

"Sorry," he said and there was a flash of hurt before he grabbed his fork and stabbed his salad.

"No, I am, it surprised me..."

"Don't worry about it." But his smile was flat and his eyes on his food as he said it.

It was too late. That flat smile and flash of hurt wiggled its way to my chest.

The very last thing I wanted to do was hurt him.

Ever.

TWENTY-TWO
MAX

I was the fool who started the game. I'd like to say I couldn't help it, but I wasn't an animal who acted on pure instinct. Although, there definitely was a part of me that might have become an animal around Kimmy. It happened the moment I caught sight of her in that dress. She stole my breath and squeezed a vise around my chest, right where my damn heart was located. A hundred thoughts raced through my brain as I saw her walking down that aisle. Her smile. The sunshine making her eyes even bluer and her hair shinier than usual.

She was damn gorgeous. So much more than a body too because for the last day, we'd done nothing but stay in bed, ordering room service, and then diving right back into bed. Or into the whirlpool tub at my villa. Or the wall. I still hadn't had her on the kitchen table but there was time.

Sitting at the table, next to her, inhaling the coconut and mint and whatever the hell else she had that made her smell gorgeous, I'd wanted to drive her as crazy as her body in that dress drove me.

Leave it to her to match my game, though, and now I was sitting next to a woman who would let me fuck her eighteen different ways in the privacy of our villas but froze at a simple kiss on her cheek.

I got it. We were around family. What we were doing was fun and she probably didn't want to answer any questions about us any more than I did, and that was mostly because there *wasn't* an *us* and there wasn't going to be an us.

I wasn't ready to have that conversation. Hell, we'd already had it. *Twice.*

Still, it stung when she pulled away, immediately searched for who might have seen like I was some loser instead of someone she'd be proud to be seen with.

Kimmy hates athletes.

Right. That was further confirmation. As if I needed it slammed into my already sore head.

I turned to Maverick and Mason. Carrie and Gretchen had forgone sitting at the table for the wedding party and were with their husbands which left seats for Abby and Anna, who I still, for the fucking life of me, couldn't tell apart.

I sure as hell spent the rest of dinner trying though, while Kimmy and Bridget talked.

I wasn't avoiding her. I just didn't know what to say to her.

Hey, we could do this long-distance thing, right? Wanna give it a go?

Even if I wanted it, what was the point? She'd made it clear last night where her priorities were. They were so different than what I envisioned when I saw my future, I wasn't sure I could get over that part. I wanted a wife. Kids. At the very least, I wanted someone who lived in my same damn zip code.

No matter how I sliced or diced it, there were too many things in our way, showing me this wouldn't work.

Sure, we enjoyed each other and had fun, but hell, I didn't need more friends.

I wanted a woman exactly like Kimmy.

And she'd made it clear she didn't want me. Not in that way.

Which sucked. Seriously sucked.

"Hey," she said, and her hand slid to my thigh.

Where the touch before was gentle, this one was comforting.

Where before, I'd used the tablecloth for cover to keep what I was doing to her private, now it felt like we were hiding. My thigh tightened beneath her soft touch and a riot stirred in my brain. Did I want to end this and have her stop touching me before I went and did something stupid like fall in love with her?

Or did I want her all over me, for as long as I could have her?

My dick enjoyed that idea immensely.

Which was probably why I pushed my chair back to the table and like the first night I met her, I stood and held out my hand. "Want to dance?"

The smile I received was blinding. "Any time, hotshot."

Exactly what I'd hoped to hear.

SHE HAD her hands on my chest, and we were swaying back and forth. The night we first met, I showed off my formal dance moves. Tonight I didn't want the distance and space separating us. Fortunately, Kimmy slid right into my arms and my hold like we actually wanted the same things. My hand was cupping her at my chest and my other held her lower back. I drew circles with my thumb against her dress as we slow danced with most of the other couples.

"Your parents are looking at us," I whispered, smiling down at her.

She didn't so much as flinch. "So let them. We both know the score here and I'm an adult."

"Right." That hurt more than it should have but I kept it hidden.

And truly.

Fuck this.

I was a competitor. I literally found my success in winning

games for a living. I'd never been one to back down from a fight in my life, and maybe those fights had only been with my brothers, for a starting spot on a team, or for the puck on the ice, but there was no way in hell I was sitting back and letting *whatever was supposed to happen, happen.*

That wasn't the kind of guy I was. Never would be.

Didn't mean I had to tell Kimmy about the change in rules, though. At least, not yet.

"We only have two more nights here." Tomorrow was the wedding. We all flew out the day after.

Her bottom lip pushed out. "I know. I'm not ready to leave."

Her fingers pressed against me, gripping my hand holding hers tighter. Perhaps we *were* close to being on the same page... at least in the same game.

"There's one place on this island where I haven't been yet, been saving it for you."

"Where?" Her eyes widened and she rolled her lips together. "Oh..."

"The beach," I murmured. My dick grew hard at the thought, pressed against her stomach. "Any chance we can sneak off there tonight while everyone is here?"

She scanned the restaurant, and for a brief moment, panic flared that she'd say no.

Instead, she smiled up at me. "I'll meet you there in twenty minutes. Just let me say good night to my parents."

She slipped from my grasp before I could double check, but hell if it wasn't sexy watching her walk away.

That dress fit her like a glove.

It'd take a miraculous feat of nature to prevent me from sprouting a hard-on during the wedding tomorrow. No wonder why grooms and groomsmen always stood at the altar with their hands in their pockets.

FURTHER PROVING she was all on board with this idea, Kimmy didn't need twenty minutes.

Good thing because I arrived in ten, with only a towel wrapped around my waist. At least, it was supposed to be a towel. It never failed to amaze me that hotels didn't take into account the potential size of guests when purchasing linens. One quick, harsh breeze could have it falling to the sand.

Although that worry fled as soon as Kimmy's shadow and then the rest of her stepped into the clearing of the beach near the sole, pale light at the bench where you were required to leave your belongings.

She arrived in fifteen, a beach bag in her hand and a towel wrapped around her body.

Almost looking exactly like she did that first night, except this time, she wasn't sneaking past my villa—she strolled with the confidence she probably carried into her courtrooms to battle deadbeats and abusers.

I briefly remembered what Marshall had said about Ricky and her job. Ignored it when she kicked off her sandals.

"You're early."

"So are you." She set down her bag on the bench.

"I couldn't wait." No reason to lie about it. Not anymore. If I had forty-eight hours to convince Kimmy we could do this... or at least *try*... then I had to bring my all-star game.

She came toward me on the sand, gaze dropping to my stomach, lingering there before dipping lower and quickly rising back up. "Neither could I."

Her voice was husky, and I figured once I plucked the towel from where it was tucked in between her breasts, I'd find her small, pale pink nipples hardened into needy little points. Her tan lines from this week would follow the swell of her handful-sized breasts and her lower area would point me right to where I wanted to be inside of her.

"Fuck," I groaned, already hard from looking at her, and hell. Let her look all she wanted. And touch. And taste.

I flicked the tiny corner of my own towel at my hip and let it fall to the ground. Let her see what she did to me in less than two minutes. "Every time I see you it hurts, you're so pretty."

She giggled and shook her head. "That *does* look like it'd hurt."

I wrapped my hand around my length and stroked slowly. "Only because I get so damn turned on whenever you're around."

"So it's my fault?"

She took a step toward me and reached out, covering her hand with mine. I quickly flipped our hands so it was her skin on mine and I stroked harder, faster, taught her how I liked it until we were both mesmerized by the tan skin of our hands, our entwined fingers sliding up and down my shaft.

But not so mesmerized I forgot about her damn towel. I reached out with my other hand and met her gaze. "This okay?"

"Always."

And then it was us and skin and moonlight and sand and rolling waves, absolutely nothing separating us except for salty air. Which I quickly closed the gap on and tugged her into my arms, slammed my mouth to hers, and kissed her with the fervency of a man who was not going to say goodbye in forty-eight hours.

If she wasn't ready for my words, I'd let my actions do the talking for now.

His kiss was different. More desperate, more fierce, and I loved every single punishing second of his mouth on mine and our tongues twisting together as we continued working him with our hands together.

"Just so you know, I'm not fucking you on this beach." He pulled off my mouth and trailed kisses to my jaw, back to my ear, and down my throat before reversing the direction.

"No?"

"No." His hand tightened around mine. "But we are going to get off here, first me, and then you're going to show me exactly what you did that first night."

"Oh..." A delightful shiver of excitement coursed through me. Every time he got a little bossy my core tightened and grew wetter. "Then perhaps I should stop using our hands."

I dropped to my knees and watched his jaw fall in surprise, but it quickly changed as I sank my mouth around his tip, trailed my tongue all over his shaft and down his length. I played with his heavy, large balls and drew his head into my mouth.

His jaw snapped close, his head fell forward and his hand

came to the back of my head. Not controlling, but there was a slight sting as he grabbed my hair and moved with my tempo.

"Fuck. So good, Kimmy. So damn good." I worked him quickly, then slowly. I wanted to savor this moment of him kissed by the moonlight and brought to his knees by me. I wanted to remember everything about this night, quickly becoming our last.

Mostly, I wanted no adventure we could do together left undone.

His hips bucked as I gagged around him, so deep, and still not close to having all of him. My other hand worked his base, wet from my spit and his precum, and as I tried to take more, I swallowed around him.

"Fuck," he grunted again. Cursed and praised. He told me I was such a good girl and I was doing so well and he was so close to coming and all the praise shot sparks of pleasure to my own wet sex but where last time I'd taken care of myself before, but tonight I wanted to do it just for him.

Let him see how much he drove me wild.

Let him see how even though I was a master at my own self-care, I was pretty damn certain he was better.

"Shit, Kimmy. I'm going to come."

I hummed my approval, took him deep again, and forced my eyes to look up. I met his gaze over the ripples of his abs and his hard, square jaw, took him as deep as I could through blurry, watering eyes, and right as his movements quickened, I opened and took him deeper, swelling around him.

"Shit shit shit." He chanted more curses. More praises.

And he came down my throat like a man possessed. Or perhaps... a man obsessed, and hopefully it was with me.

When he was done, I lingered on his hardness, ensuring all of him was cleaned up before I slid back.

I wiped my eyes and Max was there, pulling me to my feet where he brushed tears off my cheeks with his thumbs while he brutalized my swollen lips with his.

"You're so damn incredible," he murmured, and then lifted me, until I had no choice but to wrap my legs around us. He carried me toward the water, still breathless from his climax, and once we neared the edge of the sea's lapping tide, he settled us down.

"Your shoulder," I muttered because I'd felt it that time. That hitch of pain when he lifted me.

"Is fine," he grunted.

He sat on the beach and spun me around so I was in his lap. His knees bent, he widened them and draped mine outside of his.

"What are you doing?"

"Want to see you and the water and the moon while you get yourself off."

"That's…"

"Sexy. I know. I have good ideas."

I laughed, bit down on his forearm that was wrapped across my chest, bracing my back to his chest, and laughed harder when he cried out.

"Baby," I teased.

"Man," he grunted, as caveman as they came.

"Same thing." I shrugged and his teeth bit into my shoulder, surprising me and I echoed his earlier cry.

"Now who's the baby?"

He kissed where he bit and hummed, a finger running over what I assumed would be teeth marks. "Not hard enough to leave a mark for tomorrow, but damn if I don't want to do that to you."

My pussy spasmed at the thought and since I was sitting on him, he must have felt my lower body tremble.

Max chuckled in my ear and leaned back, reclining us with his hands bracing up on the sand behind.

"I feel so exposed," I muttered as I saw every inch of me, opened and spread out for him.

"You're safe with me. Always will be."

It was a heavy promise for a man who'd be walking out of my life in two days, but I pushed that thought down. "I know."

I turned as much as I could and kissed his shoulder. Then I twisted, the move difficult from how wide he had my legs but I was able to lift my chin and brush it along the column of his throat. "Do you know what I thought of that night when I thought of you?" As I asked the question, whispering my secrets against his skin, I trailed my hand over my breasts and tugged at my nipples.

"What?" The gravel was back in his voice and I grinned against his skin.

"I wondered what kind of man you were, in bed. If you'd be bossy. Specifically, if you'd boss me around. It got me so hot."

"You like it when I take control."

"I love it." And my hand slipped down my stomach to meet my other where my bundled nerves were swollen, pulsing, and wet. "Oh God," I groaned, flinching at that first, soft contact.

As I did, he cursed against my cheek. "Shit. This was a bad idea. I want to fuck you so bad right now. Touch you. Taste you. You're so damn delicious, so sweet."

I moved my fingers to his praise and compliments and even though he wasn't touching me, his dick grew harder again, brushed against me with every roll of my hips.

"That's it. Two fingers, show me how you like it, Kimmy, so I can make it the best you've ever had."

"You already have," I rasped, my head now pushing against his shoulder.

"Slide them in deep and add a third."

I listened. He knew exactly what to say to drive me absolutely crazy. I cried out, biting down on my bottom lip, moving my fingers to his command inside me with one hand, my finger around my clit throwing me over the edge.

I came like a rocket, and he quickly wrapped an arm around me. Without that, I might have face-planted into the sand.

"Jesus, you're beautiful," he murmured, voice thick. "So damn sexy. Always, Kimmy. I hope you know I'll always think that about you."

And it sounded like goodbye. Or a promise. I wasn't certain and the haze of my climax was clearing, muddling my thoughts, everything but my surroundings until I shattered in a cacophony of noises and cries and bright lights behind my closed eyelids.

"Shit, I can't believe we just did that," I said once I slipped fingers from inside me. He took my wrist and brought it to his mouth, humming in pleasure as he darted his tongue out. He cleaned the taste of me off my fingers off and nipped my fingertip.

"It will be a memory I'll never forget."

His eyes were no longer heated. They'd softened along with his smile. Perhaps it was the post-orgasm haze. Perhaps it was more.

Either way, I turned on his lap and pressed my hand to his cheek and kissed him softly.

"Me either," I admitted.

I wouldn't forget a single moment of this week with him.

"Do you know what I want to do now?"

His hands brushed up and down my thighs before he wrapped his arms around my stomach. He held me to him in such a gentle way and swayed slightly while we watched the dark sea. "I have a few ideas."

"Of course you do. But I'm not talking about those." I twisted so I could kiss his chin. "I want to watch you play."

"Play?"

"Hockey. I don't know anything about it."

His arms around me squeezed me tighter, and I was pretty sure gravel was in his throat again. "You want me to teach you about hockey?"

"Yeah. Can you?"

"I've got some game film on my computer."

"Can we watch them?"

"Only if you stay naked."

I laughed and held up my hand for him to shake. As soon as he pressed his palm to mine and that familiar electric tingle shot up my arms, we shook. "Deal."

"FOR SOMEONE who was a nervous wreck last night, you certainly have your composure today," I teased Bridget from beneath the scowl of the hairdresser who was having to re-blowout and straighten my hair.

In my sex-crazed haze last night, I'd let Max carry me back to his villa where he promptly tossed us both in the shower. Not thinking clearly, I'd completely forgotten to twist my hair into a chignon to keep it out of the water and as soon as I realized what I'd done, I'd shrieked, terrifying Max so bad he almost slipped right onto his ass.

Fortunately, he saved himself and we didn't have to maneuver the rest of the night around icing his tailbone.

Unfortunately, I had to face the wrath of the hairdresser when I called the resort this morning to see if she could get me in earlier so my mass of hair wouldn't delay the wedding.

Good thing for Max, he'd gotten to see me with curly hair. From the way he continued touching it, fisting it and then splaying it out across his chest I'd made him happy.

Bad thing for me, three hours into my appointment and the hairstylist was still scowling at me. Also pretty sure she was jabbing the bobby pins into my hair unnecessarily rough.

Lucky for her, I was still high on sex with Max that morning, so I wasn't ripping her a new one for being unprofessional... it'd been an accident for the Mother's sake.

"Of course I'm not nervous. I'm marrying Marshall today."

She winked at me and got a slap on the wrist from her makeup artist. Right. We were supposed to sit still like porcelain dolls for *hours*.

I mean, had these ladies ever worked with women? We talked. A lot.

Another rough jab of a pin hit my scalp and I flinched, and

then cried out when the tight grip on my hair was pulled by my maniacal stylist.

My hands clenched into a fist and I shot her a scowl.

She... the irritating woman, grinned at me.

And winked.

"So things with you and Max are good?" Bridget asked, with her eyes closed while the stylist applied shadow to her lids.

"They're what they've always been. A week of fun." I ensured I didn't move a muscle while I spoke and gave up the pretense. Marshall clearly knew. We hadn't fooled Bridget at breakfast. I was leaving tomorrow. There was no point in hiding anything anymore.

Fortunately there were no errant stabs of pins to my scalp.

"That's it?"

"What do you want me to say, Bridget? That we're falling in love after a week? That's ridiculous."

"I knew with Paul in three hours."

"Unhelpful, Gretchen," I drawled.

"Same. I mean, maybe not three hours but the second date for sure with Brad."

Bridget opened her eyes long enough to smirk at me. Pretty sure she was silently saying *See?* "The first time Marshall met Nathan I knew."

"That's not love, it's lust," I muttered, and I was pretty sure the stylist who despised me was nodding along with me.

"No," Gretchen said. Her hand settled on my knee and I focused on her in the mirrors in front of us. "I knew lust. I knew chemistry. There was absolutely something different the night I met Paul. It was instant. This connection where within moments I already felt closer to him than anyone else I'd ever met. That conversation flowed like we'd been best friends, soulmates separated at birth or something and found each other. It was the most insane thing, but I knew. He told me he always knew within that first week too. Said he would have proposed then if he wasn't scared I'd laugh my ass off and he'd lose me."

"It is possible," the woman doing Bridget's hair chimed in.

Great. Like I needed further interference here.

It was *five* days. I couldn't be falling in love with a man I barely knew.

But I did know him... he wasn't only an attractive man. He was a good man. I'd never been able to tease someone so easily or be teased without feeling like their words were more barbs than playfulness. I'd never felt like I could sit and talk to them for hours, or find peace in them sleeping next to me. I'd never felt comforted by their presence while they were next to me and I was reading. I'd never been so interested in their lives. How they lived. All Max and I had done this week was *talk*. None of it the usual superficial stuff like favorite colors and movies, especially after the other night.

But these women were crazy. Had to be.

There was no way I was falling in love after five days.

Was there?

The sun was at our backs, making sweat drip down my spine. Next to me, Maverick wiped sweat off his brow.

The parents were all seated. The bridesmaids and bride would be walking down the aisle at any moment. Yesterday's gloomy weather was long gone, and in its place was the sun, beating down at our backs through our white dress shirts. My ass was burning through the navy dress pants we had on, and I couldn't wait until the ceremony was over so I could remove my matching navy tie.

I tugged at it, tried to get air beneath my collar, but it was no use.

Close to me, Marshall was doing the same, although based on the constant fidgeting he wasn't purely fighting the heat.

"Getting cold feet?" I asked, which was an odd saying, especially since ours were bare and burning hot against the wooden makeshift altar.

"I don't want to screw this up for Bridget," he muttered.

Malcolm pressed his hand to Marshall's shoulder. We'd done the pep talks, the couple shots of tequila to loosen ourselves up, but apparently, Malcolm had one last piece of wisdom to give.

"Just don't sport a woody when she walks down the aisle. Trust me. You never live that shit down."

I snorted and covered the sound of my laughter with a cough. "Nice, Malc."

"Seriously. I'll show you the pictures. Shelby still mentions it."

Marshall lifted a hand. "I don't need to see those. *No one* needs to see those."

"I'm just sayin'... be prepared in about forty-five seconds to start reciting Max's hockey stats or something equally boring. That's sure to deflate anyone's erection."

"Hey." I knocked my elbow into his side. "I would think statistics would only increase your excitement."

He rolled his eyes and rocked to his heels. "True. Numbers are easier than people."

"Not helping at all, assholes," Marshall said and the music changed, signaling the arrival of the bridesmaids. "Fuck. This is it, huh?"

"Enjoy every second," Malcolm said in a whispered rush as our little sister came into view. "Trust me. Enjoy every damn second of this and tomorrow and the day after and you'll be fine."

Morgan stepped into view first. And shit. Our sister looked gorgeous. If she ever pulled her face out of a book long enough to meet a man, she'd have five brothers watching their every move. But it wasn't her in a long dress similar to the ones they wore yesterday that had a lump growing in my throat. It was Malcolm's words. Because as Morgan came down the aisle and I waited to see Kimmy, it was *her* I was thinking of.

I'd enjoyed every single second of my time with her this week and was refusing to count down the hours until I had to say goodbye to her. Last night, sitting in my villa with her curled up while I explained hockey to her, my role on the team, and told her about my teammates was possibly the most intimate encounter with a woman in my life.

Even when she'd pulled the laptop off my thighs and climbed

over me, I *almost* hadn't wanted that moment to end. Granted, that particular moment led to other fantastical moments permanently seared into my brain.

But it was no longer about the sex, not completely.

There was something so incredibly alluring about Kimmy, the way she spoke, the confident way she knew exactly what she wanted. Hell, her drive and her career, the passion and excitement she'd shared when she told me about her job... all of it tied up in a perfectly wrapped gift I wanted to savor forever.

"Holy shit," I whispered, choking on my own breath as she appeared.

Her hair, once again straight, forced me to press my lips together so I didn't laugh. The dress was the color of the water as it met sand, light teal or a pale blue I didn't know, but against her freshly tanned skin from the week and the smile on her face, she appeared more elegant and more regal than any other moment.

"Nice," Maverick next to me teased. "Good call."

"Shut up," I told him under my breath.

I couldn't tear my eyes off her as she walked down the aisle. Couldn't help myself from imagining her walking to *me* at the end of it. It'd never happen, not if she didn't believe in marriage, and hell, not if she didn't want to see me after this, but no way in hell was I going to back down from trying to convince her for more either.

There had to be a compromise somewhere between marriage and never seeing her again, and I was determined to find it.

Our eyes met as she neared the altar and, if I wasn't mistaken, her already pink cheeks darkened. I looked at her, let her see every rush of emotion I was currently experiencing and held her gaze until she stepped off to the side.

I couldn't tear my eyes off her, the way she dipped her chin and whispered something to Bridget's friend I didn't know... Carrie, I thought. I was still looking at her when she slid her eyes back to me. They caught again, and this time she gazed at me and I swore—

freaking swore—hell, I'd bet my next year's salary on it, that she was feeling the same way as me.

I'd never connected with someone as deeply as I did her, from the first second of contact. Hell, every time we touched, there was a spark. A push to get closer. It wasn't chemistry. I'd had that. I'd reveled in cheap chemistry.

This was different. Deeper.

As her blue eyes sparkled in the sun, brighter than the ocean waters or the crystal clear sky, as they shined on me, I knew.

I'd do *anything* to make this work.

Distance and time and commitments be damned.

KIMMY'S HAND was warm and in mine as she opened her sliding glass door.

I hesitated before following her inside. This was our last night. Tomorrow I'd hop the first puddle jumper flight back to the main island and board my plane for Miami before having a four-hour layover and returning to Vegas.

Kimmy would go to California.

The distance wasn't unsurmountable, it was the question of her feelings for me. Neither of which I wanted to bring up now and risk ruining our night. If by chance, she only gave me one more night with her, I was going to make it worth it.

Her brows puckered. "Are you coming in?"

"Yeah." I cleared my throat, pushed down all the thoughts that'd been constantly swirling since I realized how much she'd come to mean to me in such a short time.

The wedding went smoothly, although I wasn't sure I'd ever let Marshall live it down when he got all teary-eyed saying his vows to Bridget. But then he had to go and give a ring on a gold chain to Nathan, promising to do right by both mom and son, and even my eyes turned misty. The reception was a blast, the food excellent, the wild dancing and drinks top notch.

But through it all, I'd counted down the minutes until this moment, right here, both of us a little tipsy but not drunk.

If I wasn't mistaken, Kimmy had as much on her mind as I did, which had left the walk back to her place quieter than usual.

"Drink?" she asked, moving to her fridge.

"I'm good." I'd need water later, but tonight, I simply wanted *her*.

As she opened a bottled water, her soft smile turned to me. "Tonight was great, but I'm exhausted."

"Me too, and I'm on an early flight tomorrow."

She drank her bottle, and I watched as her throat moved, remembered how good that throat felt swallowing my dick, and cleared my throat.

I wanted to take tonight slow. If she was up for it.

"How tired are you?"

"Not too tired for whatever you're thinking."

"Reading my mind now?"

She twirled her finger in front of my face from across the counter. "Your face says plenty. It's your *thinking about what I want do with my tongue* face."

A laugh rushed from me. "My tongue? You think I was thinking about what I was going to do to you with my tongue?"

Although she wasn't too far off.

"You know what I mean."

"I was thinking about your throat swallowing my cock, if you want to be specific. I suppose there's a tongue involved."

Water spewed from her mouth, hitting me on the chest.

"Oh my God. I'm sorry."

I wiped it off, both of us now laughing. "I probably deserved it anyway. Do you know what I'd like to do first?"

"Now I'm afraid to ask."

I walked around the end of the counter. Her hair was gorgeous.

There were some twists with her hair and they were pinned back, but most of it was down. It was curled, but it wasn't her kind of curled. I reached out and tugged on one so it bounced. "I'd really like to see you in your natural hair one more time."

She swallowed and her eyes grew heavy. "One more time. Right."

And yet she said no more.

"For me?" I asked, and a lump was growing in my throat again.

"I can do that. As long as you help me tug out the two hundred pins in my hair first."

"I can do that."

She spun, putting her back to me, and while I pulled out each and every pin in her hair until there was a massive pile on the counter, we talked. About nothing. About everything. We drifted into conversation about some of the cases she'd worked on. The things she'd seen. I bent down frequently and kissed her shoulder when she grew emotional.

"Do you want to join me?" she asked, reaching back to unzip her dress. I stilled her hand.

I did. Dear God, I wanted that.

But then we wouldn't have slow either.

"I'll jump in when you're done. I don't want to hurry anything tonight."

She grinned at me as she twisted her neck. "Okay. Then unzip me?"

"Gladly."

I WAS ON THE BED, feet kicked up, only in my boxers when Kimmy finally stepped out of the bathroom. She hadn't joked when she said it took her hours to do her hair. I'd poured a quick cup of coffee to ensure I was awake and thank God I did.

The sight of her in a towel wrapped around her small frame? That hair?

The timid smile on her face as she caught sight of me?

Perfect. Absolutely perfect.

I rolled to my side and patted the bed next to me. "Come here."

She didn't hesitate. She came my way with that confident stride and halfway to the bed, dropped the towel.

Hell *yes*.

"You're the sexiest woman I've ever seen," I told her as she placed a knee to the bed.

She grinned and shook her head. "Not even close."

I grabbed her hips and yanked, rolling to my back as she squealed. A burst of heated pain sluiced down my arm and I gritted my teeth. "Then you don't know what I see."

She was laughing now, head tipped down, creating a curtain around us and her hands were at my chest, playfully running her thumbs over my chest. My nipples.

"And what do you see?"

I skated my hand up her arm, cupped the back of her neck, and brought her down to me until our lips met. "Perfection. Gorgeous, confident, sweet, and sassy perfection."

She hummed against my mouth and then I took hers, kissing her in slow, soft strokes, stroking the fire between us until she rolled her hips, showed me her need.

Carefully, taking care of her and my shoulder, I rolled us again so she was beneath me I settled my weight on top of her, propped up on my elbows so I didn't smash her, and with one hand, removed my boxers until I could kick them to the floor. "There are so many things I want to do to you, so many ways I think of taking you, but tonight, I want you slow. I want it hard, and I want to make it so good for you, you never forget the feel of me deep inside of you."

I mumbled it at her throat, her jaw. I whispered all the things I wanted to do, the places I wanted to taste, the areas I wanted to touch so the map of her body was embedded in my palms.

And then I did everything I promised. We didn't fuck. We didn't have sex. I made love to Kimmy long into the night. Until her throat was hoarse from her cries. Until she pushed me off and pleaded, "no more, I can't take anymore." I made love to her until her scent was permanently ingrained into my brain, and my gut ached at tomorrow being the last time I could ever see her.

I turned to kiss her one last time, counting them down because the end could be soon.

"Please," she whispered, reaching for me. And even though she was the one who said she couldn't take more, she asked for *one more* time.

I made love to her once more, until we both crashed from exhaustion.

FUCK. I rolled over and slapped at the alarm app on my phone. It was on a quiet beep, but that didn't matter. I'd trained myself long ago to not need a loud, obnoxious sound to wake up to.

It was morning. Time to pack and board a plane and fly all day and it was time to say goodbye.

"Damn," I groaned and scrubbed my hands down my face. Kimmy was next to me, sleeping on her side, but I knew the moment I grazed her jaw with my finger she was awake, too.

"I need to get going."

"No." She was barely awake, eyes hadn't even opened but she still pulled me down on top of her. "Not yet."

"I need to catch the flight."

"What time is it?"

"It's five. My flight's at six-thirty."

"Oh shit." She opened her eyes and wiped hair off her face. Thank *God* I'd asked her to shower. All those untamed and crazy curls were definitely a sight I was going to miss seeing every morning. "I'm on that flight too. I can't believe I forgot. I totally—"

God, she was cute. I kissed her to silence her and when I pulled back, she was less sleepy but still soft. "You have an hour. It's okay."

Bonus to me. If she was on my flight, we didn't need to say goodbye yet.

"I need to get back to my villa and shower and pack. Why don't I come back for you when I'm done and we can take the taxi to the airport together?"

As much as it could be called an airport when it only had two tiny planes.

"That'll work."

"Good. I'll see you soon."

She reached up and slid her hand to the back of my neck, up to the longer part of my hair on top. "I wish we had more time."

We had all the time in the world, she just didn't see it yet. The fact she didn't want to let me go said enough. For now. "Let's talk when we're awake, okay?"

"About?"

I kissed her instead of answering. "I'll be back in forty-five minutes."

Her eyes narrowed and her lips pushed out. "All right, hotshot."

Every second that ticked on my watch felt like doom. We were quiet, drinking our coffee and managing not to spill any in our laps on the bumpy ride to the island's airport. As the plane took off, I'd reached over and grabbed Max's wrist. It was windy, and we were thrown back and forth while the pilot took off until he finally stabilized in the air.

When I went to let go, no longer at risk of throwing up that coffee, Max flipped his hand and held mine back.

How was I going to say goodbye to this man? Because we were now going through security, slipping back into our sandals. We'd barely spoken and yet what was there to say?

Goodbye stuck to my throat like glue and every time I thought the words, my stomach churned. Silly, right? Yet what were we supposed to do? Exchange numbers and hug like we'd made a new friend?

A giggle escaped my throat and I slapped my hand over my mouth.

"What?" Max asked, threading his belt through the belt loops of his light blue shorts. "Are you laughing at me?"

"No." I shook my head, still laughing. "I just realized we don't have each other's phone numbers."

His amber eyes darkened for a second and then he dropped his head, chuckling along with me. "Seems like something we would have done earlier if we'd been in the real world, huh?"

Right. Because we weren't in the real world when we met. It was a vacation. A fling I frequently reminded him. A fantasy every single woman dreamed of—a great sexy hook-up with a man who knew where to find a clitoris.

"Do you want it?" he asked.

"Want what?" My brain was muddled by the sex thinking.

"My number."

"Oh. Sure. I mean, if you think—"

"I want you to have it."

"Okay then." My cheeks were hot. Burning. Embarrassment rolled through me in a flash of fire, making my fingertips hot and tremble when I handed my phone over to him. "Code is JELLY."

His head had bent at my screen, a view of the California coast I hadn't seen in a year. "Jelly?" he chortled, peered up at me through his dark lashes.

I confirmed with a nod. "Jelly."

His fingers moved on my screen. "Care to explain that one?"

"Who would guess it?" I asked and seconds later, his phone dinged in his hand and his screen lit up.

"You have a point." He handed me my phone back and smiled as he pulled out his own. "But for some reason, I think there's more to it." He gave me a scrupulous look and gestured to my phone. "Look."

I peered down at my messaging app, still open. "Hotshot." I rolled my eyes. "Of course that's your name."

"Could be stud muffin."

"Absolutely no."

"Sex king?"

"Do you want me to throw my phone at your face?"

His smile stretched ear-to-ear. "You won't. You think it's too pretty to mess up."

He had a point. "Fine. You're right on that one."

"I'm always right." He bent to grab his carry-on backpack and pulled it over his shoulders. Both of us had checked our larger suitcases when we arrived, so I just had my purse and my business laptop bag with me. "So, what time does your flight leave?"

"Nine thirty-eight."

His eyes widened. "Are you connecting in Miami?"

"Yeah." Wait a second. "Do we have the same flight back home?"

My brain must have been seriously sex muddled to not consider this before. What were the odds? I knew my parents weren't leaving until this afternoon so they could help Bridget's parents clean up and get Nathan back home. It hadn't occurred to me we'd be on the same flight back to the States.

Max gave me that panty-melting smile one more time and threw his arm over my shoulders. "Looks like you're not getting rid of me yet."

I was already dreading the moment I would.

MAX DRAGGED me into a pizza place. Yep. At seven-forty-five, I was walking into a pizza restaurant.

At my ridiculous expression, he explained, "I have to go back to low-carb as soon as I get home. This might be my last pizza for the next six months."

Fortunately, they served breakfast pizzas, all served buffet style so while Max loaded up his tray with three all-meat pizza slices, one supreme, two cheese, and what looked like a Margherita, I slid one slice of a sausage, egg, and cheese onto my tray.

"So, a low-carb diet during the season for you?"

"Yeah. I eat a shit ton of fish, salmon mostly, and other lean meat. Boatloads of vegetables. I have to, though. I'm getting old to still be in the league. I mean, hell, one of our newest players is so young he can't even legally drink yet."

"Seriously? Wait... Arlo?"

"You remember."

I remembered everything about the night he told me about his team while we watched game film. About last night. The entire week.

"I'm a lawyer. A good memory is a key component." I blew it off and felt the sting of his disappointment, but what was he expecting? Me to throw myself at him? Beg him to call me and come see me? If I'd had any hope of that being a possibility, it was shot to hell and back before listening to him talk about his season, the intensity of it, how often they had games, and how much they were on the road.

If we lived in the same city, sure. But that wasn't possible for either of us.

"Right." He bit into a slice of pizza, a quarter of it fitting into his mouth while I picked at a chunk of sausage.

I ate my breakfast slowly while he inhaled his at breakneck speed. The man couldn't only chow down on what was essentially a large pizza by himself, it seemed he did it in a matter of minutes.

Which meant we'd have to walk to our gate.

Say goodbye.

Damn. We should have thought about this earlier. I didn't want our last moments to be in an airport around strangers. Emotion rose in my throat and I swallowed it down, forced it the rest of the way with the last bite of my pizza.

"Do you cook?"

"Me?" His brows jumped. "Of course, yeah. Why?"

"I don't know. You're a single guy. Most men I know don't."

He leaned in with a look part salacious, one hundred percent wicked. "I think we both know by now I'm not like most men you've met."

I squirmed. How did he do this to me? Turned on over pizza at too damn early in the morning.

He sat back in his, looking supremely satisfied.

"No. You're not," I admitted.

"And yes, I cook. Mom always taught us boys how to do things like that before we moved out but especially for me. As soon as I reached high school and the pros were a long-shot possibility and I started taking my training really seriously, Mom did a lot of research into what I should be eating for maximum performance. She not only made me choose the menus, but I had to go shopping with her. Then she taught me how to cook everything."

It sounded like something my mom would do.

"Dancing and cooking. She made sure you guys could handle a home with a partner."

He was chewing on another bite, one of the last two slices, but his expression turned thoughtful. "You're right." He wiped his lips with his napkin. Shamelessly, I followed every pull and tug of those delicious, full lips. I'd miss them, definitely. "Made us all clean, sweep, and mop toilets, everything. We hated it, but she always said we wouldn't be one of those men who let their wives do all the work inside the home or play the *oh I'm too stupid card*, as she called it."

Of course she did. Because she probably expected her boys to get married. Have wives. Grandchildren. The typical, suburban house I'd never once considered being part of my future.

But now…?

I pushed that down, but it was getting harder, souring my stomach every time I did so.

"I wish I would have had more time with her this week. She sounds wonderful."

Max gave a little shrug. It was entirely possible I imagined the shimmering of hope in his eye. "Maybe you'll get to someday."

"Yeah. Maybe."

His grin blinded me.

Then made me promptly want to cry.

How had this man become so important to me? How had he slid through my walls, my no-athlete mantra and become someone I didn't want to walk away from?

More importantly, did I have the guts to bring it up first?

We were four hours away from each other. I'd looked it up even though I'd been to Vegas several times.

Maybe once a month we could squeeze in a weekend? Or I could go to him a night during the week? Change my schedule a little bit. I didn't *always* need to be the one burning the midnight oil. It'd be a change. A compromise on my end for sure, at least during his season, but that was long.

It could work somehow... couldn't it? If we wanted it badly enough?

Did he, though?

That was the question.

"HEY. Watch my bag for a second? I have a question about my connecting flight."

I looked up from my e-reader and then down at his backpack. "Yeah, of course."

"Cool." He bent down, kissed my forehead, and while he walked away, I was too busy swooning over that kiss to take advantage of staring at how good his ass looked in his shorts.

Boarding would start in a few minutes. We'd already glanced at each other's passes on our phones. Of course, Max was sitting in first class. I was only a few rows back in economy, paying extra for more legroom, not because I *needed it*. I hated feeling like a sardine. It was always my luck I got stuck next to either the massive talker and oversharer, a swoony, doe-eyed couple in love who made out the whole time, or a snorer in desperate need of an APAP machine.

Admittedly, when I needed to use the tray table, I also had to scoot to the front of the chair like a child to reach it.

My bottom lip found its way between my teeth, and I nibbled, debating what to do. I only had three hours left with Max and even though I'd been pretending to read, I hadn't read a word. Because we'd talked. Like we always did. We talked about growing up in Ohio. He told me about the small beach town in Virginia where he grew up.

I told him about law school, the LSAT. He grilled me on what life was like for me, in a firm, as a woman in a field still mostly dominated by men. The *thoughtfulness* of that question alone.

"How are you treated?"

Good. Bad. Like an assistant, which actually happened more often than sexual harassment or innuendos. It was the patronizing and dismissing that bugged me more than anything, even if I got so used to it I rarely corrected men anymore. Being called sweetheart by sixty-five-year-old men, or darling, or even once *kiddo*, was so commonplace I barely recognized it anymore. Unfortunate, but true.

"Thanks," Max said and grabbed his bag, sliding back into the seat next to me. His knee knocked into mine playfully.

"Everything okay?" I slid my e-reader back into my bag. I'd have all the time in the world to read all by myself in the months ahead.

"Perfect." He grinned at me and that smile quickly dimmed. "Listen, there's been something I've wanted to talk to you about."

Oh Mother. My heart leaped inside my chest. "Yeah?"

"Thank you for flying *American Airlines*. We are now boarding flight AA three-two-one to Miami. As a thank you to those who are currently serving, we are now seating active military and any passengers needing special assistance."

A rush of people pushed to their feet. I never understood it. The plane didn't take off earlier because everyone stood in a line, crowding in like cattle when they were in group nine while the plane was only boarding first class.

The harsh reality slammed into me, and I turned back to Max. My hand landed on his knee. "What is it?"

Because please, please let him insinuate something... anything.

"Your birthday."

"What?" I jumped back in shock.

"When's your birthday?"

"That's what you wanted to talk about?"

He glanced back to the line that was quickly moving. He was first class. I wanted a hug. A kiss.

I wanted to never let him go.

"No." He shook his head. "That's not it, but we have time for the rest. Right now, I want to know all your favorite everythings but most importantly, your birthday."

Shock must have hit me. Around us, everyone was standing, crowding into their lines. "Why?"

"Because I don't want to miss it." He leaned in then and brushed his lips to my cheek. "Now that I have your number, this isn't goodbye. You know that, right?"

I wasn't sure I ever wanted there to be a goodbye again. I was already nodding, breath hitching and getting caught in my throat. "I'd hoped so."

"Good." His hand slipped to my cheek, cupped my jaw, and then he brought our lips together. He kissed me softly, no tongue, but no less intense until someone's throat cleared behind us. He pulled back and bent so our foreheads pressed together. "Birthday."

"October fourth."

"Ten-four." He grinned. "Got it. Take care, Kimmy. I'll see you soon, okay?"

He stood, grabbed his backpack and then he was maneuvering through the lines and crowds so quick, I was still stunned in my seat, watching him leave.

That was *it*?

TWENTY-SIX

MAX

I was rolling dice and playing a game I wasn't sure I'd win. A part of me felt like a dick. I should have said something. Manned up and grabbed my balls and told her what I wanted.

But truly, it wasn't until breakfast when I mentioned my mom I felt that this could go in my favor. As if the fates putting us together wasn't enough. Like it'd been a coincidence we ended up on the same three-hour connecting flight. I had a forty-five-minute layover, which meant I'd need to haul ass to my next flight. Kimmy's was two hours.

Doubts assailed me. I should have talked to her two nights ago on the beach. Last night.

This morning.

I should have said what I was feeling any time, as soon as I thought it.

But I was afraid. Yeah, big old *player*, Max Mikolajczyk, was afraid of her rejection. No other woman would compare. The feelings I had around her would never be the same with anyone else.

I knew it to the depths of my soul. I knew it more than I knew I wanted to play professional hockey when I was ten.

And while I didn't want to play games with her heart, I wanted to ensure when I took my shot, she couldn't walk away. We could figure out all the details of our circumstances thirty-five thousand feet in the air.

As long as they—the stranger, not Kimmy—said yes.

My knee was bouncing and I couldn't sit still. I'd talked to the gate agent and tried to sell her with my offer. As long as they said they'd change seats, she'd make it happen. But it hadn't yet, and most of the plane was full. First-class service had already brought me warm towels and offered me a mimosa, which I declined in lieu of water.

My whole plan to wait could absolutely, one hundred percent blow up in this soft leather seat and leave me looking like a fool because if the person wasn't interested, I wouldn't have time to tell Kimmy what I was thinking.

What I wanted.

What I wanted with a desire that wouldn't die, far past my hockey career.

"Excuse me, Mr. Miko...?"

"Miko-why-check," I said, saying my name exactly how it sounded. It was tricky. The flight attendant who had her hand on the corner of the chair in front of me nodded.

"Mr. Mikolajczyk. We have a passenger who wants to speak with you?"

"Yes. Where?"

"She was late, incoming connection from Puerto Rico was delayed. But she says *yes*, if that's what you wanted to hear."

Abso-fucking-lutely it was. "Yes. Do I need to do anything?"

"No, sir. She wanted to thank you personally."

"Of course."

Fortunately, first class was full but the one seat next to me was empty. And I felt more relieved by that when a woman turned the corner, a baby on her hip, tired purple circles beneath her eyes.

"Gracias. Gracias, señor."

"De nada," I immediately said, almost the only Spanish I

knew outside of *thank you* and *sir*. "De nada," I repeated, and stood from my seat with my water in hand. "Please." I turned to the flight attendant. "Will the seat next to me stay open?"

She shrugged. "I'm not sure. I can check the log, but I don't know off the top of my head."

"No worries." I stood and grabbed my backpack out of the overhead compartment. I should have thought of that earlier. Just moved Kimmy up to first-class with me.

But hell.

I knew her, even if I had done that she wouldn't have liked it. If she wanted first class, she would have done it on her own.

"Gracias," the woman said again. She had one hand over her infant's ear to protect him from noise, a boy, I assumed due to the all-blue sleeper.

"You're welcome. Please. Have a seat. I can get your bag." I pushed it under the seat in front of me, and once she was seated, I told the flight attendant. "If you can take tips, please, there's a special one for you if you take care of her. She looks like she needs it."

"Yes, sir." She nodded. Wasn't exactly an answer, but whatever. I had bigger fish to fry.

I needed to convince a woman who argued for a living to take a chance on a guy she'd rarely see.

Time to shoot my shot.

KIMMY PAID no attention as I stood in the aisle outside her seat. I should have found an overhead bin to store my bag, but the closest ones looked full, so screw it.

I dropped into my seat and kicked my bag beneath the chair in front of me. *Damn, economy sucked* when you were as tall and built as me.

My knee hit hers and she shifted, letting loose an irritated sound as I touched her.

Because of course she would.

"Sorry," I said, and I was already smiling at her as she pulled her face out of her e-reader thingamabob.

It fell to her lap.

"What are you doing here?"

I shrugged shamelessly, because that's what I was. Shameless. Especially when it came to Kimmy.

"I wasn't ready to say goodbye."

"Max..." Her jaw almost hit her e-reader and then her eyes welled with tears.

A crying woman was a bad thing, right? My stomach twisted.

Then she smiled, and her eyes glistened with tears, and what I hoped was joy.

Leaning in, I slid my hand to her cheek. Screw the woman at the window next to her, who was trying *really hard* to look like she wasn't paying attention to us. "I know. It was a week, but it was a hell of a week and it's one I'll remember for a really long time, so don't hate me if I want a few more hours with you, okay?"

"I could never hate you." She leaned in and gave me a soft kiss. Resting her hand on my thigh, I held her against me, until she snuggled up with her head on my shoulder and slipped her hand to my thigh. "Thank you."

The flight attendants came to the front, and outside the window, the stairs we'd used to board the plane were pulled away as the plane started backing up.

Ignoring the safety procedures, I lifted the armrest between us and tucked Kimmy in close to my side. "I want to see you again after we get back home."

Her hand on me squeezed and she lifted her head off my shoulder. "How?"

"I have no idea, but I know today can't be the last time I see you." I shifted then and cupped her cheeks in my hands. "I like you. A lot. I know it'll be difficult. We'll both be busy, but I also think we're worth it."

"I..." Her eyes widened and she bit down on her lip. "We want different things. Long-term. I want to see you, I do. I'm afraid eventually one of us will get hurt."

"There's a risk in any relationship. I'm asking you to take that risk with me. And you can have time to think if you need it."

Hell, I hoped she didn't need it. My heart was thumping like a racehorse against my chest.

She closed her eyes and turned so her lips brushed along the heel of my palm, my inner wrist. Sparks ignited and I shifted in my chair.

I did *not* need to be sporting a hard-on a three-hour flight.

"No," she finally said and peered up at me.

A screech of a record blared inside my brain. "No?"

She grinned and leaned forward. "No. I don't need time to think about it. I can't imagine never seeing you again, either."

"Thank Christ," I muttered and slammed my mouth to hers.

The kiss was hot and searing, definitely risking that hard-on I was so worried about. I pulled back before we could take it too far for where we were.

And shit.

That wouldn't happen for a long ass time, because now we had to figure out when in the hell we could see each other again.

TWENTY-SEVEN
KIM

"You're an idiot."

"Excuse me?"

My assistant, Ethan, stared down at me, shaking his perfectly gelled in place black hair. "You heard me. You're an idiot. If Theo was having meetings with his doctors, meetings that could decide his *future*, I'd be doing whatever I need to get to him."

"We're not like that." Because we weren't. Not Max and I. Not yet.

It'd been two weeks since we got off that plane in Miami and went our separate directions at the airport to our connecting flights.

Two weeks of daily phone calls and nightly FaceTime calls.

Two weeks of not being able to touch him, to taste him.

I was *dying*.

And tomorrow, he was coming to me. We'd planned it because it was his free weekend and until his season started, he'd spend most of the time traveling to me. I'd go to him when he had home weekend games, the rare weeknight he'd have a day off. My schedule was now color-coded and blocked until Thanksgiving since I'd downloaded his schedule and gone through it with a Sharpie marker.

He'd laughed his ass off when I admitted what I'd done, saying, "Damn. You must really like me."

I hadn't been able to deny it.

But tomorrow was huge.

Max had an appointment with his doctor tomorrow and his coach. Then the team's general manager and owner.

He'd already had CT scans done when I finally convinced him to talk to his doctor about his headaches that didn't stop when we returned. He'd also had an MRI done to see if he needed shoulder surgery.

Tomorrow, his fate for the first half of the season, if not forever, would be decided.

I wanted to be there for him, not stand and pace in my office and then my home, worried about him driving to me afterward.

Because Mother... what if it was bad news?

He'd confessed how much Charlotte's words way back when had messed him up. How hockey was all he'd had for a long time. What would he do without it? It'd been a bad night, and I hadn't been able to hold him or distract him from his fears.

Ethan slapped his hands to my desk and all five-foot-ten and one-hundred and thirty slim pounds of him glared at me. "Go home. *Pack.* And then go to him."

I stared at him. My blank phone screen. My calendar currently pulled up on my computer to see it filled with meetings and consults and depositions...

Ethan shoved me back and slapped the cover of my laptop closed.

"What the fuck?"

"I've *got* this. It's a *day*, Kimberly. Go the fuck home and fucking pack."

I could do that. But should I?

"What if he doesn't want me there? I mean, if it's bad news?"

"Then he doesn't care enough or appreciate you enough to see how awesome you are."

My chin trembled as Ethan continued to glare at me, dropping his hand from my now blank screen and stepping back. "If you care about him, be there for him. If he cares about you, that's all he'll want *if* it's bad news. But he could still be okay."

"Of course he'll be okay." Because somehow, over two weeks, I stopped caring that he was a professional athlete. I'd changed. He changed me. Now, I only wanted Max to have everything he possibly wanted and for him, it was hockey. Which meant he'd have it.

Ethan's lips quirked. He'd never once hidden his sexual orientation in the office. Hell, he still wore the same black eyeliner he had the day he interviewed for me. Some days he wore other makeup, including mascara, some highlighter. He'd taught me how to do the perfect cat's eye and the current trending winged eyeliner look.

Today, his own was smudged, evidence of stress. Probably caused by me.

"I should go see him," I said with an affirmative nod.

If Max got bad news, he'd want his own things. His friends. His teammates, maybe, but he was a social guy. Driving through the desert for hours, alone, would be hell.

"Then go."

I grabbed my keys and my purse and glanced at my laptop. So much work to do.

Ethan scowled. "I have *got* this."

"And I've got dinner with you and Theo, on me, when I get back."

"Agreed."

He stood in front of my laptop while I gathered the rest of my things like he was afraid I'd run off with it.

He wasn't entirely wrong. The thought I had of stopping burning the midnight oil hadn't quite happened.

But I could take a weekend. A day off. No harm, no foul. Ethan would take care of me.

"Can you—" I had a new consult in the morning.

"As soon as you're gone." Lucky me, having a mind reader as my assistant.

"I love you. You know that, right?"

"Psssh. Obviously. I'm loveable. Theo says it all the time."

I chuckled, leaned in, and kissed his cheek. Ethan wasn't just my assistant, he and his fiancé were the closest friends I had. "I'll call you when I get there."

"A text is fine, and I'll be tracking your phone anyway."

Of course he would.

"He'll want me there, right?" Because, dear Mother, I was a nervous hen right now. But what if I got to Max's place and he *didn't* want me there. What if....

"If he doesn't, he's a fool."

Right.

I would just need that tattooed somewhere visible so I could remember it. Good gracious. How had it come to this? Three weeks after meeting Max and I was a complete nervous wreck.

"Okay then. I'm going to go home and pack and hit the road. I'll see you Monday."

"Tuesday, if you need it. I'll clear everything until then."

"You're a saint."

Ethan smirked. "Oh no, honey. I am most definitely no saint."

I PULLED INTO VEGAS, more specifically Max's condo building's parking lot nearing seven o'clock. Like clockwork for the last two weeks, he called me right at seven. I hadn't intended to arrive when he would be calling me any moment, but considering I had no way to actually get into his secured, locked building without him, it was fortuitous when I walked up to his building, and his name appeared on my screen, requesting a FaceTime call.

My heart leaped into my throat and my hand shook.

I'd worried for hours about whether or not I should surprise him, or let him know I was headed this way. The surprise seemed fun, up until this exact moment where I was at risk of puking outside his building.

I pressed the green button on my phone and kept my head down in case he recognized the background.

"Hey there," I said, biting my bottom lip.

I glanced up at his building. The double doors. He'd given me his address once when I asked where he lived. It was a nondescript brick building. Basic. Together we'd Google mapped it and he'd described the street view to me, the coffee shop he stopped at. The smoothie place where he was a regular and went far more often.

"God, I can't wait to see you tomorrow." His thick brows tugged in. "Where are you?" He was used to seeing me on my couch, glass of wine in hand right after I walked through the door, or more often than not, still at my office.

"Um." I glanced up and scanned the sidewalk. People passed me, looking curiously at my small suitcase before discarding me and going on about their way.

"Outside," I admitted.

"Outside where?"

"Um." I slowly lifted my phone, turned, putting my back to the coffee shop, and held up my phone so he could see it.

Confusion twisted his features before shock set in. "You're outside my fucking building. No fucking way. What is that, a green screen?"

"No." I laughed and since his smile took up almost the entire screen, I figured this was a good thing, so I tapped the button to show him the front of his building. "I need the code to get in."

I'd been surprised when he didn't live in a building with a doorman or better security. But he said most of the people who lived in this building were young professionals. There were two apartments a few levels lower than his that the team owned, setting up new players for their first twenty-eight days when they were traded or drafted until they could find longer-term homes.

Max had always said he'd like the area so much he didn't want to leave. So he moved to the top floor.

"You're fucking kidding me. Let me see your face again."

Still laughing, I tapped the double-arrow button again and the phone shook while I set it on my face. "Is this okay? It was just, with tomorrow and everything...."

"Get your ass inside. Now."

He gave me the code. My finger shook so bad entering the eight-digit number it took three tries but then I was in the small lobby. Nothing special although it was updated and spacious. A sign for the fitness room and pool would take me in one direction. The mail toward another.

Straight ahead were the elevators.

"I can't believe you're here." The room moved behind him, a blur of the blues and grays on his walls and then colors I didn't recognize.

"I didn't want you to have to drive tomorrow—"

"Ethan forced you to leave work early, didn't he?"

His eyes had darkened when I mentioned tomorrow. If he wanted to avoid it, I could go along with him.

"Yeah," I admitted, and the elevators dinged.

I expected to step onto the elevator and find it empty but instead he was there, standing at the back of it. Phone held so close to his face that I hadn't realized he'd gotten on the elevator to come down.

My feet froze at the threshold.

Two weeks.

Two incredibly long weeks since I'd seen Max, and he looked better than ever.

"Are you going to get in, or will I have to make you?"

Hmmm... the idea had merit.

He made a move to push off the back wall and I hurried before he could get me.

I didn't need to end up with my ass in the air over his shoulder when anyone could walk up and get a flash of my red thong. I hadn't changed my clothes, still in a skirt suit from earlier. The blazer had been tossed to the back of my Jeep, and my blouse was sleeveless, gray with a slight shimmer to it.

Max currently stared at me like I was naked.

As soon as the doors closed, his hands were on my cheeks. Lips pressed to mine. He took me by surprise and I clung to him. Phones clattered to the floor and then I was being moved, my back hit the wall, the gold rail dug into my lower back.

"Shit," he gasped, and then delved his tongue inside my mouth.

My entire body lit up with pleasure and excitement. Needles pricked along my arms, causing goose bumps and my toes curled into my red heels.

"I can't believe you're fucking here," he muttered against my mouth before inhaling and then kissing my forehead.

He wrapped me in a hug and held the back of my head to his chest. "Thank you."

Any remaining worries melted to the floor as I wrapped my arms around his waist and held him back.

I didn't realize how badly I'd needed to see him, feel him again until I did, but once my hands connected in the back and we breathed each other in, I didn't want to be anywhere else.

She was here. In my goddamn basic living room, drinking bottled water, looking like she goddamn belonged in my life and space so perfectly, I was almost terrified to speak for fear of ruining it.

It'd been hell when I'd had to say goodbye to her two weeks ago at the airport.

Even more hellish when I questioned every single time I called whether or not we could make this long-distance thing work with such demanding careers.

That she'd made the effort proved everything I needed to know.

She wanted me as much as I wanted her.

"I'm not sure if I should throw you to my couch, take you to my bed, or take you out for dinner since I'm guessing you're starving."

She turned to me. Pink lips quirked up at a corner. Her hair—goddamn, I missed all that hair more than was reasonably sane—was pulled up off her neck, a huge mess gathered at the top of her head.

She lifted her hands, and her fingers went to the top button of her blouse. It shimmered from the sunlight of my floor-to-ceiling windows behind her.

My stomach clenched as she freed one button.

As she went for the second, my dick took notice.

At the third, she shook her head and said, "Stay right there."

Shit. I hadn't realized I'd moved, but I was now three feet closer to her.

"You're kidding me."

"Nope." She popped the *P* at the same time another button came undone. "I think we should order in... and then you can have me, however, wherever you want me."

Oh, fuck *yes*.

My hands curled into fists as she gently tugged her blouse from her skirt. She had on heels. Bright red. No way they were the ones she liked to wear to court because I knew she didn't have it today, but they were no less sexy. The skirt was skin tight, and as she wiggled that blouse from her waistband, I caught sight of her stomach and groaned.

"God, I missed you," I told her, for maybe the fifth or fiftieth time in the last ten minutes.

"I missed you too."

"I want to move."

"Not yet," she teased. Her voice had turned throaty.

"I thought you liked it when I was in charge."

Her head tilted to the side and she grinned. "Maybe I've changed some of the things I like lately."

Another button freed. The fucking teasing peek of a red bra beneath her blouse.

Dear sweet Jesus. Please let her underwear be matching.

My delicious, pint-sized minx in matching underwear and heels made my dick get harder.

"Like what?"

"Athletes." She grinned and pushed off her blouse. It fell from her shoulders, down her arms and fluttered to the floor.

I didn't see where it landed. I was already moving. Screw her commands. As soon as I got my hands on her, she'd give me exactly what we both loved.

She squealed as I grabbed her hips, flipped her around, and then bent her over the back of the couch. "Hold on, Kimmy."

"You were supposed to stay still." She was laughing, losing all the heat and bossiness in her tone.

Her hands had curled around the back of my leather couch to brace her fall and I covered them with my own.

I found the tiny zipper at the back of her skirt and tugged it, the quiet hiss of it being pulled down amplified by Kimmy's quickened breathing.

It fell to the floor, a halo around the red heels and that matching thong I'd hoped to see revealed in all its glory.

Red. Lace. Her round ass so damn perfect. I cupped her ass and slid my hand up her back. She shivered beneath my touch and turned her face so I could see her.

Lust glistened all over her. She licked her lips as I found the hair tie in her hair. I quickly undid it, careful not to pull at her hair, and then her thick mass of curls I'd missed so damn badly, thought of while I jerked myself after we got off our FaceTime chats, fell down her back and over her shoulders like a curtain.

I was rock hard. Granite. My dick was visible through my athletic shorts. I'd worked out all day, slowly, watched the rest of the team practice, and scowled at all of them who could be on skates while I was still side-lined.

My fate would be sealed tomorrow.

But my future, I figured, was secured the moment Kimmy decided to get in her Jeep and come to me.

"Stay there," I told her, covering her hands with mine and giving them a quick squeeze.

"Why?"

I spanked her playfully. "Because I said so."

I grabbed my phone from where I'd gathered both of ours from the elevator floor and tossed them to the kitchen counter. After pulling up my DoorDash app, I set the screen on my couch so she could see it.

I kissed her shoulder and trailed my fingers down her spine until they dipped in the crease of her backside. I pushed aside her thong and found her sex dripping wet and both of us groaned as I slid a finger inside of her. It'd been too long, and the first feel of her wet heat pulsing around my finger was almost enough to send me over the edge.

I murmured against her skin. "After you tell me what you want to eat, I'm going to drop to my knees and eat you."

MORNING CAME TOO EARLY. Not like I'd had much sleep, but even after I wore Kimmy out, first bent over the couch, then in my bed after we ate dinner, and again when we showered, she fell asleep draped over me.

I stayed awake until exhaustion and worry finally tugged me under around four in the morning.

Now, my alarm was going off, beeping quietly on my nightstand, and Kimmy stirred.

Her hand grazed my stomach, and I stopped her movement.

Today was going to be hell.

The only silver lining on an otherwise gloomy freaking day was that she was here. For me. To support me.

"I want you to come to my meetings today," I said, whispering at her temple. I knew she woke quickly with little lingering in bed because she'd told me, but I'd also noticed it on the beach.

Hell, if only we could go back there.

A few more weeks where the real world didn't matter.

Where my head didn't still pound occasionally and my shoulder didn't still sting if I moved too fast.

None of it were good signs, and as much as I was trying to be optimistic, doing everything I was supposed to, I was finally becoming a realist.

I'd just suffered my fourth concussion in a matter of years. I'd looked into it after I got home.

Coach Vik's face pinched every time I rubbed my temples. My physical therapist, as well as one of the team's doctor's assistants, had started to seemingly enjoy spouting off stats of symptoms and risks of CTE.

"Are you sure?"

The only thing I was sure of was that there wasn't a chance in hell my team would put a guy at risk of brain injury out on the ice again. The league had cracked down in recent years on head injuries. Twenty years ago, they'd do it. Now? No chance in hell would they risk the bad publicity. One wrong slam onto the ice. One wrong hit into the boards and the entire organization could be front and center on *Good Morning America*.

In the worst way possible.

"I'm sure."

"Do we need to leave soon?"

Kim sounded awake, ready to hit the morning running, tackle the obstacle in our path. I'd learned a lot about Kimmy in the last two weeks. Topping the list was that she didn't leave a lot of time in her life for relaxing.

"Not quite yet." I rolled, taking her with me so she was straddling me. God, I loved the way she bounced on my dick. The way her eyes rolled back as soon as I started sliding inside of her.

Her hands pressed to my chest and a smile broke out on her face. "What are you thinking?"

I rolled my hips and showed her exactly what I was thinking. I was already hardening, and the tip of my dick pressed against her ass as she rocked against me. "Of how good you feel wrapped around me. How much I want you."

"Yeah?" She slid down my body and wrapped her hand around my dick. It jumped in her hand as she stroked me slowly.

"Always," I groaned as she tightened her grip and moved her hand just the way I loved.

"Are you sore?" I asked, head pushing back into the pillow while my hips arched up toward her.

"Not bad."

God, I loved that. Loved she felt me long after I was inside of her.

She stroked again, gathered moisture from my tip, and used it for better lubrication. "I want to fuck you until you scream."

Screw my neighbors.

Kimmy chuckled and lifted onto her knees. With her hand around my dick, she guided me to her. "Then do your worst, hotshot."

As soon as I entered her, she gasped. Heat colored her cheeks and her eyes fluttered closed. "Oh God. That's always so good."

She stayed there, letting her body accommodate the stretch and burn of me before slowly sinking down.

"Condom," I grunted. "Wait."

"No. I trust you." As she said it, her hand pressed against my chest for balance.

We'd already talked about me being clean, her being on the pill, but I hadn't not used a condom since that one time on the sand. Even last night I'd used them.

"Are you sure?" I grabbed her hips, stopping her from further moving.

"Sure I trust you? Of course I am." She was being glib.

This wasn't the time. Even so, her trust meant everything given her dislike of athletes.

"If you change your mind—"

"I'd tell you. Now..." She rolled her hips, taking the rest of me deep inside of her and sounds I didn't know I could make escaped my throat.

"Fuck, that feels good."

"Are you going to be a man of your word and do what you promised or am I going to have to do all the work."

This fucking vixen.

"I'm always a man of my word."

I flipped her, rolled us over, and slammed back inside of her tight, wet sheath. Her scream bounced off the walls as I took her hard, fast. I spread her legs wide, drank in the way her body took me so beautifully.

"So fucking perfect," I grunted, staring at her tits.

I dropped one of her legs, grabbed her hips, and pulled her to me as I took her even harder, rolling my hips to set her off faster.

"God, yes. Max. Please." Her hands went to my headboard to brace herself, and I took long, deep strokes, driving her crazy while she pleaded for more and made sure every neighbor knew my name.

She came, clamping around my dick like a vise and all the self-control I had couldn't have held me back.

"Fuck. Yes. Keep coming," I grunted, pressed my thumb to her clit and kept her orgasming going as my balls drew tight with the need to release. I came, shooting deep insider of her while her pussy clenched around me.

"Holy shit, you're good at that," she rasped, peeling a hand off the headboard and running it through my hair. "So freaking good."

I kissed her shoulder, her chin, until my mouth was at her cheek. "I think every time I'm with you might be perfect because I'm falling in love with you."

The words were out before I could suck them back in. I blamed the orgasm. The fear of what was coming. And I expected Kimmy to jolt in surprise.

Instead, she huffed a laugh, turned toward me, and pressed her lips to mine.

"Good," she whispered, lips kicking up into a smile. "Then we're falling together."

TWENTY-NINE
MAX

The high of the morning only lasted until we climbed into my Suburban and headed toward the team's training facility. The guys would be there doing their morning skate practices and working out. After this morning's declarations to each other, Kimmy and I got up and brushed our teeth. I used the bathroom and took a quick shower.

While she was on the way to take hers, I'd wrapped an arm around her, flung her into the air and back to the bed where I gave her two more orgasms, took another one for me, and then showered and rinsed off with her while she washed her hair.

I could have stayed in that shower and watched her forever, but instead, I'd dropped to my knees while she conditioned, gave her one more orgasm and then made breakfast for us.

"Can I meet any of the guys?" she asked, and while she wasn't twiddling her hands with nerves, there was a hitch in her breath that showed she was nervous.

"Of course. Dominick and Joey are usually in the gym or getting done by now." The two of them had started working out together every morning last summer and it stuck. I usually saw them headed out when I was headed in for physical therapy, but we were getting there earlier this morning.

"And Alix?"

"He'll be there." He'd already told me he was going to be at the meeting, even if he had to sit outside.

Knowing him, he might take this harder than me. I'd had six weeks to get used to the idea, even if the truth of it didn't start sinking in until I got back from Tunstago Bay.

"What's your coach like?" she asked, and this time she was quieter. Growing more worried.

I fought the urge to slam the car into a U-turn and drive the hell away.

Today was going to be the hardest day of my career, bar none.

"He's a fair man. A good coach who cares about us players, but I don't think he cares so much on a personal level. Just wants the wins. That's not to say he's an asshole or anything."

"But he's not family to you."

"Hard for him to be better than the one I already have." I reached out and took her hand in mine, squeezed. I hoped she knew she was now included in that.

"Your family is pretty great."

"You're pretty great," I teased and laughed when she made a barfing sound.

Her laughter died when I turned the corner, the team's security gate looming in the distance and growing closer.

"Fuck. Today sucks."

"It could still be okay."

"I know." It absolutely could be. My shoulder could be better, which it was, but it wasn't perfect. My surgery could finally be scheduled. But my head... what would be the cost of another concussion?

And was I still willing to risk it?

Hell, a month ago, six weeks ago, I refused to have this conversation. Refused to acknowledge it as a possibility. Nothing had changed in my life in the last six weeks. Not my love for the game and the high of skating onto the ice to the roar of thousands. Not my excitement for being a part of something so few got to experience at a professional level or my dedication to be the best. Nothing changed except the woman beside me, supporting me, and encouraging me.

Which meant *everything* changed.

I flashed my credentials to get past the security guard, parked in the underground parking garage, and once I turned off my Suburban, I sat there.

There'd be no more pre-game workouts or early morning skates.

There'd be no more meals or playing soccer or hacky sack in the halls with the guys.

There'd be no team dinners.

They'd move on. Grab a new player during the draft or call up someone from the minor team.

I'd be replaced in less than thirty days, and fuck... what was I *doing?*

"Max?" I jolted at Kimmy's voice, the concern lining her eyes and the worry in her tone. "Are you okay?"

"Yeah. I'm all right." I would be. Eventually.

I climbed out of the Suburban, Kimmy's worry a heavy blanket that followed me to her side of the vehicle and held her hand while she jumped down.

She smiled but it fell flat when I stepped into her, backed her into the side of my SUV.

"I need you to know something."

"What is it?" Her free hand settled at my bicep.

"I meant what I said this morning. I'm falling in love with you."

She blinked, and then her smile returned, this time genuine, and I swear her eyes watered a bit before she leaned forward and rested her forehead on my chest. "I'm falling in love with you, too. Whatever happens today, we'll face together."

Always.

I'd known this girl for three weeks. Had only spent seven days with her. Now, I couldn't imagine a life without her.

Like hell I'd scare her off with that now, though. Hell, she'd just admitted she was starting to like athletes... we'd approach marriage versus long-term commitments later.

"Come on." I kissed the top of her head and squeezed her hand. "Let's get this over with."

As soon as we entered the practice hallway, the smell of home assaulted me. So maybe it was the mixture of cool cement and sweaty socks, but for me, it'd been the smell I loved for almost my entire life. What was different, however, was the silence.

Other than the air-conditioner humming in the vents, there wasn't the chatter of janitors. There wasn't the slam of weights dropping to the floor after a deadlift echoing from the weight room, and when we passed it, the room was jet-black.

Empty.

"I thought you said—"

"Maybe they finished early. Or are working out at Joey's or something." It was rare, but it happened. He'd turned his pool house into the perfect workout room complete with a floor meant to imitate the feel of ice. It kicked ass.

Something else I'd probably no longer see much of.

I blew out a breath and headed toward the elevator. Coach's office was on the sixth floor and the elevator ride took a decade.

"Ready?" Kimmy asked, glancing up at me. The worry was heavier than ever in her eyes.

"Ready."

The doors opened and we stepped off. Her hand in mine began to sweat. Maybe it was mine.

Maybe it was the fact that every single player from our first line was standing outside the coach's office, dressed in their jerseys, arms over each other's shoulders. Behind them, fanned out... the rest of my fucking team.

"Fuck." My head fell and I pinched the bridge of my nose. These assholes.

We'd stood in support like this for Dom when he had to address the media last spring about his family.

Apparently, it was what we *did* now.

"I hate you all," I muttered and on beat, they all smiled at me.

"Wow," Kimmy said. She was doing worse hiding her emotion and surprise than I was. Tears streamed down her cheeks and *fuck* yes. This was why I loved her. Because she felt something and didn't hide it. She was right there, crying in a roomful of strangers all because they were important to me.

Because *I* was important to them.

"We love you too," Alix said and stepped forward among the team. Dom followed.

I knew the asshole had a soft spot for me. "You *do* love me," I said to him.

"I hate you less than most," he fired back and came right to me, threw an arm around me, and slapped my back. "Good luck."

"Jesus, you're going to make me cry."

"Then I really will punch your face."

I shoved him off me. He'd been threatening to do that to me since he joined our team. I always knew he wasn't a bad guy even if half the team hated him at first. But then we learned his background, his family. I'd always suspected there was something deeper to him than being another asshole with a chip on his shoulder.

I hadn't been wrong at all.

"You guys didn't need to be here," I said, but hell, I was glad they were. "First, meet Kimmy." I smirked down at her as she smiled at me. It shook from nerves.

Her cheeks blared hot pink.

She'd never been prettier.

"My girlfriend," I finished.

"Awww…" they sang almost on cue. A couple guys from the third line stood in the back and made kissing faces at each other, making everyone laugh.

Dicks. All of them.

Fuck, I'd miss them.

Alix held out his hand to Kimmy. "It is nice to finally meet you. He talks about you… too much, I think."

"You ass." I shoved his shoulder and then clasped it. "Did you plan all this?"

"Nope." His eyes slid in Dom's direction.

Holy fucking shit. I grinned at the guy, looking almost as nervous I had felt up until this moment.

"Don't even say it," he muttered and then lost the fight on his grin. "And as soon as you can, I promised Holly I'd invite you to dinner. She misses you."

"Right." A frog clogged my throat, making breathing difficult. Talking worse.

Kimmy stepped closer to me and slid her arm behind my back.

My silent supporter.

"This is Dominick," I told her.

"It's nice to meet you."

"Good man you have here," Dom said. And hell… I'd go through this all over again to get that compliment from him.

Kimmy rested her head against my arm. "I know."

Movement came from behind the guys, and then Coach was there.

At once, any happiness fled into the shadows, ducked under tables, and hid behind curtains.

"Max. You made it."

"Surprised you made it through this riot in one piece." I held out my hand to his and shook it.

"Animals, all of them," he agreed. "Who's this?"

"This is Kimberly. My girlfriend," I told him. I'd have to find a better word for that. Girlfriend was too young. Partner too serious. Fiancée or wife sounded best, but I had a lifetime to get her to change her mind on that.

Or not.

Didn't quite matter to me either way.

They introduced themselves and I caught sight of the team doctor standing back near the team. He had files in his arms along with his iPad and my throat thickened again.

"We should move this to Vik's office," he said, and while he gave nothing away, it didn't matter.

"There's no need. I'd like to talk to you about my shoulder, definitely, but I have something I'd like to say first... and since everyone is here..."

I dropped my gaze to Kimmy. Her brows puckered adorably on her forehead. Maybe I should have given her a heads up. I hadn't expected her to surprise me though and had planned to tell her everything once I got to her place tonight.

Hopefully she liked my surprise too.

More—I hoped she liked an unemployed boyfriend.

"What is it, son?" Vik asked.

"Max," she whispered.

"It's okay," I whispered back and pressed a kiss to her forehead. "I'm okay."

At that, understanding dawned and her chin trembled. "Are you sure?"

No way could I be a hundred percent sure. But I was as close as I could get. I'd had a decade-plus of being able to do what I absolutely loved.

The risk now was greater than the potential reward.

"Yes." I kissed her again, lingered, and noticed vaguely no one made a sound. Not even a childish kissing noise or sound.

When I pulled back, I brushed a tear off her cheek and turned to the team. My pseudo-family.

My coach.

"I'd like to take this moment to announce that effective immediately, I'm retiring from the sport of hockey."

EPILOGUE

KIM

Nine Months Later

TURNED OUT, Max's headaches bothered him more than he ever let on. That last minor concussion he got while rock climbing took months to heal. Even now, he was more sensitive to light. He forgot basic things, would stop in mid-sentence, shake it off and change the subject.

Turned out, he wasn't some dumb jock who was living in full denial, just halfway so.

He told me everything after we left the training facility that day. How he'd researched CTEs, their minor symptoms, symptoms he'd realized he'd already been showing. Symptoms he could no longer ignore even if he wanted to.

He'd told me he always said hockey was everything to him, that he wouldn't leave the sport until they carried his dead body off the ice, but then he realized he changed.

He grew up.

He fell in love.

Did I feel guilt some days that he essentially threw in the towel for me? A woman he'd known a short amount of time? Hell, regardless of how long we knew each other, I'd feel that guilt. That weight. The need to prove he'd made the right choice.

So yes. Absolutely.

Until I realized, I'd do the exact same thing for him if necessary.

That was how fast and hard our love hit. For all my eye rolling the morning of Bridget's wedding nine months ago, laughing as the women joked about love at first sight, they were right.

From the moment I met Max, I knew he was different.

It took me about two weeks after announcing his retirement to realize he was my everything.

Now, I was pouring him a glass of red wine, me a glass of white, and trying to imagine how in the hell I lived in this small bungalow tucked away in San Bernardino without him.

Yeah, he moved in with me immediately.

Then he enrolled in college. Turned out most universities would accept a retired, professional athlete months after the deadline to enroll. He could only take online classes right now, but he was kicking ass halfway through his second semester at Cal State at San Bernardino where he was majoring in Education.

He wanted to teach middle school math.

Every time I pictured him in a classroom of twelve- and thirteen-year-olds, I grinned. He'd be an awesome teacher.

I stepped out back, the spring air crisp and cool, and took the seat next to him.

"How's it going?"

"Good." He reached for his glass of wine and sat back, pushing glasses up to his forehead.

Yeah... he needed those now, too. Helped his eye strain and his headaches which were now happening at a much more *normal* rate and cause.

They only made him sexier.

He let out a sigh that made me sit up straight. I knew him well enough now to know his sounds. His grunts when he was working out. The tick of his teeth to tongue when he was concentrating on school. The clicking sound he made while trying to work through a new play with the kids.

This one wasn't a good one.

"What is it?" I asked and took a healthy sip of my wine to prepare myself.

It could be anything.

A muscle jumped in his cheek. "I got a call from Coach Vik today."

"Your old coach?" A chill slid through me. No. There was no way he'd go back to playing. Not after everything he told me. Not after I did my own research.

He chewed the inside corner of his bottom lip and nodded. "It's nothing."

"It is. What did he want?" I pushed toward the edge of my seat. There were few times I saw Max this uptight. Right before finals that first semester.

Right before his team lost their championship game and were down by one, had possession of the puck with twenty seconds to go and couldn't tie it up. He'd found a rec hockey league, volunteered to coach. Apparently eight-year-olds lost their damn *minds* when they heard a former pro player was their coach. Parents too.

I lost track of the hours I found him on FaceTime with Dominick, both of them giving each other shit about whose youth team was better, who had better plays, grit, speed, and spirit. *Hours.*

"Not to play." He pressed at my frown line with this thumb, smiling as he rubbed away the tension there. "He said our old assistant defenseman coach is leaving for Wisconsin."

I held my breath. *Our.* He said *our* like he still considered himself on the Vipers team. Which really said everything.

He pressed his lips together and looked off toward the back fence.

"And?" I prodded.

"And he wants me to take it." He shrugged like it was no big deal. Like he hadn't spent a second considering it. But if I knew Max, he was already drafting plays. Planning training schedules. Running through the line-up of current players, including some guy from Seattle who had been traded for his spot.

"What'd you say?"

"That I'd think about it. Talk to you about it."

"What are you thinking?"

"That I love kids and had a blast coaching them this year."

"But..." Because while he had, I already knew where this was going.

"It's not the same. Not the same challenge. It doesn't give me the same fire."

I sipped my wine and waited. He'd have more to say.

"I can't move back there and be away from you. I can't imagine..."

"Do not give up something you dream of and love for me. Not again." There was that guilt.

"It wasn't for you."

We'd had this argument slash discussion multiple times. I conceded this time without a fight.

"Would you enjoy it?" I asked instead.

"I guess that's the fear... what if I don't? What if I do something like that, jump at it, and it's still not the same."

"Max..." I sighed, set down my glass, and climbed into his lap. He was a giant goofball with a heart of gold and sometimes—sometimes, he put too much pressure on himself to be this *amazing* man he missed the fact he already was. "Maybe nothing will give you that same passion as hockey, but that doesn't mean it's not your purpose. Even a small fire is better than ashes."

"Your career is here. Your *purpose* is here."

"And our *life* is together."

He shook his head, brows furrowing. "I can't ask that of you. To uproot everything for me."

"Why not? Don't hockey wives and girlfriends do it all the time? Any professional athlete's spouse or partner? Isn't that part of the deal?"

"You're not dating a player. You're dating a retired player."

"I'm *living* with the man I'm going to spend the rest of my life with. You will *always* be more important than a job."

He shook his head and blew out a breath. God, sometimes I wanted to hit him.

Not *hard*, just hard enough to knock sense into him. He'd spent his entire career thinking he only had one thing to offer.

Hockey.

How he could doubt everything else he gave me, support, encouragement, a partner in every sense of the word. Compassion. Passion.

"Let's imagine a scenario."

For a second, the darkness in his eyes lightened. "Of you on a beach? Naked? I'm in."

He squeezed his eyes closed and grinned, showing all teeth.

"No." I kissed his cheek. "What if I got a got call from a firm in New York? The *best* firm in the entire country. The whole wide world. Let's say they called to make me partner. Should I take it?"

"Of course." Man, I loved the way he loved me.

"What about you? What if you were teaching? Would you come?"

"Of course. There are schools all over."

"Then.... the same could be said for—"

"I get it. I get it, I do, it's different. I moved *here* because this is your passion. This is your career. And I'm asking you to uproot that."

I pressed my hands to his cheeks. "Is that what you're asking? What you want?"

His hands brushed my thighs, long, gentle sweeps that left me squirming in the chair.

After several long moments, he lifted his head and squinted. I shifted right to block the sun from his eyes. "What if I am?"

"Then it means I need to start studying for the Nevada bar exam."

A bright, shining smile hit his face. "Yeah?"

"We have a life to live together. Chasing each other's dreams. Supporting each other. The location doesn't matter as long as I have you."

"I love you. You know that, right?"

"Every day for the rest of my life."

Married or not.

Because we were both changing—

And with Max, I might not, someday, be as opposed to it as I once was.

But we'd see.

We had all the time in the world.

THANK YOU for reading Shot Taker! I hope you enjoyed it. If you're still loving the Vipers as much as I am, stay tuned this fall for Kane's book. It's a wild adventure you won't want to miss! You can pre-order Goal Chaser here: https://amzn.to/3xnM9JM

DON'T MISS a single sale or new release announcement. Join my newsletter and you'll be the first to know whenever something exciting is happening!

THANK YOU

HUGE thank you to Nina and all the incredible women at Valentine PR for throwing your full enthusiasm and support behind me and these books. I've loved working with you and can't wait to see what the future brings us.

Ellie and Virginia, as always, thanks for putting up with my mess and spit-shining each manuscript until it sparkles. Thank you especially during this crazy time in our world for your flexibility and your extra hard work.

Shannon, you're the best. Always. Forever. Your talent is astounding and I'm thankful I can call you a friend.

To my Sweeties! I love you ladies and your excitement for my books!

To all the bloggers who devote their time and passion into reading books, book tours, release events, leaving reviews, promoting and pimping – you are all rockstars! Thank you for all the love over the years.

My family— I love you all to the moon and back. I don't know what I would do without you in my corner, cheering me on every step of the way. Your support is everything to me and I love you all with all of my heart.

To my girl crew— Tamara, Lauren, Niccole, Cassy, and Bree. What would I do without you ladies? Thank you for blessing me with your friendships. My life is a hundred times better with y'all in it, and a gazillion times more entertaining! To the SteelP! May we forever reign.

And last but definitely not least – to you the reader. I'm blown away with every release how much you adore my books. You have made my dream a reality and I hope I can cheer you on with yours. Please don't forget to leave reviews on Goodreads or whichever retailer you've purchased this copy from. It helps us so much!

ABOUT THE AUTHOR

Stacey Lynn likes her coffee with a dash of sugar, her heroes with a side of bossy, and her wine a deep shade of red.

The author of over forty romance novels, many of which have been best-selling titles, she loves being able to turn her vivid imagination into a career that brings entertainment and joy to her readers. Focused on sports romance and emotional, small-town romance, she also loves stretching herself in different genres.

Born in Texas and raised in the Midwest, she now makes her home in North Carolina and loves all things Southern. Together with her ultimate tall, dark, and handsome hero, she has four children. Her life is a chaotic mess that fights with her Type-A, list-making, neurotically organized preferences and she wouldn't have it any other way.

Subscribe to her newsletter so you can stay up to date on all her new releases. www.staceylynnbooks.com

OTHER BOOKS BY STACEY LYNN

<u>Las Vegas Vipers ~hockey romance</u>

Final Shot (free on all retailers)

Game Changer

Dream Maker

Rule Breaker

Shot Taker

Goal Chaser – September 2022

Secret Keeper – December 2022

<u>Ice Kings Series ~hockey romance</u>

Playing With Fire (free on all retailers)

Playing To Win

Scoring Off The Ice

Hooked One Her

Hard Checked

Fighting Dirty

<u>The Rough Riders Series ~football romance</u>

Dirty Player

Filthy Player

Wicked Player

Cocky Player

<u>Love and Lies Duet ~angsty slow burn, romance</u>

All the Ugly Things

All the Beautiful Things

Love and Honor Duet ~angsty, romantic suspense

Twisted Hearts

Unraveled Love

Love In The Heartland ~small town romance

Captivated By You

This Time Around

Long Road Home

Before We Fell

Crazy Love Series ~small town romance

Fake Wife

Knocked Up

28 Dates

Weekend Fling

The Fireside Series ~small town romance

His to Love

His to Protect

His to Cherish

His to Seduce

Tangled Love Series ~erotic romance

Entice

Embrace

Enflame

The Luminous Series ~BDSM romance

Dominate Me

Crave Me

Long For Me

Just One Series ~rockstar romance

Just One Song

Just One Week

Just One Regret

Just One Moment

The Nordic Lords Series ~MC romance

Point of Return

Point of Redemption

Point of Freedom

Point of Surrender

Standalones

Remembering Us

Don't Lie To Me – billionaire romance

Try Me – A Don't Lie To Me Novella